Scott knew wh~~_____~~
before h~~_____~~

And he opened it anyway, ~~_____~~
persistence," he growled. ~~_____~~

"We brought lunch." Mercedes held out a large paper bag that smelled of Mexican food. A meal wasn't going to sway him. He was about to tell her that when Mercedes pushed past him into the living room, dragging Gemma, his half sister, behind her.

"Mind if we invade your kitchen?"

"Yes. I do." The kitchen wasn't fit for any visitor, let alone this woman who, he would bet, groomed her kitchen as well as she groomed herself. Say whatever else you wanted to about her, she did make herself pretty and smelled nice to boot. Like...springtime. He couldn't say what that meant exactly, except the scent took him back years, to a time when life was easier. Lighter. He scowled.

"Here's fine, then." Mercedes shared a conspiratorial look with Gemma and helped herself to the couch and coffee table.

Mercedes must have found her stubborn, pushy mojo overnight. Wasn't he lucky?

She was average height with nicer-than-average curves. Her dark wavy hair was everywhere, though she'd tried to control it by pulling the front parts back in a clip. Her calculating smile at Gemma highlighted prominent cheekbones and drew his attention to her glossy lips.

If she hadn't been so bent on steamrolling him into being this girl's knight in shining armor, he might have considered getting to know her on a more personal level.

Short-term, of course.

Dear Reader,

Thank you for picking up the fifth The Texas Firefighters book! If you've read any of the earlier books in the series, you may remember mentions of paramedic Scott Pataki. Scott seemed like a good guy, so I thought I'd give him his own story.

He is a good guy, but he's in a bad place. A dark one. And he believes the only way to save himself from the things that are eating away at him is to escape San Amaro Island.

It's a bad time to get involved with someone. Anyone.

When his pregnant half sister, someone he'd never met and never wanted to meet, shows up and brings Mercedes Stone with her, involvement is inevitable. That doesn't mean he's not going to fight it for all he's worth, though.

I hope you enjoy *Island Haven.* If you're inclined, please let me know what you think of Mercedes and Scott at amyknupp@amyknupp.com. To read more about my other books, visit my website at www.amyknupp.com, or look me up on Facebook.

Happy reading,

Amy Knupp

Island Haven

AMY KNUPP

TORONTO NEW YORK LONDON
AMSTERDAM PARIS SYDNEY HAMBURG
STOCKHOLM ATHENS TOKYO MILAN MADRID
PRAGUE WARSAW BUDAPEST AUCKLAND

Recycling programs
for this product may
not exist in your area.

ISBN-13: 978-0-373-60713-6

ISLAND HAVEN

ABOUT THE AUTHOR

Amy Knupp lives in Wisconsin with her husband, two sons, five cats and a turtle named Scuttle. She graduated from the University of Kansas with degrees in French and journalism and feels lucky to use very little of either one in her writing career. She's a member of Romance Writers of America, Mad City Romance Writers and Wisconsin Romance Writers. In her spare time, she enjoys reading, college basketball, addictive computer games and researching island havens, preferably in person. To learn more about Amy and her stories, visit www.amyknupp.com.

Books by Amy Knupp

HARLEQUIN SUPERROMANCE

1342—UNEXPECTED COMPLICATION
1402—THE BOY NEXT DOOR
1463—DOCTOR IN HER HOUSE
1537—THE SECRET SHE KEPT
1646—PLAYING WITH FIRE*
1652—A LITTLE CONSEQUENCE*
1658—FULLY INVOLVED*
1702—BURNING AMBITION*
1748—BECAUSE OF THE LIST

*The Texas Firefighters

Other titles by this author are available in ebook format.

Don't miss any of our special offers. Write to us at the following address for information on our newest releases.

Harlequin Reader Service
U.S.: 3010 Walden Ave., P.O. Box 1325, Buffalo, NY 14269
Canadian: P.O. Box 609, Fort Erie, Ont. L2A 5X3

For Justin...you know why.

CHAPTER ONE

LAST NIGHT WAS GRUESOME.

Scott Pataki poured himself a glass of whiskey, straight up. So what if it was a quarter after eight in the morning?

Eyes closed, he downed half the glass, trying to expel the gory images from his paramedic shift. The motorcycle-and-cement-truck tangle had been bad enough. Grisly. Closed casket for sure. But to follow that up, not fifteen minutes after they'd gotten the ambulance cleaned and restocked, with a suicide call...

Thirty-six more days was all he had to make it through. Then he would finally escape—if he was lucky, before the job ruined him completely.

He swigged down the rest of the liquor, set aside the glass and headed to the hallway, unsnapping his jeans as he went. Before he could reach his bedroom, the doorbell pealed through the quiet. He swore and resumed his path to the shower but heard the sound again not twenty seconds later.

"At 8:26 a.m.?" he muttered, glancing at his

watch. "Should be illegal to bother someone at this hour."

He retraced his steps to the living room. If he didn't get rid of whoever was out there right now, chances were they'd only come back in a few hours and interrupt his sleep. If he still had the ability to collapse like the dead and ignore it, there'd be no problem. But these days his sleep was as bothered as his waking hours.

Jaw clenched, he whipped the door open, planning to celebrate ridding himself of the unwanted visitor with another shot. Two if it was a religious zealot trying to save his soul.

If the teenage girl on his front step was a religion freak, they were getting younger. And tougher.

"Hi," she said, sizing him up. Vaguely familiar, restless-looking hazel eyes stared at him expectantly. Obviously she'd gotten the wrong apartment.

"Can I help you?" he said impatiently.

"You're Scott Pataki, right?"

"That's me."

That she knew his name didn't faze him. He was a paramedic. He met scores of people. He didn't recall seeing this girl before, though.

"I'm Gemma Lawrence." She said it almost as if she was challenging him.

He looked her over thoroughly, racking his

brains for a connection. She was only a few inches shorter than his six feet, with messy, coarse-looking dirty-blond hair that hung to her shoulders. Her face was bare of makeup, except for the dark eyeliner she'd look better without. Her sloppy, oversize sweatshirt was not only stretched out and wrinkled as though it'd been slept in for a month straight, but it was all wrong for the weather. The temperature on San Amaro Island this stifling June morning was already close to ninety-five degrees. Ripped, faded jeans and orange camo tennis shoes rounded out her out-of-season getup.

"Dale Pataki is my father," she added.

Oh, hell, no...

Son of a bitch, yes. The eyes. That's where he knew them from. Once you filtered out the too-heavy eye makeup, they matched his own father's. The realization reared itself like a rabid pit bull that'd worked its way out of a too-small backyard kennel.

Scott fought the urge to slam the door and act as if the past sixty seconds hadn't happened. Just as he'd been doing for ten years.

Make that three shots.

"Why are you here?" he asked.

She glanced to the side, probably at one of his crazy-ass neighbors down the way, then back at him. "Hot out here."

"That's summer in Texas for you." Chitchat

about the weather wasn't going to win him over even if she hadn't just uttered the name of the man that made his blood boil.

"Can I come in?"

He eyed her warily, then inadvertently looked in the direction of the shower and bed he ached for. This problem wasn't going to go away until he handled it. He stepped aside to let her in, glancing at his watch. "It's past my bedtime. Make it quick."

As Gemma swiftly entered his apartment, chin up, he noticed the overstuffed backpack hanging from her shoulders and the black purse with metal accents that was big enough to hide a small child in.

"Do you have a roommate?" she asked, looking around the living room, taking a couple of steps toward his video-game system at the other end. She seemed to be scoping out the place.

"Not anymore. What do you want…Gemma, was it?"

She whirled around and pegged him with a determined, measuring stare. "Yes. Gemma. I always imagined you being friendlier."

He'd never imagined her being anything. Never thought of her as a real person. "Are you going to tell me why you're here?"

She looked at him for another moment then became unusually interested in the thumbnail on her right hand. As Scott's patience slipped, she raised her long lashes again as if daring him to look away first. "I need a place to stay."

"Why would you think you could stay here?" Scott uncrossed his arms and did his best to remain calm as she wandered to the window. In the silence, he fought an inner battle against the rage his father's name stirred. Why today? He wasn't sure he could handle that particular memory lane anytime, but today of all days, after his worse-than-usual shift, he was at the end of his rope.

When she didn't immediately answer his question, he fired more at her. "Why aren't you at home with your mom? Fort Worth, wasn't it?"

Her shoulders jerked slightly, as if she'd been absorbed in her thoughts. Seconds ticked by.

"My mom kicked me out." Her tone was indifferent, cool. She walked over to the old couch and sat. The only sign that she wasn't totally at ease was a subconscious rubbing together of the fingers and thumb of one hand. With the other hand, she touched her abdomen purposefully. "I'm… pregnant."

Pregnant? He glanced at her belly but between the army-green sweatshirt that sagged over her and the way she was leaning forward, he couldn't see any telling bump.

Though she looked mature for her age, she wasn't much more than a child herself. Her skin looked soft and fresh, undamaged by the sun. Her eyes told a different story, though.

Scott opened his mouth to speak but couldn't figure out what to say to her announcement. Instead, he lowered himself to the arm on the opposite end of the couch and chewed on his dry lip, at a loss. Anger he could handle, but her revelation dampened that from a bottled-up rage to more of a slow, steady boil. Sympathy was tempering it, in spite of himself.

"Your mom kicked you out because you're pregnant?" he asked unnecessarily.

Gemma nodded. "In theory. Personally, I think she's just been waiting for an excuse. Which works for me because I planned to leave after graduation anyway."

"Did you graduate?"

"Close enough. The ceremony's tomorrow. I don't know how much you've heard about my mom, but she's not terribly reasonable."

"I haven't heard anything about your mom." Nor did he want to. "How pregnant are you?"

"Twenty-eight weeks."

He calculated the months in his head and looked again at her middle.

"The sweatshirt covers it and I'm relatively small, I've been told, because of my height, but I assure you I wouldn't make that up."

"Where's the father?"

Where was he coming up with these questions and why was he asking them? This was so far from being his problem and still…he couldn't throw her out. Yet.

The thing was, she damn sure couldn't stay here.

"He's not in the picture." Her answer came quickly.

Scott had several things to say about Daddy-O leaving her high and dry, but he reminded himself again this wasn't his problem. His concern was finding a place for her to go, someone to help her. He was in a bad state himself, but maybe not as coldhearted as he and everyone else thought.

"Why did you come here?" he asked, softening his tone.

He'd been aware, painfully aware, his dad had a child with another woman, but until now, she'd never had a face. It'd been easier to hate her before.

"We're in the same boat. It was you, our honorable father who I haven't talked to in almost four years, or the street. You win."

He tensed at the blunt reference—the use of *our*—to the reality that had caused him to walk away from his so-called family ten years ago. It didn't bear thinking of, not now with this stranger sitting in his apartment. Not ever. "Why would you even come up with the idea of showing up here?"

He'd never once had any desire to meet his dad's other family.

"You live on an island. We're practically family. Sounds ideal to me."

"We're not family." Scott had once been perfectly content being part of a family of three— just him, his mom and his dad. Then he'd found out the truth. Now the word *family* had very little significance to him.

"Half." She had a way of sounding removed from the argument, as though she didn't have any stake in it, and yet, there was a contradicting edge beneath her words.

Scott swore as he shot to his feet. "Come on."

"What?"

The unveiled spark of hope that flitted over her face got to him, but he wasn't going to be her solution or her savior. Couldn't.

"I'll buy you a bus ticket to get home." He didn't have much cash available, but he could spare a little if it would get her back where she belonged—and give him some peace. "Your mom is probably worried about you."

He expected her to protest, but she stared at him for several long, heavy seconds, all traces of toughness gone from her face. She rose wearily, straining under the weight of her backpack, and he wondered how long it'd been since she'd left home.

Shaking his head, he reminded himself of who she was and led her to the door. A stop at the ATM was all he could do for her. His father's love child wasn't someone he could handle charitably, now or ever.

Sometimes the person you pinned your hopes on wasn't cut out to be a hero.

CHAPTER TWO

MERCEDES STONE WANTED to wrap this beautiful girl in a hug and protect her from the crazy world. Didn't matter that Gemma seemed fully able to protect herself—at seventeen years old, she shouldn't have to.

She and Gemma had sat together for the better part of two hours on the pillow-covered love seat at Ruby Herman Women's Services, founded by none other than her grandma, where Mercedes volunteered every other week. Four hours a month wasn't much, and someday Mercedes would do more, but for now, Gram needed her at home. People like Gemma were the reason Mercedes burned to be more involved at the shelter, and ultimately to become the director. Helping women in need was much more her calling than her paying job of social-media marketing.

Gemma had shown up in the middle of the afternoon after pocketing the cash her half brother had given her and tracking down the shelter on foot. Though she'd been reluctant to tell her story at first, Mercedes had eventually gotten her to talk more. To let some of it out. The girl, who had gone from defensive, crossed arms to leaning on the back of the love seat as if she needed it so she could stay upright, described herself as a loner. Mercedes was sure she'd been holding so much inside for so long that she wasn't far from bursting.

Gemma had kept her composure better than Mercedes, who'd become teary. She couldn't help it. No one should have to deal with such a combination of bad luck, tough circumstances and crappy parenting. How could her mother send her away during the hardest time of her life, when she needed love and support the most?

Mercedes turned her Honda CRV in to the parking lot on Miller Street that Gemma indicated. "This is where your half brother lives?"

The building, squeezed between two larger condominiums in the center of the island, was in need of upkeep. It was tough to find any place on San Amaro Island that was low-rent, but this neighborhood was about as close as you could get. And that wasn't necessarily a good thing.

"This is it. He's in 6A."

Mercedes parked and turned off the engine. "You're sure you want to try again?"

"At this point, I don't have a lot of options. I hope he's done with his nap, though, otherwise I probably don't stand a chance."

The clock on the dash read 7:22 p.m. At the end of their session at the shelter, Gemma's growling stomach had snagged Mercedes's attention. She'd discovered that today Gemma had consumed only a pint-size jug of milk and a bag of mini chocolate-chip cookies. Needing to get dinner for her grandma, Mercedes had taken Gemma home with her and made grilled cheese sandwiches for the three of them.

Though Gemma had been reserved, she'd come out of her shell enough to answer Gram's questions as they'd sat around the kitchen table, eating. Gram had been thrilled to meet one of the people her shelter was assisting. Her ability to form a bond with reluctant women was what had made her so successful, and something Mercedes strived to imitate.

By the time Mercedes had called one of Gram's daily caretakers for an extra shift so she could get Gemma settled somewhere, Gemma had loosened up considerably and even hesitantly hugged Gram on her way out the door.

"You said he was going to bed at nine this morning," Mercedes said lightly. "If he's still in bed, he gets more sleep than a cat."

Gemma stared at the apartment building in silence, looking as if her mind was spinning. Plotting. Unfortunately, based on what Gemma had said about her half brother's temperament, plotting might be exactly what was necessary.

"Okay, let's go charm this guy." Mercedes spoke with forced confidence, but she knew all too well how it felt to be alone, and hated that Gemma was in that dark place.

They walked across the steamy lot to the building that, like many on the island, boasted an elevated first floor in case of flooding. When they reached the top of the first flight, Gemma took a left and headed to the end of the outdoor walkway.

A radio blared from a unit on the opposite side. As Mercedes and Gemma arrived at apartment 6A, a woman flung open another door down the way, yelled something peppered with a fine variety of swearwords then slammed the door shut.

Mercedes watched the sloppily dressed woman hightail it down the steps as Gemma knocked.

When Gemma's half brother finally opened the door, two impressions struck Mercedes right away. One, he worked out regularly. Two, this guy lived hard.

He was shirtless, his body lean and muscled. It was impossible not to admire his well-defined abs, pecs, arms. When she managed to drag her gaze upward, she registered his dark hair shaved down to almost nothing, as if he had better things to do than deal with too much of it. Though she doubted he was much older than she, his face carried the lines and roughness of either living or witnessing too much trauma.

His disarming blue eyes, hollowed out by shadows beneath, penetrated hers for a long moment. There was an endearing little-boy sleepiness in them—until he caught sight of Gemma, standing to Mercedes's left. The chill that instantly veiled his entire face was startling. Intimidating.

"You? Again?" He directed the accusatory questions to Gemma.

"Hi," Mercedes said, stepping forward as if to protect the teenager. "Mercedes Stone. I'm with Ruby Herman Women's Services." She extended her hand and was surprised when he shook it, albeit brusquely.

"Scott Pataki." He turned back to Gemma. "I thought I put you on a bus this morning."

"You dropped me off at the bus depot," Gemma clarified, unruffled.

"I gave you a hundred bucks."

"I'll give you the money back." She opened her purse and started digging around in it.

"Gemma came into the shelter this afternoon."

"So I gathered." He took the cash Gemma held out to him and shoved it in his back jeans pocket. The movement caused his arm and chest muscles to flex and shift almost artfully.

Mercedes yanked her attention back to his face.

"We'd like to talk to you, if you have a few minutes."

"Be my guest." His manner as he shoved the door open wider wasn't quite as cordial as his words.

Mercedes shot a questioning look at Gemma. The teenager had mentioned that Scott wasn't overly friendly, but Mercedes hadn't expected the blatant hostility. This was the brother Gemma wanted to bunk with?

Gemma avoided her silent question as she led Mercedes inside.

The living room was small, sparsely furnished, and cluttered, with a single bare window. The couch and coffee table seemed to be for show— it was obvious the other end of the room was more lived-in. In the far corner, a flat-screen TV that was practically bigger than Mercedes's SUV loomed at an angle. Two low chairs that resembled bucket seats sat a few feet in front of the screen. Various electronic components, empty beverage cans and video-game cases littered the floor in between.

"Gemma tells me you're a paramedic," Mercedes said. She and the girl sat on the couch, as Scott directed. He remained standing. "I think I recognize you from the fire department awards banquet last month. I was there as Faith Peligni's guest."

He'd caught her attention from afar that night, as he'd accepted an award. Something about his eyes, even from a distance, drew her in. Now that she was closer, she could see there was a haunted edginess to them.

Scott nodded. "Faith's okay. Look, Gemma and I talked this morning. I don't know exactly what you want from me, but I can't give it."

"Gemma's traveled a long way to get here. She needs a place to stay for a few nights. We were hoping you could help us out with that."

"Why can't she stay at the shelter? Isn't that what it's there for?"

"We're at capacity, unfortunately. Your fire department friends came after us once when we had one person more than allowed. Threatened to shut us down. We're pretty careful now. I put her on the waiting list for a bed, but that could be weeks."

"What do you normally do when people show up and you're full?"

"Whatever we have to in order to find a place for them. First, we try to track down safe relatives or friends. Sometimes we work a deal on a hotel room. The director has been known to let women stay at her house in extreme circumstances. They come to us when they're desperate for help. We can't just say, 'sorry, the inn's full.'"

"And that's where you think I come in."

"Technically, you do fit in the 'relative' category."

"And you think I'm a safe option?"

Mercedes tilted her head, attempting to hide how much his comment took her aback. He was messing with her, she realized as she scrutinized him. If he presented any true, intentional danger to Gemma, he wouldn't have said that. But the minute she was out of his sight, she'd get the lowdown on Scott from Faith.

"I think you want me to believe you're worse than you are," she said.

"Paramedics are supposed to save lives," Gemma said. "Not endanger them."

"That's the idea, anyway," he said, turning away, looking longingly toward what Mercedes assumed was the kitchen. He shook his head slowly before facing them again. "I'm not your guy. I'm leaving town soon."

"How soon?"

"Next month."

"Where are you going?" Gemma asked, a quiver in her voice a sign she might be losing her cool for the first time since they'd arrived.

"Taking a job on a cruise ship as a scuba instructor. Can't get here soon enough." He didn't sound excited, exactly. More...desperate. As if he was running away.

"We're just asking for a few days, Scott. She's pregnant and exhausted. She's your half sister."

His jaw tightened. His face hardened into a wall—a wall that Mercedes realized immediately she wasn't going to be able to get through tonight.

She was determined to find Gemma a comfortable place to live, but this was not it. Not right now.

If Scott didn't want his half sister to stay with him, she wouldn't.

"Okay," Mercedes said, straightening.

"Okay what?"

She halted. "You don't want her here. We'll be out of your hair." She didn't bother to hide her annoyance.

"Where are you taking her?" Scott asked.

"She can stay with me."

Gram wouldn't mind, and would've been the first to invite Gemma to stay. Between the two of them, they'd brought home countless "strays," as Mercedes's friend Nadia had affectionately called them over the years. Both human and animal. Helping those in need had been her grandmother's way of life for as long as Mercedes could remember.

Scott chuckled in disbelief. "Really?"

"Of course, really."

"All this is in the normal scope of your volunteer work?"

Irritated by the doubt in his voice, she said emphatically, "There is no 'normal.' My role at the shelter is to assist those who come to us in any way I can. Even if I wasn't a volunteer, I can't imagine turning Gemma away." She smiled at the teenager and touched her forearm affectionately, wanting to make sure she didn't feel like a burden of any kind. "I'd think you would understand that, being in emergency medical services."

He stared at her, arms crossed, unswayed by her words. Mercedes shrugged and gestured to Gemma, noting the determination on her face.

She also couldn't understand how Scott could reject Gemma, who was still a child in some ways and yet faced such grown-up circumstances. Mercedes would ensure that she was taken care of. If that meant Mercedes and her grandmother had a new roommate, then it was time to make up the guest bed.

As SOON AS THEY WERE GONE, Scott unleashed a vulgar word into the accusatory silence of his apartment. He entered the kitchen and eyed the bottle of liquor on the counter. Taking a swig straight from the bottle, he closed his eyes as the liquid warmed his throat. It wasn't enough, though. He needed to burn off…something. Rage. At the women who thought he had some kind of duty to take in a complete stranger. At his deceiving, faithless father. At himself, for being unable to bring himself to help a girl who so plainly needed a break.

Scott pounded his fist on the counter, making the bottle rattle. He carried it to the bar and settled on a stool to drink away the anger.

If he didn't, it was going to eat him alive.

CHAPTER THREE

MERCEDES CLOSED HER LAPTOP, sank into the pillows propped against her headboard and groaned to herself, exhausted. It was ten after four in the morning. Higgans, her lazy but devoted orange tabby, yawned and stretched at the foot of the bed, displeased with the disturbance.

She'd finally caught up on emails—a bunch for work and a few personal ones. She had to start getting to bed earlier, but it seemed she couldn't make real progress on anything—housework, correspondence, even some of the nonpressing elements of her job—until after ten. Daytime hours were filled with client phone calls and the occasional meeting, planning and carrying out social-media marketing plans, taking care of her grandma and fielding unplanned curveballs. She was perpetually thankful she worked from home and could be flexible. In fact, after Gram's stroke, she'd put several months of extreme effort into making that a reality.

She reached over and set her computer on the floor by her bed, too tired to put it away properly. Normally she worked at her desk in the dining room she'd converted into an office, but she hadn't wanted to creep around in the wee hours and disturb Gemma, who'd fallen asleep as soon as Mercedes had gotten the guest bed made up.

She turned out the light and relished the sudden darkness. As she rolled over, she heard a faint noise somewhere in the house. She froze and tried to identify what she'd heard.

The back door clicking shut, she realized.

Her pulse kicking up, she rolled out of bed, more awake than she'd been for hours. She hurried down the narrow staircase and veered off toward Gram's main-floor bedroom. Before she got to the slightly open door, she could hear her grandmother snoring, and her shoulders relaxed some, figuring the noise must have been Gemma.

She crept to the back door and pushed the curtain aside to look out through the screened-in porch to the backyard. It was too dark to see anything, but the door was unlocked. Mercedes let herself out and scoped the pavement surrounding the modest swimming pool. Gemma sat on the edge in her pajamas, her back to Mercedes and her feet dangling in the water.

"Hey," Mercedes said in a hushed voice, crossing the few yards between them. "Couldn't sleep?" When she arrived at Gemma's side, she sat cross-legged next to her.

Gemma shook her head. "Cats."

"Oh, no, did they wake you up? Wasn't the door closed?" Higgans was in Mercedes's room but it was hard to guess where Spike was prowling.

Gemma sneezed twice and nodded. "I'm allergic."

"You didn't tell me!" Mercedes said. "I'm sorry. They've always claimed the guest bed as their domain. It must be full of hair, even though I changed the bedding."

"Dander," Gemma corrected. "It's okay, I should've known. I can't be in a house with a cat without sneezing my brains out, sometimes wheezing. I was too tired to care. Hoped I'd be okay."

"And I have two of the beasts. You don't stand a chance. I can clean everything, vacuum everywhere. As soon as Gram wakes up in the morning."

Gemma shook her head. "It wouldn't do any good. My mom moved us in with a guy, charming jerk that he was, a couple years ago. He had one cat and I tried cleaning everything in existence. Believe me, that was a job, but it didn't work. I was on allergy pills 24-7. It's nice of you to offer, though."

"That's awful." Mercedes's mind spun as she tried to come up with a solution. Though they hadn't discussed how long Gemma would stay, she'd assumed it would be longer than half a night. She sensed Gemma wasn't done with her half brother, but the last thing Mercedes wanted was for her to feel more pressure. There had to be a way to make staying here work, short of giving up her pets. "We could get a new mattress, get rid of all the old bedding. Keep your door closed…"

Gemma sniffled and leaned forward to dip her hands in the cool water. "There's no way to get rid of all the dander, no matter how clean your house is. It spreads. Gets in the ductwork." She sneezed three more times and followed it with a mild curse.

"Frustrating." Mercedes threw her head back and gazed at the stars, cradling her knees to her chest. "I'm sorry, Gem. We'll figure out something for you."

For several seconds Gemma kept her eyes on her hands, still gently splashing. "I know Scott has room. He used to have a roommate, so there has to be a second bedroom. He just needs to be convinced to give me a chance. That would buy me a month."

Mercedes stopped herself from saying the first thing that came to mind—namely, that Scott wasn't nice and she couldn't understand why she'd want to live with him.

"You're a seventeen-year-old girl and he's—"

"A twenty-eight-year-old paramedic with a chip on his shoulder."

"That sums him up pretty well. He must have a lot of things stressing him out."

"One of those things we have in common—a jerk of a father who screwed us over."

"Scott doesn't come across as the type who's going to sit and discuss what upsets him."

"Which works perfectly because I'm not, either," Gemma said. "I've wanted to meet him for a long time. I've come all this way. I'm not going to give up so easily."

"Why is he so important to you?" Mercedes managed to keep her voice nonjudgmental. "You've never even talked to him before yesterday, right?"

Gemma was quiet for some time. Pensive. "My family has been a mess since I was born, thanks in part to my dad. Scott was in the same situation and was able to walk away. Make his own life. I want to do that, Mercedes." There was steel beneath her words. "Ever since I learned of his existence, I've admired him for getting out. Envied him."

"After meeting him, I'm thinking living with him might not be as rosy as you've always imagined."

"No." Gemma shook her head adamantly. "I

don't expect rosy. I don't know… Maybe I kind of like the idea of having an older brother."

The words were understated, but the loneliness that drew her features downward yanked at Mercedes's heartstrings. She sensed it was difficult for this girl to admit needing anyone or anything.

"Feeling alone is hard," Mercedes said. "I'd loan you my sister anytime." She tried to lighten the mood a little.

"How old's your sister?"

"Four years older than me. Thirty-one. We're not very close. She's making her annual visit to Texas in a few days. And in truth, I wouldn't do that to you."

Gemma pulled her hands and feet out of the water and lay on her back on the pavement, gazing up at the sky, her jaw set. "Maybe I'm being dumb wanting to go back to Scott's, but one brush-off from him isn't enough to scare me away."

Mercedes lightly brushed Gemma's arm as she studied her. "It's not dumb if you really want to get to know him."

"I didn't find out about Scott and his mom until I was twelve," Gemma said. "My dad didn't live with us and only spent a few days a month with us. They told me it was because of his computer-sales job. That he had to live in Houston because of it. My mom has never been a stellar parent and I used to cling to his time with us. Never questioned the oddity."

"I can understand that. My dad died when I was ten," Mercedes said. "Motorcycle accident. After that, I would've given anything to have him back even part-time."

Gemma rolled to her side on the pavement and faced her. "That's rough. I'm sorry to hear that."

"Thanks. It's been a long time." Unfortunately, time had never made that hole in her life go away. "So what happened when you found out the truth?"

"Ugly, ugly blowup. I was pissed at the world. Hated my mom—would you believe she knew he was married the whole time? I detested my dad and wanted nothing to do with him. But when I found out about Scott…" She sat up a little clumsily because of the extra weight in her belly, bracing herself on her hands behind her. "I imagined him as an ally."

She smiled forlornly and Mercedes realized that was the first time she'd seen even a hint of a grin on Gemma's face. She really was a pretty girl when you got beyond the sullenness and stress. Especially once she washed off the dark eyeliner.

"After that, I kind of stalked him online. Found a bunch of mentions of him in old articles about his high school sports teams. Later as a para-medic, first in Houston, then here. Kind of crazy, I guess."

"No."

"I built him up in my head as having the ideal life."

"There's no such thing."

"I know that," Gemma said. "But I'd like to give his way a try." She sneezed and took a tis-sue out of a pocket in the hoodie she wore over Gumby boxers. "He might have a mean bark but I'm betting he's okay when you get past that."

"You could be right." Faith, Mercedes's fire-fighter friend who worked with Scott, had said as much when Mercedes had questioned her. "Are you sure you want to deal with the bluster, though?"

She nodded. "I need a place to live." She stated it as simply a fact, emotions aside. "You don't have to go with me. I've got this," Gemma said.

"I'm not letting you go by yourself."

Gemma tilted her head in surprise, stared at her as if waiting for her to rescind the offer, and that's when it really hit home how used to being alone Gemma was…how she expected to fight her battles on her own.

No more. She was seventeen and, though she seemed several years older, not quite a legal adult.

Everyone else had left her to her own devices. That wasn't okay with Mercedes.

"I don't know that he'd be my first choice for a roommate, but if that's what you want, we'll convince him to let you move in."

Gemma let that soak in, bit her lip against a grateful smile and lowered her gaze to the ground. After a few seconds, she looked back at Mercedes. "You know, I debated for over an hour whether to walk into the shelter yesterday or not. It's not really my way. But you are one pretty cool chick, Mercedes."

Mercedes squeezed Gemma's arm and tried to ignore the jitters the thought of going back to Scott's elicited. Yes, he was an intimidating guy, but that wasn't it. Not entirely.

There was something about him that…got to her. In spite of his efforts to scare everyone away, or maybe because of them, something about him intrigued her, beyond her general tendency to get involved when someone seemed troubled, as he most definitely did. It must have something to do with those eyes.

At this point in her life, when her first responsibility—very willingly on Mercedes's part—was to her dependent grandmother, she couldn't afford to be intrigued or sidetracked by any man's eyes or troubled soul or anything else.

But this wasn't about her, Mercedes reminded

herself. And if taking care of Gemma meant facing Scott Pataki again, she'd do it. No problem whatsoever.

CHAPTER FOUR

SCOTT KNEW WHO WAS AT the door before he answered it. And yet he opened it anyway. "You get an A+ for persistence."

"We brought lunch." Mercedes held out a large paper sack that smelled of Mexican food and said Ruiz's on the side.

Food wasn't going to sway him. He was about to tell them that, when Mercedes pushed past him into the living room.

"Mind if we invade your kitchen?" She was too cheerful as she stood distractingly close.

"Yes. I do." The kitchen wasn't fit for any visitor, let alone this woman who probably groomed her kitchen as well as she groomed herself. Say whatever else you wanted to about her, but she did make herself pretty and smelled nice, to boot. Like…springtime. He couldn't say what that meant, exactly, except the scent took him back to a time when life was easier. Lighter. He scowled at the thought.

"Here's fine, then." Mercedes shared a conspiratorial look with the teenager and helped herself to the couch and coffee table.

She must have found her stubborn, pushy mojo overnight. Wasn't he lucky?

She'd dressed casually today, wearing short jean shorts and a white tank with the women's shelter logo on it instead of the preppy tailored clothes she'd had on yesterday. She was average height with nicer-than-average curves he couldn't help noticing. Her dark wavy hair was everywhere, though she'd tried to control it by pulling the front parts back with a clip. Her calculating smile at Gemma highlighted prominent cheekbones and drew his attention to her glossy lips.

If she wasn't so bent on steamrolling him about being this girl's knight in shining armor, he might have given thought to getting to know her on a more personal level. Short-term, of course.

"We got a baker's dozen plus chips and salsa. There's plenty for you," she said.

"I'm not hungry," he lied. "But don't let that stop you."

They missed the sarcasm completely…or didn't care that they weren't welcome. Gemma, lacking the awful eye makeup today, curled up on the near end of the couch, tucking her feet under her, and Mercedes bent over the bag to unpack it, giving him a shot of cleavage she hadn't been sporting the day before. When she straightened, she caught him getting an eyeful. She quickly darted her glance away, looking slightly disconcerted. Nervous.

"I'm starving." Gemma tossed a piece of fish that had fallen out of her tortilla into her mouth. "So." She leaned forward, chewing then licking sauce off her finger. "About your spare bedroom…"

"I never said I have a spare bedroom."

"Do you?" Gemma asked.

He had to admit a little admiration for her guts and directness. He leaned against the wall, realizing these two had every intention of drawing things out. "Yes."

"I can give you two hundred dollars if you let me stay here till you leave. Plus, I'll clean. You're going to need that before you move out." She shot a concerned look around her as she raised her food to take another bite.

"Where'd you get two hundred dollars?" he asked.

"I brought it with me."

"And yet you took my money for a bus ticket?"

"I gave it back."

He couldn't argue with that. "I thought Mercedes had come to your rescue."

Mercedes became absorbed in dipping a chip in salsa.

"That's not going to work out," Gemma said.

"She's allergic to my cats," Mercedes said as if she felt guilty. "Poor girl ended up sleeping outside on one of the loungers for half the night."

"I've slept in much worse places, trust me." Gemma brushed her shoulder-length hair behind her ear, a dangly bracelet jingling with the movement.

Both women watched him expectantly. He could feel their gazes burning into him.

What was his hang-up, really? What did he care who slept in the other room, as long as they didn't bug him? The rent money couldn't hurt. And yet...this wasn't someone off the streets with no ties to him.

"You're a minor," he said stubbornly.

"Technicality. I'll be eighteen soon. The first of August. I'm going to be a mom, Scott. I can take care of myself."

Scott pushed himself off the wall in disbelief. "Are you planning to keep this baby?"

Gemma returned his stare with a stubborn one of her own. "I am. Yes."

"Gemma needs a place to stay temporarily," Mercedes said in a rush, as if she sensed he was about to voice what a stupid idea keeping a baby was for a seventeen-year-old. "While she looks for a job and gets her future figured out. The baby is a few months down the road. You'll be long gone."

"I'm not a babysitter. For a baby or a teenager."

"We're not asking you to be." Mercedes had stopped eating after one taco. "She's been on her own for years for all intents. Gemma doesn't need you to take care of her."

Something about the way Mercedes looked at him said they expected too much of him. Hell, expecting anything of him was too much. They had no clue how just being in the same room with this girl, this part of his dad's other family, ripped him up inside.

Scott took a long look at Gemma, defiantly ignoring Mercedes's stare. He was still boggled by how similar Gemma's eyes were to his father's. The narrowness, the oval shape. The light hazel color. He dropped his gaze to her nose and lips. The nose was nothing like his father's—delicate and thin where his overwhelmed his face. And the lips...her upper one was fuller than the lower and had a distinctive bow to it. Not a single hint of Dale in her mouth—and Scott found himself fixated on that fact. Wondering for the first time about the woman who had lured his dad away from his happy family. Were these that woman's lips, her nose? Was it the dip at the top of her mouth that had caught his father's attention?

Scott stormed into the kitchen without a word. He leaned over the dirty dish-filled sink, arms propped on the counter, and worked to get the anger under control. Damn, he hated feeling like this. Seemed as if he spent more time worked up than not anymore.

It took him several seconds to focus on breathing evenly before he realized he wasn't alone. He straightened quickly and turned the faucet on without a glance at the doorway, then retrieved the last clean glass from the cabinet and filled it with water. When he'd downed the full glass, he set it on the counter and finally looked.

Mercedes, of course.

MERCEDES HAD FROZEN as soon as she'd reached the kitchen and seen Scott leaning on the sink looking…vulnerable. Not so tough. She didn't want to sympathize with him for any reason, but that glimpse of a different side of him had caught her off guard.

"Where are my manners?" Scott said sarcastically. "I forgot to offer you a drink."

She eyed the bottle of whiskey he'd left, uncapped, on the counter. It was more than half gone and she wondered just how long it'd taken him to work through that much hard liquor.

"I had water in mind," he said, "but I can pour you a shot or even a full glass if you want."

She opened her mouth to respond then stopped, reminding herself he was going out of his way to irritate her. Any trace of sympathy she'd experienced not two minutes ago was long gone. "I'm fine but Gemma needs to drink a lot."

"Thought you said she doesn't need anyone to take care of her."

The anger underlining his words was subtle but very much there. Something had set him off in the living room. She had no idea what. It certainly wasn't going to deter her.

"She's got a lot on her mind, if you hadn't noticed."

"Don't we all." He walked over to the refrigerator and took out a mini can of vegetable juice. He tossed it to Mercedes and she managed to catch it with both hands. "Give her that. You've decided I'm the scum of the earth, haven't you?"

"You've worked hard to make me believe that," she said, walking closer to him. "I'm not sure I understand why."

"Here's what you don't understand. The reason I'm not lining up to be best friends or even roomies with that girl in there…" He braced one hand on the counter and narrowed his eyes. Eyes full of something more than just anger. "I have a problem with the fact that my dad fathered her while he was married, theoretically happily, to my mother. I can't so much as look at her without all…that coming back."

He turned away, seeming to regret revealing that little bit.

"I'm sorry, Scott," she said gently as she tried to imagine what that discovery must have done to him. "How old were you when you found out?"

"Does it matter?" he snapped.

"I guess not," she conceded. "It'd pretty much suck at any age."

He met her gaze again, sizing up her sincerity. "It's ancient history."

She studied him closely, realizing there was more to him than his gruff, irritable surface. Layers more. "Maybe not so ancient to you?" she asked.

In response, he reached around her and scooted the whiskey bottle closer. He stiffened when she touched his forearm.

"Gemma's a victim just as much as you are, you know. She had no control over...anything. Your dad hurt her, too. She hasn't heard from him in four years."

His jaw tightened as he considered that. Seconds passed. A minute and more. She was about to turn and leave him alone when he moved. He held out his hand and nodded toward the veggie juice. Mercedes handed it back to him, expecting him to blow up and yell at them to leave.

Scott stared blankly at the can for a few moments, then walked past her into the living room.

Curious, Mercedes leaned against the doorjamb between the two rooms and watched. Scott sat next to Gemma, who was still shoveling food into her mouth as if unsure when she'd get to eat again, and handed the juice to her.

"Thanks, I think," Gemma said, sounding surprised. She took the can and read the label. "Is this stuff really drinkable?"

"It's healthy for the baby."

Looking unsure, she popped the top open. Smelled it, frowned and took a sip. She didn't bother to hide a shudder, making Mercedes stifle a grin. "That crap is vile."

"Maybe it's not for everyone," Scott said, leaning forward to rest his forearms on his thighs. "Cleaning this place is a big task."

Gemma watched him, the look on her face mirroring Mercedes's curiosity.

"I've seen worse," Gemma said carefully.

"You've got a month," Scott said, not looking at his half sister. "Keep the place clean for me and hold on to your money."

"You've got a deal."

The teen played it cool, but Mercedes could see her eyes spark with relief.

A full month. They could work with that. Gemma could get a job, start searching for a more permanent place to stay and begin figuring out how to provide for her baby.

"I'm not agreeing to be your babysitter or your friend," Scott said, scowling to offset Gemma's instant relief. "I'm not home much."

"Fine."

He addressed Mercedes. "I work twenty-four-hour shifts. She'll be alone a lot."

"I'll be around to help her." Mercedes pushed off the doorjamb and walked to the coffee table. "I'm not going to desert her."

"You stay out of my business and I'll stay out of yours," Scott said, turning back to Gemma.

"Where's my room?"

He leaned back, defeated in his quest to scare her away. "The room on the right of the hall."

Gemma tried to keep her poise as she passed Mercedes.

As soon as Gemma was gone, Mercedes lowered herself to the edge of the couch beside Scott, keeping a good distance between them. "Thank you," she said, fiddling with a silver band on her little finger. "I take back all the nasty thoughts I had about you."

Scott opened his mouth to say something but stopped and looked sideways at her in surprise. Then he actually smiled.

The guy had killer dimples.

Mercedes had a thing for dimples.

Luckily, his grin slipped away before she could blink and he said, "I'm going to regret this."

It wasn't hard to remember why dimples weren't everything.

IMMEDIATELY AFTER Gemma and her guard dog Mercedes left, Scott's regret set in.

Agreeing to let the teenager move in was a dumb decision. Asinine. Just thinking about it—about her, her relationship to him, her insistence on meeting him in the first place—had him vibrating with anger.

He had only a couple hours left before they showed up to move Gemma in officially. He headed toward the shower, pulling his shirt off on the way. He had to get out of here, be gone when they arrived. Stay gone for as long as possible. Gone was going to become his new motto. For thirty-five more days.

Why the hell had he caved?

Because the woman with the long, alluring hair had worn him down with the line about Gemma being a victim just like him. He hadn't realized his dad had left Gemma's family, too. That'd taken him by surprise, but still. One weak moment.

Gemma had some screwed-up idea that they could be friends. She hadn't said so, but there wasn't a doubt in his mind.

Wasn't going to happen.

Letting her move in was his good deed of the day. Hell, the year. He was behind a few. That was all it was, though. He wasn't getting friendly with anyone. Wasn't going to make any ties. The job on the ship was the best thing that'd happened in a long time. He'd been a lone wolf for ten years and didn't want or need any entanglements hanging over him when he left.

When he was done showering, he threw on jeans and a T-shirt and stalked through the apartment, to the kitchen. Still agitated. Antsy.

The bottle of whiskey on the counter beckoned to him. Promised sweet oblivion.

He succumbed to the call without hesitation, feeling like the oldest twenty-eight-year-old on the face of the planet. Twenty-eight going on forty. Looked it, too.

Time to get gone, he reminded himself. But not without his good friend oblivion. He picked up the bottle and headed out of the apartment.

CHAPTER FIVE

IT'D BEEN ALL MERCEDES could do to wait until nine o'clock this morning to check on Gemma at Scott's apartment. She fully suspected the girl could handle herself okay, but that didn't alleviate the guilt Mercedes felt for leaving her to the wolf.

To avoid making Gemma think Mercedes didn't trust her, she planned to treat the teenager to breakfast.

She climbed the steps outside Scott's apartment, again registering the clamor of various neighbors and hoping Gemma had been able to get some peaceful rest. As she was about to knock on the door, she noticed it was mostly shut but not latched all the way. She tapped lightly to prevent it from popping open.

When no one answered, it occurred to her that Gemma might still be asleep. And who knew where Scott was. Maybe he worked today. She knocked again, a little harder, causing the door to inch closer to opening.

Mercedes's chest tightened as her imagination took flight and projected all kinds of bad scenarios. She checked the doorknob—maybe it was locked and whoever had closed it had merely failed to notice they hadn't pushed it far enough.

It wasn't locked. Anyone could walk in. She shuddered with the realization and eased the door open a few inches.

"Gemma?" Her voice was gravelly with fear and she cleared her throat. "Gem?"

No movement or sound came from the apartment. Mercedes eased the door farther open and stepped inside.

Her heart lodged in her throat at the first thing she saw—or rather, the first person.

Scott was sprawled facedown on the couch, his bare feet hanging over the edge. His wrinkled clothes were twisted around him.

"Scott?"

He didn't stir.

She stared at his torso for several seconds, trying to ascertain that he was breathing. She moved closer and was overcome by the smell of sour alcohol, or more specifically, the smell of someone who had alcohol coming out of his pores.

Mercedes clamped her teeth together audibly and stepped backward, unsure of which was winning—disgust or anger.

"Unbelievable," she said, more to herself than the comatose, irresponsible—

"Mercedes?" Gemma's sleepy voice startled her from behind and she spun around.

"Gemma, are you okay?"

"Why wouldn't I be? What's wrong?" Gemma's hair stuck every which way. She wore the same Gumby boxers and a black tee printed with the name of a band Mercedes didn't know.

"I woke you up," Mercedes said apologetically.

"No big deal." Gemma walked past her, staring at her roommate. "Scott?"

Mercedes took in a slow breath, trying to soothe her temper. "Good luck getting a response from him."

Gemma chuckled. "Is he alive?"

"For now. I'm seriously considering killing him. Was he home when you went to bed?" To think Mercedes had been relieved he was gone when they'd brought in the mattress they'd borrowed from Faith's parents and the rest of Gemma's admittedly few things.

"This is the first I've seen him since we brought him lunch yesterday." Gemma stopped grinning, as if realizing Mercedes wasn't as amused by Scott's state. "Maybe he came in late and didn't want to bother me by walking by my room."

"Or maybe he was too drunk to find the way to his room." Mercedes went over and shoved his feet as she spoke.

Scott slowly turned his head from one side to

the other and muttered something unintelligible. His face was an odd shade of green. Mercedes put some distance between herself and the dead-weight on the couch, recognizing her urge to do him physical harm was dangerously overpowering.

She turned to Gemma, her back to Scott. "I'm craving the breakfast platter from Egg City. Eggs, biscuits and gravy, bacon. I was hoping you'd go with me."

"Do they have chocolate-chip pancakes?"

"And blueberry, and banana nut…"

"Let me get dressed."

"Take your time. Shower if you want."

Gemma hurried to her bedroom and Mercedes turned toward Scott, unsure what to do about him but concerned in spite of herself. He'd of course passed out again.

She sat on the coffee table, facing him, eyes narrowed and arms crossed. He must have sensed her stare because his eyelids fluttered, as if they'd been cemented shut and he had to fight to open them. When he'd finally won the battle, it took seconds, lots of them, for him to focus on Mercedes and recognize her. She could tell when he did because he did some near-dead semblance of a grimace.

"We told you we didn't need you to babysit, but would it be too much to ask for you to take care of yourself?" she said, fighting to keep her voice even and her volume low enough Gemma wouldn't hear.

Scott groaned and again said something she couldn't understand. Something she probably didn't want to understand, judging by the kiss-off tone.

"Is this your usual Saturday-night fare, Scott? Or something you do nightly?" She rose from the table, paced the floor, biting down on so many things she wanted to say. She wasn't generally confrontational, but some things pushed her too far.

Behind her, Scott rustled around noisily and groaned, obviously suffering. Good. He deserved it.

She involuntarily turned toward him when he made a particularly pained sound. He was sitting up and his face had drained even of the green tint. Recognizing what was happening, she sprang into action, glancing around frantically. There—a popcorn bowl on the floor, littered with unpopped kernels. She grabbed it, dumping the kernels on the floor and flying to Scott's side with it, holding the bowl at arm's length.

He took it from her and emptied his stomach, but she didn't stick around for details. God, really?

In the kitchen, Mercedes grabbed a handful of

paper towels and dampened them with cold water. Then she found a large plastic cup in the cabinet, appreciative that Gemma had started her cleaning crusade in this room last night, and filled it with water and several ice cubes from the freezer. As she worked, she registered the sound of the shower running at the other end of the apartment. Thank goodness Gemma was otherwise occupied and didn't have to witness her unheroic half brother's disgusting antics.

When she returned to the living room, Scott was gone. So was the bowl, she noted, grateful as she'd never been before that he hadn't left it behind. The front door was still closed and she hadn't heard him leave, so she headed down the hall past Gemma's room, past the closed bathroom door. There was only one other door and it was open.

Mercedes peered into Scott's bedroom. Piles of clothes lined the floor and a stack of paperbacks towered unevenly next to the head of the bed. The queen-size mattress was one big tangle of sheets and blankets pushed toward the foot. But no Scott.

He stumbled out of what she assumed was an adjoining bathroom then, his color only slightly more human. With an angry glance at her, he continued then and collapsed onto his bed.

Concern nagged at her. Scott wasn't some low-tolerance, novice drinker. That was obvious from the bottle on the kitchen counter. It had to take a lot of liquor for him to be this messed up.

Without hesitation, she barreled into the room to his bedside. "Put this on your forehead," she said, holding out the wet paper towels.

He shifted slightly, moving only his head and only the minimum amount necessary to look up at her. When he didn't respond further, Mercedes placed the towel on his forehead herself, half expecting him to jump up and yell at her. That he didn't just reaffirmed her worry.

"I brought you some ice water when you think you can get it down." She set the cup on the cluttered nightstand and again noticed the stack of books. He wasn't the type she'd ever guess was into reading.

"I don't know much about alcohol poisoning, but…are you going to be okay?" she asked, noting he didn't budge an inch when she took her hand away from the towel.

"I'm fine," he said shortly.

"This doesn't seem like 'fine' to me."

"Go away. Not your day to save me."

She studied his pale face, trying to make concessions for how he must feel right now. It'd been years, but she'd had hangovers before. None as extreme as this, however.

"I said leave."

Who was she to argue if he wanted to asphyxiate on his own vomit? If she stayed here for another minute, she might just stick the towel in his mouth and help him.

"Enjoy your morning, Scott," she said with a falsely sweet voice as she left him alone.

A HEAVY, SUFFOCATING MASS of self-loathing weighed on Scott when he woke up later.

To say his head throbbed would be an understatement. It felt as if someone was taking a pickax to it, chipping away for a treasure. But that was the least of his misery—more urgent and unbearable was the churning in his gut. He breathed in slow and evenly to fight off the nausea.

The worst part of it, as if feeling like death warmed over wasn't bad enough, was the fact that he'd lost a large chunk of his night. No recollection whatsoever of what he'd done or where he'd been for several hours. How he'd gotten home. When. Who'd seen him being out of his damn head.

He'd left the apartment on foot, so as long as his Mazda was still out in the parking lot in the same spot, he could be pretty sure he hadn't driven. Thank freaking God. Wouldn't that be swell to have his colleagues come peel his remains up from the street somewhere.

He hadn't felt this bad in...ever. He was a guy

with fast metabolism. His hangovers, when he had them, were minor, maybe requiring a couple ibuprofen. At least they used to be.

He raised himself slowly to sit against the head-board and breathe, then he shut his eyes to stave off the vertigo effect of moving and blanked his mind.

When he eased his eyes open several minutes later, the cup of water on the nightstand caught his attention like prime rib to a homeless man. He reached for it with a shaky hand, sloshing water over the side. The ice had melted, but the liquid was still cool. Only after he'd taken several sips did he stop to think about where it'd come from.

Jesus. Mercedes had seen him like this. He hated that anyone witnessed his worst, but her, someone who had her act together, whose bad moments probably consisted of an uncharacter-istic swearword slipping from those feminine lips…that didn't sit well at all.

He looked around for the wet towel he thought he remembered, found the wad of paper towels on the mattress next to the pillow. He groaned as he carefully leaned his head back. He'd never hear the end of it, but even worse than dread was bone-deep shame.

This wasn't the man he'd set out to be.

With that thought, the taste of bile filled his

mouth. He rushed to the bathroom, disregarding the pounding of his head, and got sick again.

Afterward, he wilted against the wall, shaking from the inside out, a sheen of sweat coating his forehead and neck.

When he could summon the energy, he stretched up just enough to turn on the shower, leaving the temperature cold. Clothes still on, he crawled in, let the icy water pelt his face and wished it could wash him right down the drain.

CHAPTER SIX

MERCEDES'S SISTER, CHARLIE, had been in town for six hours now. Not that Mercedes was counting down the time of her visit or anything…yet. As usual, it'd been really good to see Charlie at the door. It no longer even bothered Mercedes that her sister refused to allow anyone to pick her up at the airport—she never had, preferring to show up in a cab. Now that Gram wasn't mobile or very portable, it worked out for the best anyway.

Gram's excitement was infectious, and Mercedes always enjoyed hearing the latest from New York and her sister's life, which had turned out so different from Mercedes's.

Now the two of them flanked Gram, who sat in her wheelchair on the screened-in porch on the back of the house. Mercedes had opened a bottle of wine with dinner and her second glass was just starting to relax her.

"So," Charlie said, holding her glass by the stem and slowly spinning it between her fingers and thumb. "I have something to run by you two."

The announcement made Mercedes sit up a little straighter in the cushioned wicker patio chair. She forced her thoughts away from Gemma and how she was faring with her hungover roommate.

She studied her sister for a hint. Charlie set her glass on the mosaic end table to her left and grasped her straight dark hair—tinted this time with reddish-pink highlights—at the nape and let it fall down her back. Mercedes had always envied her straight, manageable hair. Charlie moistened her lips, looking unsure of herself for once, and that, more than anything, put Mercedes officially on alert.

"What's up?" Mercedes said, overcome by curiosity. Her sister never ran anything by her family.

"What is it, Charlotte?" Gram was the only person who could get away with calling Charlie by her given name. She struggled to smooth out the blanket Mercedes had draped over her legs, her left hand severely limited due to the stroke she'd suffered, so Mercedes reached over and helped. It was still eighty-five degrees outside even though the sun had set, but Gram's frail body didn't hold much heat anymore.

"I've decided to move to San Amaro." The words came out in a rush and hung in the humid air surreally. They were the last ones Mercedes had ever expected her sister to say, and they didn't immediately sink in. "I was wondering how you would feel about me living here, at least for a while."

Mercedes's brain worked its way around the equally unexpected question. "Here? As in, in this house?"

"Yes." Charlie was normally so confident, but now she sounded unsure of herself. Leaning forward, she twisted her hair around her finger. "Just for three or four months, maybe. I want to buy a place eventually, but I don't want to rush any decisions. I'd rather take my time, get to know the area better before shelling out money for my own home."

Mercedes was still trying to process the idea—and the feelings it evoked—when Gram spoke. "Heavens, we'd love to have you, honey. You know you're always welcome. The guest bedroom is yours for as long as you want it."

Welcome, sure. But live here? Her New York City, jewelry-designer sister? "Why?"

"I… Well, I just thought since there's an extra bedroom…"

"I mean, why are you moving to San Amaro?" Mercedes clarified, aware of the frown her grandma shot her. "What about your job?"

"I quit, actually."

For ten full seconds, the room was quiet except for the evening sounds from the backyard—the distant hum of the air conditioner, some crickets, a lonely birdcall.

"You quit your job? At Montague?" As far as Mercedes knew, Charlie had always loved designing high-end costume jewelry for one of the most reputable companies in the industry. She'd worked her way up to the top designing position and had a great deal of influence.

"That's the one." Charlie laughed nervously. "The pressure and the long hours were getting to me. I decided it was time for a change."

"What about Jeff?" Mercedes had met Charlie's boyfriend only twice, but he and her sister had been together for three or four years and lived together.

"We split up. I let him have the apartment." Charlie tried to keep her voice void of emotion, but there was a suspicious waver in it.

"You left Jeff?" Gram said, sounding slightly scandalized.

"Something like that." Charlie again tried to chuckle, and Mercedes discerned a hint of sadness. "We...grew apart. It was time to move on."

Mercedes wondered how many more clichés her sister could throw out. "Did he leave you?"

Charlie's false happiness crashed and she hesitated, studying her fingernails, which had leopard spots painted on them. "He said he didn't love me anymore."

Mercedes leaned forward, tamping down the urge to hug her sister. "That's rough, Charlie. Maybe he'll come to his senses. Figure out he made a mistake."

"The following weekend, I saw him at dinner with one of his female coworkers. Clearly not talking about business."

"Oh, Charlotte." Gram reached out her right hand across her body, toward Charlie. Charlie took her offered hand, looking as if tears were close.

"How long ago did all this happen?" Mercedes asked, feeling helpless.

"Four weeks."

"You could have called me." Mercedes's offer was genuine, though she and her sister had never been confidantes.

Charlie met her gaze over Gram's head. "I wish I had."

Again, Mercedes tried to hide her surprise at the uncharacteristic admission. This breakup had messed with her sister big-time.

"So what do you say, Sadie?" Charlie asked with a forced smile. "You're hesitating. Are you okay with me moving in?"

Hesitating. Yes, she was. How selfish was she?

Though Charlie's weeklong visits always started out well, usually by two to three days into them, Mercedes was ready for them to be over. It was challenging for a household of two to adjust to being three, even for a short period of time.

Obviously, Charlie needed her family as she never had before. "Of course I'm okay with it. There's plenty of room."

Charlie exhaled and sagged against the back of her chair. "Thank you both."

"You didn't really think we'd say no, did you?" Mercedes asked in a gentle voice, regretting that she'd hesitated.

"I'm trying not to take things for granted." Charlie again became engrossed in her fingernails, running one index finger up and down over the nail of the other. "Jeff set something off in me. Or rather, the lack of Jeff did. Not right away. I was too in shock to think straight for the first week." She paused when her voice wavered. "It's weird how fleeting people can be in our lives. Disturbing. You know?"

Gram nodded somberly. Mercedes had had that exact thought many times. There weren't many in her life who were there for the long haul. Gram. Faith and Nadia. Most times she'd hesitate to put Charlie on that list. "I've noticed that."

It wasn't surprising they'd made the same conclusion, considering the losses they'd suffered early in life. Their dad's death. Mom's paralysis from the same accident. Mom's eventual death.

"It made me realize that family is it. Those

are the only people who stick around. And stupid me, over the years, I've put so much distance between myself and the only family I have left that we barely know each other."

"That's true." Mercedes couldn't sugarcoat that no matter how much she wanted to.

Gram darted an alarmed glance at Mercedes.

"I decided it was time to change that. So here I am."

"Here you are," Mercedes repeated, trying to quash any doubt. She didn't question that her sister meant what she was saying. But Charlie had had a giant emotional blow, big enough to make her take some drastic action. Who knew what she'd do once she'd leveled out a bit. Gotten back to "normal." Her norm had always been putting distance between them. And maybe that was the crux of her concern about her sister moving in. How long would she stay this time?

"What are you planning to do for a job?" Mercedes asked. There wasn't a jewelry market in San Amaro like the one she was used to in New York. In fact, there wasn't a jewelry market at all, unless you counted stringing shells together on a leather cord.

"You've always loved your career," Gram pointed out.

"Yes. Past tense. Loved the paycheck, too. I won't make half as much here, but I'm fine with that. I've got enough stashed away that I can make it on a fraction of the income."

"You can live with us longer than three months if you need to, you know." Gram addressed Charlie but smiled at Mercedes, her joy at having both her granddaughters close tangible.

"Thanks, Gram. I don't know what I'll be doing by then. Maybe I'll open my own gallery. Maybe I'll paint caricatures for tourists. Maybe I'll take a cooking class and open a restaurant on the beach." She laughed quietly. "I don't know. I could do anything."

"So what can I do to help you?" Mercedes asked. "Do you want to update your résumé? Want me to watch job listings? Introduce you to people? Look for houses?"

"You don't have to do anything—" Annoyance slipped into Charlie's tone, but she stopped short and took in an audible deep breath. "Okay, forget I said that. I know that's your way. I'd love your help as soon as I figure out what's first."

"Just let me know."

The three of them discussed logistics and details for several minutes, though there wasn't a lot to plan. Charlie had no intention of flying back east—she'd purchased a one-way ticket. She'd willingly left her furniture with her ex, had put the rest of her belongings in storage and would have them shipped.

When there was a lull in the conversation, Mercedes spoke up, more than ready to call it a night so she could reflect on everything in private—and organize herself for work tomorrow. Nothing worse than starting the week out behind. "It's past your bedtime, Gram. Are you getting tired?"

"I guess I am," Gram said. "Too much excitement for this old lady." Her happiness rang through her thin voice.

"Let's get you inside." Mercedes stood, released the wheelchair's brakes and maneuvered it toward the door.

"Can I help?" Charlie asked, sitting forward on her chair.

"That's okay. You relax," Mercedes said over her shoulder. "You've been traveling all day."

When Mercedes opened the back door, Spike, their oversize white cat, rushed out onto the porch.

"Spike, get back in there. You know better." The cat disappeared under Charlie's chair. "There's a job for you," Mercedes said. "See if you can get Spike back inside."

"Sure. Okay." Her sister's reply was curt.

She was the one who'd offered to help.

As Mercedes rolled Gram into her bedroom, they heard a crash and Charlie swearing out on the porch. Mercedes couldn't help grinning. "Guess Spike doesn't want to be caught."

"That cat thinks he's a wild tiger."

"Until he gets hungry." Mercedes pulled the chair up to the left side of the bed and set the brakes.

"Just leave the back door open," Gram suggested. "He'll wander in as soon as you turn my light out. Has to claim his spot at my feet, you know."

"True. This is more fun, though."

"I'm not sure Spike or Charlotte would agree." Gram chuckled. "I'm thrilled she wants to stay with us. I just hope she's okay."

"I'm sure she is. She's a tough one," Mercedes said as she helped Gram to her bed.

She worried that Gram was so thin, yet she was thankful she didn't weigh more every time they did this. The process was slow, and Gram's muscles shook with the effort, but the therapist had told them countless times that it was good for her to use those muscles.

Once they'd gotten her situated and tucked in, Mercedes went into Gram's bathroom and sorted out the bedtime pills she needed. She carried them and a warm washcloth out to Gram.

"Your sister seemed to appreciate the dinner you made tonight," Gram said, taking the cloth from Mercedes. "It's good she's moving back. I don't think she gets many home-cooked meals in New York."

"I eat well, home-cooked or not," Charlie said as she walked into the room. "The cat's in. Stubborn feline. Do you want me to get you a drink or anything, Gram?"

"I usually get her some ice water to drink while she watches the news," Mercedes said.

"Got it." Charlie saluted and headed for the kitchen.

"That's my girl. Thank you, honey."

It was stupid and petty for Mercedes to be irritated, but she couldn't help it. Whenever Charlie visited, Gram was so pleased to have her company. The New York sister was a novelty. All because Charlie had run away.

If Charlie left again, if the island didn't live up to her expectations or she decided she missed the center of the jewelry world, Mercedes would be the one, once again, left to pick up the pieces. For their grandmother.

For herself.

CHAPTER SEVEN

SCOTT WISHED HE WAS less interested in the sight that met him in his apartment Wednesday morning after his shift.

He entered quietly, expecting Gemma to be asleep. Though he wasn't going out of his way to get to know her, he could say with certainty she wasn't a morning person. Something they had in common.

When he walked into the kitchen, he halted. Mercedes was standing on the bar with her arms above her, wiping down the main light fixture, her back to him.

It'd be hard for any red-blooded male not to appreciate the feminine body before his eyes. The fact that she had barged into his thoughts more than once since the last embarrassing time he'd seen her made denying any attraction difficult.

Khaki shorts covered that nicely rounded ass of hers. She wore a plain orange tank top that had inched up to reveal a strip of soft-looking, tanned skin at her waist. Her sandals wrapped complexly up her ankles like some kind of Roman fashion statement—a strangely hot one. She'd gathered her hair in a sloppy bunch on the back of her head, and bits of it cascaded sexily at her nape.

"What are you doing here?" he snapped, reacting to the increase in his heart rate.

Mercedes startled and whipped around to face him. "It turns out Gemma has an obsessive-compulsive side to be reckoned with," Mercedes said. She reached up and wiped down the long, flat surface of the fluorescent light. "She was obsessing about dust on this thing. I don't want her climbing up here in her condition."

"I can take care of it. It's not your responsibility."

"It's just about done now." She finished and lowered herself to the edge of the counter then jumped down to the floor.

"Why are you in my apartment before 8:00 a.m.?"

Mercedes washed her hands, acting oblivious to his mood. She reached behind him for a dry towel. "I'm giving Gemma a ride to her job. Supposed to be there at eight-thirty."

"Don't you have your own job?"

"I work at home. My hours are flexible so I can take care of my grandma. Or give a friend a ride to work when necessary," she said pointedly.

"Since when does Gemma have a job?"

"You live with her. Don't you talk to her?"

"Not if I can help it. I told you she's a roommate. Nothing more." He opened the refrigerator, took out a tube of ready-to-bake cinnamon rolls, pressed the preheat button on the oven and searched in the cabinets for a pan suitable to bake them on.

"She found a babysitting gig," Mercedes said curtly.

"Good for her. She can get some practice." He found a shiny cookie sheet he didn't remember seeing before and started placing the doughy rolls in a circle on it.

"Why are you like this?" She stood with her arms crossed near the doorway, as far from him as she could get without leaving the room.

Good.

"Like what?"

Mercedes chuckled insincerely. "So unhappy. Determined to make everyone around you miserable."

"You're making a lot of assumptions based on two previous meetings."

"Am I wrong?"

"I told you the reason I don't like being around her," he finally said, keeping his focus on the rolls. "There's a lot of history that can't just be undone in a couple of days." He felt her staring at him from the side and refused to look at her.

"So why do you act that way toward me?"

Because she looked like that and smelled like that and threatened to awaken things inside him he didn't want awakened. Not now. Not when he was on his way out of town. Not ever, really.

"I don't see the point in getting closer to her or anyone when I'm leaving so soon," he finally said, arranging the last pastry on the pan.

"That's a lame excuse, if you ask me."

He bit down on a retort, recognizing she didn't deserve his wrath. Though he would never win any friendliness awards under usual circumstances, he was being exceptionally unfriendly to Mercedes.

"So you said you were going to be the scuba director in your new job?" she asked, taking two steps toward him.

"That's right."

"Do you dive often?"

Understanding that she wasn't going to cease and desist anytime soon, or at least not soon enough for his liking, he stuck the pan in the oven and turned toward her. "No. I do enough to keep up my certification."

"When's the last time you had fun?" she asked.

"Fun? Really? I couldn't tell you. When's the last time you had fun?"

She squinted pensively for a few seconds. "Just last week. I beat my grandma at Scrabble. Clobbered her, actually."

He grinned before he could stop himself, mostly because he suspected she was serious. "Sad."

She frowned and turned away and, dammit, he felt a flickering of remorse for being such an incessant asshole to her. She was probably a kind person—hell, he knew she was just by her treatment of Gemma. Then there was the way she'd tried to take care of him the other day when he'd been nearly dead from a hangover. He'd worked hard ever since to be pissed by her intrusion, but he couldn't quite pull it off. It'd been a damn long time since anyone had gone out of their way to be nice to him. Especially someone who looked as good as Mercedes.

Mercedes checked her watch. "I thought Gemma wanted to be there early today. Wonder what's holding her up."

"She's a teenage female." He leaned against the counter a few feet away, facing her. "Listen," he said, looking at the floor. "I'm sorry I was an ass last weekend."

"Oh." She seemed surprised. "It's...okay."

He scoffed. Shook his head. "It's not okay. I was—" He broke off and shook his head again. "You should've walked away the second you saw me."

"I didn't want your death on my conscience," she said with a shy smile.

"The cup of water you left may have saved my life, once I was coherent enough to notice it."

"That's…good." Looking uncomfortable, Mercedes took two long strides to the doorway and looked into the hall toward Gemma's room. She was fidgety when she turned back around and returned to the counter.

He was mildly amused that he was making her nervous. She seemed to handle him better when he was acting like a jerk. Though making her uncomfortable wasn't his objective, he pressed on. "What I'm trying to say is thanks. For…you know."

"I didn't do much."

"Did more than most people would do for a stinking hungover jerk."

She ran her fingers back and forth over the edge of the counter, meeting his gaze. "I'm trying to find a way to argue that." A grin tugged at her lips. "But I can't."

He closed the space between them and put his hand over hers, surprising them both. He pulled it away quickly, but not before registering the jolt of pleasure that shot through him at the smallest touch of her baby-smooth skin. He cleared his throat and took a step away. Without looking at her, he said, "I'm embarrassed you saw me like that."

Before she could say anything, a sturdy knock sounded at the door.

Scott frowned then walked past her to answer it. He was still mumbling to himself about the stupidity of touching Mercedes when he flung the door open and momentarily had the power of speech stunned out of him.

As seconds and half a lifetime ticked by, Scott's mouth went dry. Rage was unleashed in him as suddenly as if he'd been struck by lightning as he stared down the man who'd ruined his family.

His father.

"Scott." The single word seemed amplified, the voice familiar and yet aged, gravelly around the edges.

Scott noticed his own jaw was clamped shut hard and his hands shook with anger. He gripped the doorknob with all his strength and tried to formulate words.

"It's me. Your father."

"I know who you are." He was surprised at how calm his own voice sounded. "The question is what the hell you think you're doing here."

There was movement in the hall behind him, but Scott barely registered it. Couldn't care less who it was, as his primary objective was either getting his father the hell out of here or cutting him down to make him hurt.

"I came to take my daughter home," his dad said. "Gemma. Is she here?"

Scott stared at his father. The man looked like hell. His hair, once brown, was gray, verging on white in places. Frown lines gave him the appearance of jowls, and he'd put on a good thirty to forty pounds around the middle. His brown eyes were flat. Tired. He looked more similar to Gemma in Scott's memory than he did in person. His dad cleared his throat, obviously ill at ease. As he damn well should be.

"Takes a lot of nerve—or stupidity—to show up at my door after all this time."

His dad looked to the side, maybe at whoever was standing several feet behind Scott, then rubbed his finger absently down the side of his large nose. "I'm not going to get into the past with you right now. Where is Gemma?"

Scott was torn. If he handed over Gemma, that'd get her out of his hair, but it was what his father wanted. The father who hadn't taken anyone but himself into consideration years ago, who hadn't once tracked Scott down since he'd left. When faced with that choice, it hit Scott that Gemma really wasn't much trouble. She'd stayed out of his way for the most part. Though he barely knew Gemma, Mercedes had mentioned this man at his door had also walked out of the teenager's life. Why should he be allowed to waltz back in whenever he felt the need to be a parent?

"She's not here."

"Don't lie to me," the older man said, his voice lower, quieter. "I have sources that assure me otherwise."

Scott narrowed his eyes, trying to discern what his dad meant by that. "Have you stooped to spying? Guess that shouldn't surprise me. You were always big on the covert life."

"I'm concerned about Gemma, son—"

"Don't," Scott interrupted in a dangerous, barely controlled voice, "ever call me that."

"As I said, I'm here to take her home." His dad managed to sound as if he was reasoning with a small child.

Hatred pulsed through Scott as it hadn't in... years. "Leave. Now."

"Scott," the older man said. "I know you don't want to see me—"

"You don't know the half of it."

"She's underage."

"She's better off on her own than with you."

"I'm her father. I have the right to see her."

"You gave up rights when you walked out of her life."

"It's okay, Scott." Gemma's steely voice came from just behind him, but he didn't turn away from his dad. "I can talk to him."

It'd be easier for everyone if he simply slammed the door in their father's face.

"Really," Gemma said more softly.

He dragged his stare away from Dale and looked at Gemma, questioning her silently.

"Gemma, honey?" Their dad tried to see around Scott, who didn't budge.

Gemma nodded at him and stepped toward the door. Scott backed off reluctantly, not more than a couple feet.

"Look at you," their father said, his voice full of pride that just about sent Scott through the roof.

"What do you want?" Gemma asked, managing to sound bored and inconvenienced.

"Can I come in?"

Gemma glanced over her shoulder at Scott.

"You're the last person I want in this apartment," he said, his arms crossed.

"It's his place," Gemma said dismissively to their dad.

"What are you doing here, Gemma?"

"What do you care?"

Their father averted his gaze, shifted his weight from one side to the other. Finally, he summoned the courage to look her in the face again. "Are you okay?"

"I'm fine."

"If you're fine, then give me five minutes to talk."

She looked at Scott, her brows raised.

"Fine," Scott said. "Five minutes."

Dale shrugged and attempted to smile at his daughter.

Gemma ignored the overture and stepped back a couple of feet, giving him room to enter. "Right here is fine, but I'm not leaving with you."

"Privacy?"

Gemma nodded at Scott, assuring him she could handle this. Scott reminded himself that "this" didn't concern him one way or the other—protecting Gemma had just been his automatic reaction to go against what his father wanted. What did he care if she followed him home like a puppy?

From the kitchen doorway, Mercedes said, "We can wait in the other room." She sent him a meaningful look, but he wasn't sure what she was trying to tell him.

With a shrug, Scott followed her into the kitchen. He paused at the bar, pressing his hands on the counter, still shaking from the inside out with the urge to lash out at the man in the living room.

Mercedes lightly brushed her fingers on his upper arm. He frowned at her hand, pushed off the counter and strode away.

"I'm staying here," Gemma said from the living room.

"Your mom told me. About your problem."

"It's a baby," Gemma clarified, making no effort to hide her dislike of Dale. "Not a problem."

"Why didn't you call me, Gemma?"

"Why would I?"

"Because I'm your father."

Scott bit down on a hateful comment, only so he wouldn't miss any of the conversation.

"Sending Mom child support doesn't make you a father."

A lengthy pause came from the other room and Scott imagined his dad doing the guilty weight-shift thing again. "I'm sorry, Gemma. Sincerely. I did wrong."

"Understatement of the millennium."

Scott exchanged a look of admiration with Mercedes at the ice in Gemma's tone. He turned away and nodded once emphatically.

"I didn't think you'd want to hear from me."

"I didn't," she said coldly. "That's just what a dad is supposed to do. Obviously your children are out of sight, out of mind."

Scott started toward the living room to back her up, but Mercedes held her hand out and stopped him with a touch to his forearm.

"That's not fair," their father said angrily.

"Don't talk to me about fair."

"I get it. You're mad at your mom for kicking

you out, and probably me, too. I'm trying to make things right here, or at least to start—"

Scott couldn't hold himself back any longer. He shot out of the kitchen in a rage.

"You don't get a damn thing!" he said as he rounded the corner to the living room. "You have no idea what it means to be a parent a kid can rely on. Gemma doesn't need you. I can't stand the sight of you." He opened the door. "Get out."

The older man scowled at him. "I'll leave for now. At least I've seen her with my own eyes. But I'll be back."

"Don't bother," Scott said with less volume but just as much hatred. "Out."

Their father looked at Gemma, but she was paying more attention to her watch.

"Give it some thought, Gemma. You can come home with me instead of staying here…" His glance around said he wasn't impressed by the environment. "I'll be in touch."

"Save yourself the trouble," she said before Scott could.

Their dad gave Gemma a lingering look that she ignored, then walked out the door. Scott slammed it after him. It didn't make him feel any better.

"I'm going to be late," Gemma said, avoiding eye contact with either him or Mercedes, who stood in the kitchen doorway, as she rushed to the hall. She returned within seconds, oversize purse in hand.

Scott was still catching his breath, as if he'd been in a physical battle.

"Let's go," Mercedes said to Gemma. She eyed Scott as if she wanted to say something to him, so he stalked into the kitchen and counted the seconds until they left him alone.

He exhaled when the front door closed behind them. The need to crush something pulsed through him. Good thing he couldn't afford to sacrifice his security deposit, otherwise he'd punch a hole in the flimsy walls.

Without conscious thought, he grabbed the new bottle of whiskey from its spot on top of the refrigerator and unscrewed the top. He opened the cabinet for a cocktail glass—what a convenience to have several clean ones waiting for him for once—and filled it with beautiful amber-liquid fortification.

As he lifted the glass toward his mouth, he froze. He narrowed his eyes at the whiskey as he caught a whiff of the spicy sweetness.

Don't want to be that guy. Don't ever want to repeat last weekend.

His hand shaking, he slowly emptied the glass in the sink. Without giving himself the chance to reconsider, he followed suit with the bottle, washing the thing's entire potent contents down the drain. He strode to the metal waste container and dropped the bottle in, savoring the loud clank of glass on the nearly empty can. Too bad it didn't shatter.

That chapter was over. He wasn't going to let his son-of-a-bitch father drive him to finish himself off.

Feeling as if he'd been turned inside out and twisted, he headed for the shower, hoping to cool his anger with icy water instead.

CHAPTER EIGHT

"DID I JUST HEAR WHAT I think I heard?" Rafe Sandoval asked as he and Scott walked out of the emergency department at the hospital toward their ambulance.

"What did you think you heard?" Scott opened the driver's door and climbed in, feeling as though he weighed three hundred pounds.

Rafe slid in beside him and cranked the air conditioner to High the second Scott started the engine. "Thought I heard the Wicked Nurse of the West say we did everything we possibly could for that guy and that she wouldn't have done anything differently."

Scott leaned his head back, the adrenaline of the call wearing off, leaving him drained. "You heard right."

"Coming from her, that's huge."

"Yeah." He had trouble making himself care about what the nurse had said. It didn't change the results of the call.

He closed his eyes for several seconds, wishing he could find a dark corner and curl up in a ball. Rafe was the person in the department he was most comfortable with, after working the majority of shifts with him for several years. "It's shit, isn't it?"

"What is?" Rafe asked. Both of them stared straight ahead.

Scott shook his head, fighting the black mood that always seemed to be hovering just over his shoulder, waiting for a moment like this to close in on him. "We can do everything by the book, give it our *A* game, hit the vein the first try, get the tube in right away, and they can still up and die."

Rafe's fingers beat a frantic rhythm on his thigh and Scott would bet he was jonesing big-time for a cigarette. He'd given them up cold turkey a week and a half ago. Scott leaned over and opened the glove compartment in front of his partner, glad for the distraction. The pack of gum was still there. He took it out and offered a stick to Rafe.

"Thanks, man." He stuck the gum in his mouth. "Just got to focus on the fact that we did everything we could and we did it right. Hold on to the ones that do make it. That twenty-year-old girl last week, for example."

Scott nodded halfheartedly. The twenty-year-old girl meant nothing to the family of the guy they'd just dropped off. That Scott sometimes had better luck on calls—luck was what it was starting to feel like, anyway—wouldn't make losing him any easier for the family to swallow.

He put the ambulance into gear and started for the station. They had one hell of a mess to clean up in back.

"You ever want to get out?" Scott asked as he drove.

"Every other hour or so."

"What about the hours in between?"

"That's when I'm thinking about a smoke so hard I could cry like a girl."

Scott chuckled and pulled past the fire-station driveway to back in.

"You've been doing this for how long?" Scott asked.

Rafe paused, calculating in his head. "Sixteen years, counting Denver. Damn if that doesn't make me sound old."

"This job makes me feel old."

"Some can keep with it. Some can't."

The idea that he couldn't bothered Scott. On paper, he was good, all things considered. Things like statistics and making the right decisions under the gun. And yet, he had to get out. "Wonder why that is."

"Perspective," Rafe said confidently. "Big part of it."

"I must have the wrong damn perspective then."

"You kidding me? You're taking the opportunity of a lifetime. What could be better than traveling around the world as the scuba king? If I didn't have the best wife in the world, I'd tell you to have your buddy set me up with a job on that boat, too."

It was strange how you could come across someone at just the right time and it could change everything. That was exactly what had happened three months ago. He hadn't seen Tim Markum, his high school football teammate, since he'd left Houston. Hadn't even thought of him, as he'd tried to block out memories of anything having to do with his hometown. Though Scott didn't frequent the Shell Shack, the bar the majority of the department hung out in regularly, he'd chosen to go there that night—the night Tim happened to be in town. Truth be told, he probably wouldn't have spoken to Tim if the guy hadn't talked first. It turned out Tim was a cruise director for one of the largest cruise companies in the world. Scott had mentioned how much he'd like to get away from the island and see the world, and Tim had taken it from there. Scott's scuba experience and Tim's connections had sealed the deal.

Thank God.

Twenty-nine more days and he was home free. Done with trauma and death.

"I NEED SOME OF THAT in my life." Nadia Hamlin absently stirred her Sandblaster with a straw as she watched a trio of men walk toward the entrance to the Shell Shack.

Mercedes twisted on her bar stool to follow Nadia's line of sight, then exchanged an amused eye roll with Faith Peligni.

"No," Faith said, her dark hair falling over her cheek as she shook her head adamantly.

"No?" Nadia frowned with exaggeration. She crossed her arms, drawing Mercedes's attention to the five rings she wore today. Status quo for Nadia. "Are you challenging me?"

"Absolutely not," Faith said.

"Challenging you is a sure way to get you to do something," Mercedes added.

"Maybe."

Nadia and Faith were Mercedes's closest friends. Pretty much her only friends, but she was a firm believer that sometimes quality was much more important than quantity.

She'd met them just after her mom died, when she'd moved to the island. It'd been the end of summer, right before her senior year of high school, and Mercedes had been numb and anything but social. These two had sensed she needed a couple of girlfriends more than anything and had been persistent in inviting her to hang out with them. She and Nadia had become room-mates in college, while Faith pursued firefight-ing. They didn't see each other nearly as often anymore, maybe once a week if they were lucky. When Charlie had suggested Mercedes get out of the house for a couple of hours this evening, she'd called these two—once she'd stopped resisting the idea of leaving her sister in charge.

Now Mercedes joined Nadia in checking out the three men. They were definitely noticeable in a good way, generating plenty of attention from women of all ages as they noisily approached the counter. Mercedes narrowed her eyes as recognition flickered. "They're firefighters, aren't they?"

"Bingo."

Nadia turned her head toward Faith with new enthusiasm. "Which means it'll be easy for you to introduce me." She made no secret that she was checking all three of them out as she sipped her conglomeration of alcohol. "I recognize the one on the right."

"You've met him," Faith said.

"Penn, isn't it?" Mercedes asked. "From the beach?"

"That's him. Tie-dyed swim trunks," she said to Nadia. "That might jog your memory."

"Ah, yes." Nadia twirled a strand of blond hair

around her finger. "I remember the tie-dye well. Who are the other two?"

"Middle one is Cooper and the other is Dylan, a new hire."

"Dylan looks too young, Cooper's okay, but Penn…"

"No." Faith waved when Cooper turned around and spotted her. "Why bother? It's not like you ever go out with a guy more than twice."

"After once or twice, the novelty wears off," Nadia said sincerely. "You have your firefighter—excuse me, fire *captain*. Don't go all selfish on us. Mercedes could use one, too. How long has it been since you've gone on a date?"

Mercedes thought for a couple of seconds. "More than a week."

"More than a year, more like it," Faith said.

"See? Way past due. Which one do you want?"

Mercedes laughed and shook her head. "None. You guys know I don't have time."

"You know," Nadia started, and Mercedes groaned to herself, guessing where this was going. "It's admirable that you're taking care of your grandma. She's lucky to have you."

There was a *but* in her tone and Mercedes took a swallow of her margarita as she waited.

"But don't you think your grandma feels bad about preventing you from having a life?"

"I have a life. I'm here with you guys, aren't I?"

"Only because your sister forced you out of the house," Nadia said.

"I know you guys don't understand," Mercedes said. "Gram took me in when I had nobody. I can't just send her off to some rest home because I want to go out and have a good time."

"We do understand," Faith said. "I just wish I had an answer for you, because you can't give up a social life and, as much as I hate to agree with Miss Social Extreme here, a dating life."

"Gram won't be here forever." Mercedes's throat swelled up at the thought. "I'll have plenty of time for myself later."

"I'm glad you're taking advantage of your sister's visit, anyway," Nadia said.

"I didn't tell you. Charlie's moving in with us."

"What?" Nadia set her drink down hard. "Details, please."

Mercedes told them what she knew of Charlie's story.

"It's great that she'll be close by," Faith said. "Isn't it? If nothing else, maybe you can get out of the house a little more often."

Mercedes hesitated.

Nadia narrowed her eyes at her. "You can get out of the house more. It will be my mission."

Mercedes forced a smile. "It's hard to leave Gram with my sister. She hasn't been there. She doesn't know what to do."

"She can learn."

"Yeah." Mercedes nodded halfheartedly. "I guess so."

"Seems it was a good thing the girl from the shelter is allergic to cats," Faith said, grinning. "Otherwise, she and your sister might be battling for the spare bedroom."

"Where did you say she went?" Nadia spoke to Mercedes, smiling across the room at God-knew-who. She was acquainted with just about everyone on the planet, it seemed, and her friends were used to her always having an eye on the rest of the room.

"She convinced her half brother to let her move in."

"Half brother Scott Pataki," Faith emphasized to Nadia. "The paramedic."

"Ooh?" The way she drew out the word was vintage Nadia. She had a thing for men in uniform.

"That's who you should introduce Nadia to," Mercedes said jokingly. She ignored the little twinge in her gut at the idea.

"I'm sticking with Penn."

"Penn isn't yours to stick with," Faith said dryly. She addressed Mercedes next. "What do you think of Scott?"

"He's grumpy, irresponsible and selfish." Mercedes nodded triumphantly. She wasn't being fair to him, she knew, but these two would jump to the wrong conclusion if she said anything in the least bit encouraging. Like her belief that he was fighting some personal demons, for instance.

"He's a good guy," Faith said. "Maybe going through a rough patch. You said yourself there's an ugly history between his family and Gemma's."

Mercedes nodded and rested her elbows on the table. "His dad made an appearance when I was there to pick up Gemma the other day." She explained what little she knew about the situation.

"That is messed up," Nadia said. "He's got cause to be a little grumpy. Maybe some TLC from a good woman would help."

Mercedes threw her wadded-up napkin at her friend.

"He's leaving town, anyway," she said, then eyed Faith carefully. "I don't know if that's common knowledge at his job yet."

"It is. He's given his notice. They've already hired his replacement."

"That's perfect," Nadia said. "He's leaving. No strings attached. Have some fun."

"Not everyone needs to date as much as you seem to," Mercedes said.

Nadia looked contrite. "You know I'm only half-serious with it. What I am serious about, though, is wishing you could find happiness. You deserve it more than anyone I know."

Faith nodded and Mercedes, overcome by affection for these two women who'd gotten her through so much, didn't know what to say.

"And if not long-term happiness, then at least a good time for a few nights."

"I'll drink to that," Faith said. She held her glass up and Nadia followed suit. Mercedes went through the motions just to get them off her case, but she wasn't feeling it at all.

CHAPTER NINE

MERCEDES DIDN'T REALIZE when she stepped out
from between her car and another that she was
taking her life in her hands. She jumped back to
safety between the parked cars when some moron
in a sports car zipped through the parking lot less
than five feet from where she'd been.

Her heart still in her throat, she headed across
the lot toward Gemma and Scott's apartment,
scowling at the stupid car with its stupid vanity
plate that read SHOCKR.

She was only surprised for a second or two
when none other than Scott Pataki stepped out of
the silver Mazda RX8. Looking smug, he joined
her as she walked.

"How old are you?" she muttered without looking straight at him.

"Saw you the whole time. Wasn't going to hit
you."

"Shocker, huh?" she said.

"Defibrillator? Shocking the patient?"

"I get it. Double entendre much?"

He didn't answer. Seemed to be absorbed in his

thoughts. He wore a frown as they crossed the lot and looked...sad. Which was a change from his usual angry.

"Are you okay?" she asked. As soon as the question was out of her mouth, she realized the odds of him answering were slim. She watched him out of the corner of her eye as they continued walking. When he shrugged, she turned her head fully, wondering if she'd imagined the response. Encouraged, she dared to ask more. "Rough shift?"

He pierced her with a direct hit from those blue eyes then looked toward the ground again. "Some nights it seems like everyone dies."

Mercedes did her best to hide her surprise that he'd replied. "That must be rough."

"It gets to you." He shook his head. They reached the outdoor stairway and started upward. "Pretty soon, you're going to have to start paying rent here."

Mercedes pushed her hair behind her shoulder. "I'm not here that much. You just happen to run into me every single time."

"Guess I'm used to being alone."

"Maybe that's part of your problem." She strived not to come off as judgmental, thinking she really needed to learn to think about what she said before blurting it out.

"One of many," Scott said, and she was struck

again by how depressed he sounded, instead of grumpy or irritated even when she gave opinions he hadn't asked for. "So why are you here today? Taking Gemma to work?"

"Today's my riding day."

He unlocked his apartment door and she followed him in. "I didn't see a bike out there. Motorcycle or other."

"Horses. I drive to a stable in the middle of nowhere every other Saturday. One of Gram's longtime friends comes and stays with her while I'm gone. Of course...Charlie's here now...."

"Do you own a horse?"

"I wish. Maybe someday."

"I haven't thought about horses for years." He threw his duffel bag down by the couch.

"You ride?"

"Did when I was a kid. Couple times a week."

Gemma walked out of the kitchen toward them, pulling a section off an orange then sticking it in her mouth. "Interesting," she said, looking between the two of them without hiding her curiosity.

"I'm glad you're up," Mercedes said, pretending she didn't understand Gemma's comment and pulling her into a one-armed hug. "I thought with all the stress of the past week it might do you some good to come to the stable with me."

"Stable?" Gemma glanced doubtfully at her

protruding belly—it seemed to have popped out this past week—then back at Mercedes.

"Not to ride," Mercedes clarified. "You're absolutely not allowed on a horse until that baby's born. But it's a pretty drive and the farm is peaceful. Quiet. You could bring something to read and sit in the shade."

"And breathe in the calming smell of horse dung," Gemma said. She took another bite of orange, considering. "How can I say no to that?"

"I'll feed you afterward. Egg City?"

"My weakness. Sure you want to be seen with the immoral pregnant teenager in public?"

"Don't be ridiculous," Mercedes said.

There was a hint of a rare grin. "When do we leave?" Gemma asked.

Scott had grabbed a banana from the kitchen counter, peeled it partway and was stuffing big bites into his mouth as he watched them.

"You should come with us," Mercedes said in a rush, before she could consider the invitation too carefully. "Horseback riding always helps me clear my mind." She ignored the nagging feeling that she'd regret this move.

"What kind of horses?" he asked.

"They mostly have quarter horses. Beautiful ones," Mercedes said. "We could find you a gentle one they use for kids' lessons."

Scott seemed to not hear the last bit. He looked

troubled as he paced to the doorway of the kitchen and then into the living room, rubbing the back of his neck. With a final pained glance toward the kitchen, he made up his mind. "I'm in. Just give me ten minutes to shower." He picked up his bag and headed toward his room, muttering, "Gentle one, my ass."

Mercedes couldn't tell if his grumpiness was real or in jest, but she told herself it was a good thing for him to visit the country. Lied to herself that her only interest in getting him to join them was strictly for his benefit. Denied completely any fluttering of personal interest at the prospect of spending time with him. Besides, there was nothing wrong with a tiny bit of excitement.

SCOTT HAD FORGOTTEN what being on horseback could do for a person. Feeling the wind whip past him. Moving as one with such a powerful animal.

The gelding the stable owner, Maria, had chosen for him, Serrano, was strong and graceful with an edge of wildness about him. He responded well to Scott, as if they'd been riding together for years.

He slowed the animal to a trot, catching his breath and looking ahead for Mercedes and her chestnut mare. They were a good quarter of a mile up the field on the way back to the barn.

Mercedes on that horse was a thing of beauty.

The woman could ride. He could hold his own, but she rode circles around him and looked ten times more graceful doing it. Part of the pleasure of his morning had been keeping one eye on her. From afar.

At first when she'd convinced him to saddle up, he'd figured he'd let himself in for a miserable hour or two of annoying chitchat and acting as if they were good buddies. The only reason he'd given in and come along at all was because the need for a drink had been so overpowering, he'd worried he might go out and buy a bottle once he was alone.

After about three minutes of Mercedes assuring herself he had enough riding know-how to handle Serrano, she'd taken off, leaving him in peace.

Being alone with a horse was calming. Out here, the crap of his everyday life seemed distant. Less weighty.

Out here, he had a greater sense of peace than he'd had for…ages.

He was reluctant to quit when he rode toward where Mercedes waited for him. The only thing convincing him to dismount was the faint memory of the way his leg muscles would protest tomorrow. It'd been a long time since he'd used those particular ones.

He halted the horse and climbed down. Instead

of meeting Mercedes's inquisitive gaze, he turned toward the palomino and patted it on the neck. "You're a fine horse, Serrano."

"How was your ride?" Mercedes asked, absently rubbing her horse's neck. It occurred to him that she had a way with both animals and people. Gemma, for instance. Not him.

"Decent."

"Want to groom him?" she asked.

Seemed an easy way to grab a little more time to himself. "Why not?"

They took the horses inside, Mercedes leading the way to the center aisle before they headed to their respective stalls on opposite sides of the barn.

It was a lot quieter than when they'd taken the horses out. They'd arrived at the end of lesson time and there'd been kids, parents, instructors everywhere. Now a lone whinny came from the stall next to Serrano's as Scott and the horse walked by, as if welcoming Serrano back to his spot.

As Scott positioned the horse so it could eat while he brushed, an orange-and-white cat with a fluffy tail appeared on the railing then jumped down into the stall. It boldly wound its way between Scott's legs.

"Better watch out," Scott said quietly. "Serrano might decide to use you as a football."

The gelding watched him with soulful, trusting eyes and he decided then and there he'd be back before he left Texas. He'd never taken part in the therapy offered through work—telling a stranger his thoughts and, God forbid, feelings, had about as much appeal as getting kicked by a horse—but riding…that was the kind of temporary escape he could get behind.

He lost track of time as he stroked the horse and spoke to him in a soft voice now and then. When Mercedes appeared at the stall door several minutes later, he hoped she hadn't overheard him talking nonsense.

"How's it going?" she asked, entering the roomy stall.

"Serrano thinks it's going pretty damn well."

"You're good with horses."

"It's been a long time. Guess it's like riding a bike. Where's Gemma?"

"Maria said she was on a bench in the shade, close to the trees."

She went to the corner of the stall where the cat had curled up in the straw. Scott hadn't had the chance to admire the way Mercedes looked in jeans before now and he stole a nice long stare as she bent over to lift the cat. Worn, chambray-colored denim hugged her curvy hips and ass in a way that made his body react. When she stood and faced him, the cat was in her arms, blocking his view of the plain purple T-shirt he'd kept an eye on from a distance all morning. The feline rubbed its face against Mercedes's chin, coaxing a smile from her.

"Serrano and Pumpkin are best friends," she explained. "Aren't you, fuzzball?"

She nuzzled the cat as it dug a paw into her long hair. Mercedes had had it pulled back for the ride, but now it hung freely, wild from the wind in spite of her efforts. Scott imagined running his fingers through it like the fat, lucky feline was doing with its paw.

"Has she ever been kicked by a horse?" he asked.

"Once. Pumpkin was young and got behind Serrano. He broke her hip. Required surgery, but she learned her lesson."

"She hang out with other horses, too?"

"She'll walk along the tops of the stall walls, but Serrano is the only one she likes to sleep by."

"You'd think she'd keep her distance from the one that hurt her," he said, running his hand down Serrano's neck.

He felt her staring at him curiously. "What?"

"Kind of like people." Her tone was gentle, almost nonchalant, but he knew she meant him. He wished like hell she hadn't been there when his father had come by.

The cat leaped from her arms to the railing and walked along it, out of their sight.

"Scott."

He finished tending to the horse before meeting her gaze. Being called to life-or-death emergencies was one thing, but looking a woman in the eye when she had that tone, that took cojones.

She leaned against the planked-wood wall next to the hook where he'd found the brush, her hips flexed forward and legs crossed at the ankles. "Thank you for sticking up for Gemma the other day. To your dad."

He took two long steps to the hook next to her. His dad was the last thing he wanted to think about, now or ever. And stick up for Gemma? She wouldn't thank him if she knew he'd done it out of hatred for his dad instead of support for his roommate.

"I know it meant a lot to her," Mercedes continued as he hung the brush up. "I don't think she's used to having anyone on her side."

Scott stopped short and opened his mouth to level with her. Thanks was the last thing he deserved. The words got stuck in his throat, though, and his gaze got caught up in that hair of hers. The wild, distracting curls made his fingers itch with the need to touch them. To touch her.

She studied him from behind long, beautiful lashes like he'd never seen. He was close enough he could see caramel-colored specks in her brown eyes. His gaze lowered to the subtle candy-pink sparkle on her lips and he wondered if the taste of her would match the shade.

It took one step to bring him close enough. He braced his forearm along the wall next to her head and leaned in, telling himself he only wanted to rattle her, get her mind off the subject of his father and Gemma.

The first contact was a gentle brush of his lips on hers, as if he was still arguing with himself whether the move was wise. The sample of her soft warmth coaxed a shaky breath from him and he leaned in for more. She tasted of sugared berries as she raised her hand to his nape and forced him closer. The stable and the animals around them faded to nothing as she consumed his entire awareness.

He cradled her jaw, tipping her head to deepen the kiss. As he pressed her body against the wall with his, he dropped his hand to the curve of her waist, relishing her softness. Heat pulsed through every inch of him and centered in his groin.

"Mercedes?"

They whipped apart at the sound of Gemma's voice in the distance. Lucky thing they didn't spook the horse. Their eyes met and lust arced between them. Patches of pink colored Mercedes's cheeks. It didn't take much to imagine the rest of her naked, blushing like that, in his bed. A low growl rumbled in his throat.

He saw the instant reality hit Mercedes. Otherwise known as regret. Her eyes widened and she looked away. Took a step toward the stall door, flustered.

"There you are," she said as Gemma's blond head appeared over the railing.

Gemma looked from Mercedes to Scott. "What are you guys doing?"

"Leaving." Mercedes exited the stall, hooked her arm through Gemma's a little overzealously and steered her toward the barn door.

Real smooth, Scott thought, shaking his head and covering the sting of that rejection with a forced grin at Serrano. He stood next to the horse, hand on his neck, taking in that calming smell of dung and allowing his heart rate to slow.

Kissing Mercedes, though it'd been a little slice of heaven, was a mistake. He'd do well to keep her reaction in mind and not let that happen again.

THE RIDE BACK to the island was the longest drive of Mercedes's life.

Thinking to put as much space as possible between Scott and herself, she'd climbed into the backseat of his car, letting Gemma sit next to him. That'd been a wrong decision. She'd had almost two full hours of being able to watch his every move. The flex of his biceps whenever he shifted gears. The grip of his fingers at the top of the steering wheel. The determined set of his jaw whenever he turned his head right to scan traffic.

He got to her. Just by breathing.

Dammit.

It was only a physical attraction. It couldn't be more than that because, well, he wasn't exactly Mr. Caring. The guy was a jumble of issues, and while Mercedes could fully admit she was easily sucked in to helping people solve their problems, that was not cause for romantic feelings. Especially when said problems weren't ones she could conquer.

An excruciating eternity later, he drove into the parking lot of his apartment. Sitting there waiting for Gemma to open her door and get out so that Mercedes could escape built up enough nervous energy to power a small battleship. When the seat finally popped forward, she wedged herself out in record time.

She slid into the driver's seat of her Honda, slamming the door shut in spite of the ovenlike heat. She started the engine, set the air conditioner on High and leaned her head against the rest.

Peace at last. Or as close to peace as she was going to get.

The passenger side opened and Gemma sat, leaving her door ajar.

"What's wrong with you, Mercedes?" she asked.

"What are you doing in here?"

"Food? Egg City?" Gemma stared at her, a questioning look on her face. "What happened?"

Ah, crap. She'd completely forgotten her promise. "Pancakes," she acknowledged. "Sorry about that."

She glanced toward the apartment stairs, hoping to see Scott's backside moving farther away from her. He was nowhere in her limited line of sight. Instead of a more thorough search, she threw the car into Reverse and made a panicked exit before he could appear at her window. The front wheels squealed on the pavement as she pulled out of the lot.

Gemma continued to stare hard at her, but she kept her eyes forward, acting as if driving required every bit of her concentration.

"Hey, you made me talk about personal stuff," Gemma said. "Your turn."

Mercedes drove on autopilot, trying to find words. "I... Scott..."

"He made a move on you."

She dared a look at Gemma, whose mouth twitched upward at the corners as if she fought a grin. Mercedes nodded once, biting her lip. "He kissed me." She let out a heavy breath. "How did you know?"

"Hello, obvious. Your guilty look, the way you wiped your mouth really quick, your hurry to get out of there…."

Mercedes could hear the grin on Gemma's face, and Gemma wasn't prone to smiling all that often.

"I thought he had a thing for you."

Mercedes let out a frustrated groan.

"Oops," Gemma said. "Not the time for that?"

"It's never the time," Mercedes muttered as she parallel parked in front of the restaurant.

"What's so bad about Scott kissing you?"

Mercedes put the car in Park and closed her eyes. Where did she begin?

"He's not…ugly," Gemma said.

No, not ugly. Quite the opposite. She sighed. "Killer dimples."

"I'm missing something."

Mercedes clenched and opened her fist repeatedly. If her best friends couldn't really understand her reasoning, then Gemma wouldn't, either. Mercedes knew most people didn't get her devotion to her grandma, even if they claimed they did. They couldn't fathom why she'd rearranged her whole life to make Gram's easier and to keep her out of a care home. The loyalty she felt was difficult to put into words.

"It's just…why get involved when he's leaving?" she said. A perfectly valid reason in and of itself, even if it wasn't the real one.

"Maybe he would stay if he had a hottie like you," Gemma said.

"You watch too much TV. Let's go eat." Mercedes hopped out of the car, nausea rolling through her gut. She frankly had no desire for food but would go through the motions so Gemma wouldn't feel alone during the meal.

At two-thirty in the afternoon, the restaurant was nearly deserted, so they were seated immediately. They filled their plates—Gemma with a stack of chocolate-chip pancakes and a pile of bacon, Mercedes with a small serving of fruit and a sesame bagel—and returned to their table.

"Maybe you don't want to talk about Scott, but I feel a little guilty about him," the teenager said as she poured syrup on her tower of pancakes.

"What? What do you have to feel guilty about?"

"I think our dad's visit the other day kind of messed him up."

"I think he was already messed up." Mercedes jabbed a piece of melon with her fork.

"Well, yeah," Gemma said as she finished a bite. "But it pushed him further."

"What makes you say that? Did he say something to you?"

"Are you kidding me? The most complex thing we've discussed is Pop-Tarts."

"What's his opinion of them?" Mercedes asked before she could stop herself. "Never mind. I don't want to know."

Gemma stuffed more food in her mouth and laughed.

"Maybe it's good for Scott that your dad showed up. Might force him to deal with things one way or another instead of ignoring it all."

"Maybe." Gemma got quiet again. Thoughtful. "If you want to avoid him now and don't want to hang out with me as much, I get it."

"Ha. Don't think you'll get rid of me that easily. If he tries to kiss me again—not that I think he will—but if he does, I'm prepared. I can resist him. He just took me by surprise today."

Gemma raised a brow as if she wasn't convinced, but Mercedes believed what she was saying. One kiss really meant nothing.

CHAPTER TEN

CHARLIE WAS TAKING the sisterly-bonding thing to new heights.

After dinner, one of Gram's favorite caretakers, Yoli, had shown up at the door. Way after hours. Charlie had secretly arranged for Yoli to come back after her shift ended to stay with their grandma so she and Mercedes could go out together.

Mercedes wasn't totally sold on the idea. In fact, it made her downright uneasy for several reasons, but Charlie had blown off her worries and ushered her out the door.

"I had no idea this place would be so busy on a Tuesday night," Charlie said once she and Mercedes were perched on stools at the beachside, thatched-roof Shell Shack. "I love it."

"Two-dollar Sandblasters? Are you kidding? Good thing we walked."

Charlie held up her drink expectantly. "Cheers."

Mercedes tapped their cups together, trying to show even half as much enthusiasm as her sister.

"How much did you have to pay Yoli to stay with Gram tonight?"

Charlie laughed and took a healthy swallow. "For sitting around playing Scrabble and watching prime-time TV, she's got quite the racket going on."

"You make it sound easy, but anything could come up. Even a bathroom break is an ordeal for anyone who isn't used to Gram."

"Yoli is used to Gram. You know that. She loves her almost as much as we do."

It was true, but Mercedes still felt guilty for ditching her grandma for no good reason.

"Relax, Sadie. It's a beautiful night."

"You're right."

It was a typical summer night on San Amaro Island. Hot and humid, with just enough breeze coming off the water to make it comfortable now that the sun had dropped low in the sky. The din of the thirsty crowd drowned out the sound of the waves, but Mercedes had a perfect view of them as they rolled onto shore.

She took a drink and glanced around. She spotted Macey, a firefighter's wife and co-owner of the Shell Shack, behind the bar. A couple of other firefighters' wives and girlfriends sat at the bar, as well.

The inside of the shack, if it could be called that since it was open-air, was packed. The patio looked just as crowded. She wondered if Faith or Nadia were here somewhere. They managed to go out more often than she did. Charlie had rushed her out so quickly she hadn't had time to call them. Besides, it was supposed to be quality sister drinking time, anyway.

"I don't know how you do it," Charlie said, playing with the saltshaker.

"Do what?"

"Take care of Gram. It's one thing for Yoli to come in for a few hours one night, but you're there all the time. I didn't realize how much work she is for you."

Mercedes shrugged. "I don't think of taking care of her as work."

"You've got your own job and your own life plus Gram. How do you do it all yourself?"

"I don't. We still have caretakers come in every day. Twice on weekdays, once a day on weekends. I plan all my outings for when I know they'll be there. And I can get away for short errands in between when I absolutely have to. Gram has a phone by her bed and she knows she can call me whenever she needs me."

Charlie stared at her for some time, and it made Mercedes fidget.

"It works for us," Mercedes said. "We have our system."

"I want to help while I'm staying there. More

than fetching her a glass of water. Will you let me do that?"

Mercedes studied her for a sign of insincerity but found none. She nodded. "We have our routines that I can show you."

"I'd like that. Thanks."

Mercedes took another drink and Charlie seemed to be satisfied with her agreement. At least for now.

"I've been thinking," Charlie said, scooting her stool closer so they could talk more easily. "The idea of a gallery to show my work in really appeals."

"What kind of work? Jewelry?"

"I haven't touched anything that could be even remotely construed as an accessory since I've been here and it's been fantastic. I've mostly been drawing and painting."

"I wondered where you've been disappearing to."

"The beach. The bay. This place has inspiration everywhere you look. I haven't been this productive for ages."

"There's another artist who lives on the island. I can't remember her name, but maybe I can find out and you two can get together."

"Does she have a gallery?"

"Last I knew, she had a baby. She's married

to a firefighter. I'll ask Faith her name the next time I see her."

"Thanks, Sadie. I'd love to meet her. I need some cocktail shrimp. Want anything?"

"I've got plenty here," Mercedes said, lifting her half-empty drink.

Charlie took a long swig of her own beverage and stood, smoothing down the front of her casual, drapey sundress, a style of clothing Mercedes would never be able to carry off. The least her sister could do, if they were going to be friends, was wear clothes that Mercedes could borrow. She smiled to herself, the drink starting to relax her, and acknowledged that she and Charlie would never agree on the same styles anyway. How one set of parents could produce two people who were so completely different was a mystery to her.

The breeze blew her hair slightly as she watched her sister navigate the crowd for a few seconds, then she turned back around. As she looked out toward the gulf, she noticed a man standing in the shadows on the sand. He was about twenty feet from the seawall, and his body language was what caught her eye—his shoulders sagged and his gaze was glued to the ground instead of the scenery in front of him. He seemed to not even realize he was on a beautiful beach. The guy looked upset. Lonely, maybe.

She looked away from him. Skimmed the crowd for familiar faces again. Checked on her sister's progress and saw her speaking to Macey at the bar. But she was drawn back to the beach, to the lone figure there.

He'd moved. Was heading toward the stairs just to Mercedes's right. When he walked into the light from the bar, she inhaled quickly in recognition, then hunkered down so he couldn't see her over the wall of the stairs.

Though she attempted to play it cool and focus on the water again, she was fully aware the exact second Scott reached the top of the stairs and entered her peripheral vision. She fought the need to look at him—for all of three seconds. At the moment she turned her head toward him, he looked her way and their eyes met.

He raised his brows in acknowledgment of her as he came closer. For an excruciating second, she thought he was going to walk on by. Instead, he stopped next to her, seeming almost relieved.

"Hey, Mercedes."

"Scott." Her heart started up and she stumbled over what else to say to him. Her traitorous eyes automatically went to his lips, and she remembered exactly how they felt on hers.

"I thought that had to be your hair," he said, leaning close so she could hear him over the crowd.

Hear him and smell him. She found herself breathing in deeply to get more of his faintly spicy scent. Catching herself, she straightened, increasing the distance between them.

"I'm not sure how to take that," she said, pushing her hair back self-consciously.

He met her gaze and she got caught up in the cornflower shade of his eyes. "It's a compliment. Your hair is…eye-catching. Unique."

"Then…thank you. I think." Her hair wasn't her favorite feature, by far. "What are you doing here?"

It didn't seem like his type of hangout, for one, and two, she'd never seen him here before. Not that she had much of a social life, but when she went out with Faith and Nadia, they usually hit the Shell Shack.

"They're breaking in my replacement at work," he said, indicating a loud group out on the patio close to the shack. Mercedes spotted a few familiar faces and several she didn't know. "They seem to consider it my duty to make sure he's hurting in the morning."

She nodded, and then without realizing it, she checked out the cup he was holding.

"Sprite," he said. "Want to taste it to verify?"

"It's none of my business what you drink. Especially if you're not throwing up at my feet."

Scott grimaced. "Ouch."

She instantly regretted saying it. "Sorry. That wasn't nice of me."

"Nothing I don't deserve," he said, swishing his drink around. "I, uh, gave up drinking. After that night."

She studied him at close range for several seconds, gauging his intent. Was he telling her what he thought she wanted to hear? Trying to impress her?

No. The only things she read in his face were a touch of embarrassment and a heavy dose of determination.

Mercedes nodded slowly. "Good for you, Scott. Is it...hard to be here?"

He swallowed as he glanced around the bar. "You could say that. I'm hoping to duck out as soon as everyone's too lit to notice."

He took a swig as Charlie returned and set a serving of shrimp at her own place. She slid a second conspicuous Sandblaster next to Mercedes's first one, the potent-smelling alcohol sloshing over the side.

"Looks like we've traded roles," Scott said with a hint of a grin, giving her a glimpse of those dimples. He crowded closer to Mercedes so that Charlie could get to her stool. She felt his arm graze her shoulders and shivered. Half a second later, she closed her eyes and silently scolded herself.

"Are you going to introduce me?" Charlie asked.

"This is my sister, Charlie. She just moved here from New York. This is Scott Pataki."

"Charlie?" Scott leaned toward her and offered his hand.

Mercedes spoke directly into his ear. "Short for Charlotte, but don't let her know I told you."

"I heard that," Charlie said over the crowd noise. "Very nice to meet you, Scott." She inspected him in detail, the way a mother would check out her daughter's proposed mate.

Mercedes caught her eye and shot her a warning look.

"Scott's a paramedic. He works with my friend Faith." Saying he was a friend's coworker seemed simpler and more businesslike than saying he was Gemma's half brother, or even worse, the guy she'd been up against the barn wall with. The distinction seemed important at the moment.

"Mercedes and I go way back," he said dryly, surprising her that he'd said anything at all.

"Way back," she said, aware that her sister had missed his sarcasm. "What is it, two weeks?"

"You guys have been dating for two weeks and you haven't mentioned it?" Charlie asked, sounding scandalized.

"We're not dating." Her sister was being dense on purpose. "Hey, isn't there a wife of a firefighter who's an artist?" she asked Scott, eager to change the subject.

Scott thought for a moment and then nodded. "Evan Drake's wife. She painted the mural outside the station."

"Selena." Mercedes remembered now. Her grandma had pointed out an article in the local weekly newspaper when the mural had been unveiled. "There you go. Selena Drake." She nodded to her sister and thanked Scott.

"I better get back. Duty awaits. Nice to meet you, Charlotte." The gleam in his eye as he looked at her one more time told Mercedes the mistake was intentional.

"He did not just call me that," Charlie said as he walked away.

"Scott's...trouble." She kept her tone light, as if it was all a joke, but that was truer than her sister knew.

"He's nice-looking trouble."

"Good thing you don't do trouble." Mercedes took a healthy swallow of her Sandblaster. "It'll probably be a while before you're ready to date, anyway."

Charlie dipped a shrimp into her cocktail sauce. "You never know. But I'm more interested in talking about him." She nodded in the direction Scott had gone. "What's going on between you two?"

"There's nothing going on." Mercedes hardened her jaw stubbornly and turned away—in the opposite direction from Scott—to signal the conversation was over. As she glanced around the bar, she sipped her drink through her straw. Charlie said something else to her, and maybe it was immature, but Mercedes pretended not to hear.

When she noticed the women at the main bar again, something clicked in her mind. "I think that's Selena Drake over there at the bar. Long dark hair, perfect profile. I'll introduce you before we go."

"If I had any doubt before, your extreme avoidance tactics have convinced me. If there's not something between you and troublemaker Scott, you wish there was."

Instead of denying it again, Mercedes simply frowned at Charlie and turned away as if she'd prefer different company. Which she might. Charlie moved closer once more. "Sadie, come on." Her amusement was evident, and that just annoyed Mercedes more. "What's the big deal?"

Mercedes checked her watch. Gram should be getting ready for bed now, pajamas, pills. She wondered if Yoli was handling the nighttime routine okay.

"You wonder why we're not close, Mercedes?" Charlie said, her amusement gone. "Because you shut down anyone who wants to get to know you. Really know you, beyond the face you show the world. You do it to me, always have, and I'd bet a hundred bucks you're doing the same to Scott. Because I suspect he does want to know you."

This wasn't fun anymore, if it ever had been. "It's getting late," Mercedes said with a stiff jaw, even though it wasn't quite ten o'clock. "I have to work tomorrow. I'm going home." She finished off the last of her first drink. "You coming?"

Charlie stared at her for several seconds and Mercedes saw disappointment in her eyes. For a moment, she felt guilty. Until she reminded herself that she hadn't been the one to move three thousand miles away in the first place thereby removing any chance of being close. Some things you couldn't force.

"I'm not ready to leave yet. If you'll point me toward Selena Drake, I'll introduce myself to her," Charlie said more calmly. Sadly. And that had more of an effect on Mercedes than the anger and accusations, by far.

But instead of staying and trying harder to get along with her sister, she again pointed out the slender woman with the glossy dark hair at the bar, said good-night and walked home alone. Because if the sister rules included confiding the nonplatonic thoughts in her head regarding Scott, then she was out. As long as she didn't give a voice to anything, she could still control any attraction to him. That was the only way to fight the temptation he offered and avoid letting her grandmother down.

CHAPTER ELEVEN

FOR THE FIRST time in ages, Scott climbed out of bed before noon on one of his days off. Pretty damn amazing the difference going to bed sober could make.

His body's sleep cycles were beyond screwed up from working twenty-fours every third day, but today he didn't use that excuse.

After showering, he ambled out to the kitchen for some breakfast. Gemma sat at the counter with a glass of water and a magazine opened in front of her. Though his head was clear for once, that didn't mean he did friendliness first thing in the morning. Hell, he wasn't known for friendliness at any hour. He went for his usual vegetable juice and cracked open the can, his back to her.

"Morning," she said.

He managed to grunt a reply as he rustled through the freezer in search of a package of breakfast sausage links he'd spotted the other day. The best part of this whole arrangement was the grocery deal they'd struck: he supplied the cash and Gemma did the shopping. He hadn't had so much food in his kitchen since he'd left home at eighteen.

"I didn't expect you to be up for another couple of hours."

"I'm just full of surprises," he said. "Don't want to get too predictable."

She went back to reading her celebrity-gossip magazine as if he wasn't there, which was what he preferred.

He located the sausages and took the egg carton and grated cheese out of the refrigerator, as well. As he cracked the eggs into a bowl at the counter, just a few feet away from Gemma and her magazine, he noticed she rubbed the fingers and thumb of her left hand together repeatedly, as if nervous.

Once he'd poured the eggs into a skillet and stuck the sausages in the microwave, he leaned against the counter and idly crossed his arms, waiting for the pan to heat. Gemma checked her watch, then went back to the finger-rubbing habit.

"You're fidgeting." He nodded toward her hand where it rested on the counter. It was still now, but tightly clenched. She followed his gesture with her eyes and stretched out her fingers.

"I have a doctor's appointment in a while," she said.

"Tell me it's not your first prenatal visit."

"It's not my first prenatal visit. I went regularly

back in Fort Worth. That's how my mom figured out I was pregnant. She finally paid attention to the insurance statement."

"What doctor are you seeing?"

"I'm going to the county health clinic. I don't know if I'm still on my mom's insurance. Going for the budget option."

"Won't she find out where you're living if you are?" The eggs started to sizzle, so he tended to them with his spatula.

Gemma shrugged. "Doesn't matter. She won't come after me."

She returned to her magazine and her nervous finger rubbing. It occurred to Scott that Gemma had to be one of the least talkative females he'd met. Normally he'd consider that a virtue. Something was obviously eating away at her, though, and he wanted to know what.

While the eggs and cheese finished cooking, he took the meat out of the microwave and got himself a clean plate. "Want some food?" he asked.

She didn't even look at him or his culinary concoction before shaking her head. "They're supposed to test for gestational diabetes and who knows what else. I have to fast for the test."

He busied himself piling eggs on his plate. The silence between them seemed to swell, and for once, Scott was uncomfortable with it.

"Have you talked to your mom since you've been here?" he blurted out as he shook salt and then pepper over his plate.

Gemma met his gaze. "Why would I?"

The bigger question was why did he care? But he kind of did, at least enough to be curious.

"Just wondered. My dad never tried to contact me after I left home."

"Seems to be his way." Gemma shook her head. "Not that I wanted him to. I have no respect for him."

They could start a club, he thought as he dug into his breakfast. "What's the story with your mom?"

A shield came over her face as he watched her. It was a subtle thing, an instant, a barely discernible tightening of her features, and maybe someone who didn't specialize in the gesture themselves wouldn't have noticed. It was so familiar to him that he wondered if blocking someone out like that was a genetic trait they'd gotten from their father.

"No story. She's just…" Gemma shook her head as if she couldn't find words. "Self-centered. Like a two-year-old."

He waited for her to explain more, but it became clear he'd be finished with breakfast, and maybe even lunch, before that happened.

"Why'd she kick you out?" he finally asked, slightly annoyed that for once he was being forced to play the question game to get someone else to talk.

Gemma closed her magazine and smiled, but there was nothing warm about the expression. She folded her hands on the counter in front of her. "I'm a serious disappointment to my mom." She said it with fanfare, as if quoting directly.

Scott frowned. "Because you're pregnant?"

She pursed her lips and nodded. "She's preached to me all my life about looking out for myself first—a policy she has absolutely mastered—and not trusting guys. In her eyes I blew it."

He put his fork down, crossed his arms and tilted his head. "By ending up pregnant?"

"Yes."

"Isn't that…exactly what she did?"

Gemma's acknowledgment was in the form of raised brows. "Did I mention two-year-old?"

Scott resumed eating, beginning to get a view of what Gemma's life must have been like. Not exactly rosy, he'd guess, even before Gemma had gotten pregnant. He felt a sort of kinship with her, out of nowhere. Something he couldn't explain.

"Why are you asking about my mom?" Gemma looked suddenly panicked. "Are you going to call her?"

"I'm not calling anyone." She was likely better off without her mother's drama, the way it sounded. "How long ago did...your dad leave your mom?"

"They split up when I was thirteen. About a year after I found out about you and your mom."

Without warning, the same rage he'd felt when his father had shown up at his apartment door hit him, making his chest feel tight and his appetite vanish. He fought it off, blocked out the thoughts of the past that had brought it on so suddenly.

"Who's the father of your baby?" He shoved his plate away and gave her his full attention.

She shook her head, looking as if he'd punched her.

"It's not like I'm going to know the guy," Scott said, attempting a gentler tone.

"Then why does it matter?"

He scoffed. "You're going to be a teenage mom. Last I knew it takes two to tango and I don't think you should be the only one to pay."

Ignoring him, she looked at her watch. She walked around the counter to the dishwasher, opened it and began putting away the clean dishes without a word.

Curiosity pulsed through him, but he begrudgingly accepted her need for privacy. God knew it was his life philosophy. He grabbed his half-eaten breakfast and went around to the stool next to hers to get out of her way.

They returned to their status quo silence—if you didn't count the clattering of the dishes and silverware as she put them away. She left no question that he'd upset her and she wasn't over it yet. Scott dragged her magazine over and opened it to a random page. Started reading about a Hollywood scandal he had zero interest in.

A few minutes later, he became aware that the noise had decreased. Gemma closed the silverware drawer and returned the utensil basket to the empty dishwasher, her back to him. He shoved the last sausage into his mouth and returned to the article to see how the story ended, curious in spite of himself.

"He's in jail," Gemma said quietly, still not facing him.

It took a couple of heartbeats for Scott to realize she'd gone back to their last topic—her baby's father. "Juvie?"

She shook her head and lowered it. "He's nineteen. Nothing very creative. He was caught selling drugs. In school."

Whoa.

Gemma's shoulders rose with a deep breath and she turned around without looking at him. Made her way back to her seat at his side. "I knew he was into some hard stuff but I didn't know he dealt."

Scott sized her up, trying to find a sign that she wasn't being straight with him.

"I don't do drugs," she said in a rush, holding up her hands. "I have my faults but that isn't one of them."

He believed her. "So, does he know about the baby?"

She nodded. "Does he care? No."

He didn't say anything—what the hell was he supposed to say to that? He closed the magazine and shoved it back to her place. Watched her.

"I already feel stupid enough so no need to tell me. Even if he wasn't in jail, I don't want anything to do with him. Don't want him to have anything to do with the baby. That's part of the reason I needed to get out of town. I won't ever take a dime from him. I wouldn't trust where it came from."

Yet she was determined to go it alone and have the baby.

Not for the first time, he realized this girl was no coward. Since he'd met her and found out she was pregnant, Scott had been of the silent opinion it'd be best for her to give the baby up for adoption. But now…he was beginning to see that, yes, she was taking the hardest route, but if anyone could handle it, it was her.

He scooped up the final bite of eggs with his fork and shoveled it in pensively.

Gemma stood, apparently done with the subject, and checked the time yet again.

"When is your appointment?"

"Eleven. I'll leave in about ten minutes." She began cleaning up the considerable mess he'd made preparing his breakfast. Loading dirty dishes and pans in the dishwasher.

He rose and carried his plate to the sink, rinsed it and put it in the open dishwasher. When he realized it was only twenty after ten, he frowned. "Why are you leaving so early for your appointment?"

She straightened after putting a pan in the back of the bottom rack. "It's a little over a mile. Should take me twenty to twenty-five minutes to get there."

"You're walking?"

"Yep."

"No, you're not. I'm giving you a ride."

"You don't have to—"

"I know I don't have to. In case you haven't noticed, I'm not too good at doing the things I 'have' to."

She eyed the dirty counter where he'd dripped raw egg and spilled the package of cheese. "I noticed."

"I'm giving you a ride to the clinic. And if you

don't make a big deal of it, I'll wait with you and give you a ride home."

Her slow grin made him fidget and he shook his head. "Don't make it into something it isn't. It's no big thing."

"I'm just ecstatic me and my extra twenty pounds don't have to make that long waddle. I'm going to get ready now."

The grin that played on her lips as she left the kitchen was genuine—and uncharacteristic.

He frowned at the realization that he was starting to like Gemma around the edges. That'd never been his plan. In fact, he'd intended to avoid getting to know her at all costs. He wasn't going to keep up any long-distance ties when he left. Though most people thought he was an uncaring bastard, he in fact didn't want Gemma to get hurt. It seemed she'd been through enough already.

One conversation wasn't getting involved, he reminded himself. He was giving a pregnant girl a ride to a doctor's appointment. That was all.

CHAPTER TWELVE

SCOTT HAD JUST WOKEN UP from sleeping off his shift when he heard a knock on the door of his apartment late Friday afternoon. Still drowsy, he got up, pulled a T-shirt over his head and took his time getting to the door. He noticed Gemma wasn't in her room as he passed it. He listened for her elsewhere in the apartment, but it seemed to be empty.

As he opened the front door, he was straining to remember whether she'd mentioned she was working today or not—not that it really mattered. She was an adult, or close enough.

He tensed and swore out loud at the sight of his father.

"You've got a lot of nerve coming here again," Scott said, all traces of warm sleepiness washed away by a surge of adrenaline.

"I told you I'd be back."

"Gemma's not here."

"Then I'd like to talk to you."

"I don't have anything to say to you."

"There are some things I'd like to say to you," he said.

Something about the statement set Scott's temper soaring. "Yeah? Need to assuage your conscience?"

"Just a few minutes of your time. Please." The old man's eyes were weary and he looked haggard. Beaten down.

And that set Scott off. He opened the door wider, his pulse pounding, teeth clenched. Ability to think rationally gone. He stormed into the kitchen, knowing his sorry-ass dad would follow him.

Sure enough, the old guy came in behind him. Scott leaned against the counter by the stove, his back to the doorway and his dad. He wasn't sure he could stomach looking at him.

"Son, I'm sorry—"

Scott pounded his fist on the counter and whipped around. "Don't call me that!" He was loud enough they could probably hear him on the mainland, but he didn't care. "You lost that right when you destroyed our family. You didn't just abandon us or let us down. You basically spit on our family." Scott stepped closer, taking a moment to breathe and then to laugh bitterly. "I used to think you were such a good father. I actually looked up to you. Didn't like that you had to be on the road so much for your job, but I respected your work ethic and your dedication to providing for your family. Every Friday during football season, I'd spot you in the stands, and I'd think how cool it was that you were always there for me."

"I was—"

"Don't interrupt me. I'm on a goddamn roll. All the things I admired about you were a lie. You weren't dedicated to earning a living, you were shacking up with your girlfriend and daughter. And two days after every football game, you got in your car and drove off to see them again."

"Are you done yet?" his dad managed to say when Scott took another breath.

"Not even close!" Scott took another step forward. "The first eighteen years of my life, I thought I was pretty lucky. I had a decent family. A dad who loved me. I couldn't have been more wrong, could I? Did you lie awake with your…girlfriend…chuckling over how clueless Mom and I were? Did you ever once stop to think about what you were doing? About the absolute fraud you are?"

"Every day of my life."

The quiet words stopped Scott for a second. Only a second.

"Maybe I'd believe that if you'd shown an instant of remorse in the past ten years. Ten years. You tried to tell us how much we meant to you and yet you've never tried to make amends in ten goddamn years!"

His dad stared him down, and Scott noticed the sagging skin under the man's eyes. The creases in his skin that deepened with his frown. "Can I talk now?"

In response, Scott narrowed his eyes and realized that he had nothing else to get out. For now. He crossed his arms and backed up against the counter. Waiting.

His dad's shoulders rose and fell with a deep breath as Scott's heart hammered on. "I'm sorry, Scott."

Scott's instinct was to throw that back in his dad's face, but he'd run out of steam.

"I'm going to tell you some things about what happened years ago. It won't make anything okay. It won't make you feel any better. But you should know how it happened."

Scott scoffed but gestured for his dad to continue.

"Your mother and I were going through a rough patch—and no, that doesn't make any of this any more acceptable. Just a fact. I met Lisa at a restaurant where she was a waitress during one of my many trips to Fort Worth. We didn't immediately get involved, but she was friendly. Younger than I was and paid attention to me. She listened to me."

A nasty taste filled Scott's mouth.

"I eventually made the mistake of taking her home."

"I don't need details," Scott ground out.

"That I was unfaithful ate away at me, but I couldn't seem to stay away from this younger, pretty woman who seemed crazy about me. After a few weeks, I worked up the resolve to end it. That night, she told me she was expecting our baby."

"So that made it okay not to end it?"

"Of course not."

"But you didn't."

"I didn't. And it tore me up inside slowly with every single week that passed. But I no longer knew how to get out of it."

"You're wasting your breath," Scott said. "Nothing you say is going to make me forgive you."

His father swallowed, looking pale. He nodded. "I understand that. My point is that I never ever set out to hurt anyone. I made big mistakes and they spiraled out of control. Snowballed."

Scott shook his head. There was nothing else he could say. Nothing anybody could say to make everything okay.

"I'm sorry I never came after you to apologize or try to make peace."

"It wouldn't have worked if you had."

"But I should have tried."

"Yeah. If you ever gave half a damn, I'd think you would have tried."

"It's taken me fifty-five years to own up to how weak I am." He paused, his mouth open. "I'm a coward. A hundred times over." His voice cracked with the last word. "That's not something I recommend figuring out about yourself."

"I have no plans to," Scott said, disgusted.

"No. You have nothing to fear. You're not like me."

"Got that right."

"I've always admired your strength. Your conviction."

"I don't know about that, but if so, maybe you should have done more than admire it."

"I'm…trying." His father leaned on the counter with his elbows. "I've made some changes in my life over the past few months. I have a long way to go."

Scott didn't care what he'd done the past few months or the past ten years. "You've had your say. It's time for you to go."

"I have one more thing to cover."

Scott inhaled deeply in an attempt to summon his patience. "Get it over with."

"As I've said, I've made a lot of changes. I've decided I need to be happy on my own, without a relationship, for the first time since I was in junior high school. I've been going to a therapist, figuring out what's important to me."

"Congrats."

"I'd like to help Gemma somehow. Financially, physically, whatever she needs."

Scott bit back a sardonic laugh. "Good luck with that. She doesn't seem to like you any more than I do."

"I realize that. But I'd like the chance to change that."

"That's between you and her."

"Maybe you could nudge her into considering it. She's welcome to move into my home. I bought a three-bedroom house in a nice neighborhood with good schools. I'd help her with her baby."

"That's rich."

"She needs help. She's only seventeen."

"I know that and you know that but she doesn't seem to think so."

"Try to convince her."

"I have no influence over her. If I did, I sure as hell wouldn't steer her toward you."

His father exhaled in frustration, nodded with his lips pursed. "I'll go now. No use talking to a brick wall."

"I could've told you that fifteen minutes ago and saved you a whole lot of trouble."

"I've apologized. If there's something else I

can do, let me know." With that, his dad walked out the door.

Scott pushed the door closed after him with more force than necessary. His opinion of his dad hadn't changed, but he suspected raging at the man had at least helped his spleen. If he was lucky, the old man had assuaged his guilty need to make up and he'd be back out of his life, this time for good.

SERRANO'S NICKER FROM behind him was Scott's first clue that he and the horse weren't alone.

Though his spot on the bluff made him feel like the only person in the world, he supposed it was close enough to the stables to be frequented, at least on horseback. Definitely a spot he'd want to return to, now that he'd discovered it.

The natural overlook wasn't more than a couple hundred feet high, but this close to the sea it felt like a mountain. He imagined the turquoise water just beyond his visibility as he sat facing east on the dry, grassy ground, his knees bent and arms resting on them.

He wasn't up for company, not even a polite hello. His dad's visit had kept him restless and agitated for most of the night. When he'd gotten out of bed with the sun this morning, tired of tossing and turning, he'd needed to quiet his mind. The best way to do that was out here in the middle of nowhere. Alone.

He kept his back to the interloper to make his point.

Whoever it was didn't see fit to get his point. It sounded as though another horse stopped right next to Serrano.

Scott didn't move a muscle except to clench his teeth, still determined not to socialize.

"You need to get a hat."

The familiar honey-sweet voice behind him wasn't enough to soothe his irritation.

"What the hell are you doing out here?" he asked, still refusing to turn toward Mercedes as she dismounted her horse. He could hear her rustling in her saddlebag before she walked toward him.

A tube of sunscreen landed next to his jean-clad thigh. Mercedes's worn, utilitarian boots entered his field of vision and stopped two feet from him. Surrendering to the last shreds of hope for privacy, Scott looked up at her.

Damn if she didn't make the prettiest cowgirl he'd ever seen. Light blue denim, dusty from her ride, stretched the length of her legs, hugging those hips the way he dreamed of doing, in spite of himself. She wore a thin pink button-down blouse, the top few buttons undone to reveal a fitted camisole with a lace trim beneath. The ends of the shirt hem were tied in a knot just above the waistline of her jeans and he found himself fixated once again on that strip of skin.

She lowered herself to the ground next to him and sat cross-legged. On her head was a light brown cowboy hat with turquoise bead detail at the front.

"You'd look good in a Stetson." She rested her hands behind her in the grass and braced her weight on them. "And it'd keep the sun off your face."

As soon as she said it, he noticed the blaze of the midmorning sun on his cheeks. Instead of obeying her unspoken command to apply the cream, he raised his water bottle to his dry lips and took a swig. He nodded at it. Gave her some of her own medicine. "You should have water out here. Easy to dehydrate."

Mercedes's glance darted away as if she knew he was right. "I forgot to pack any. I don't plan to stay out too long, though."

"Didn't figure today was your riding day since you went last weekend," Scott said after a lull in their back-and-forth. He'd been banking on that, in fact, when the thought that he might run into her had hit him on the drive. "You following me?"

"I needed to get away. That's the one good aspect of my sister being here. Easier to have a couple of hours free."

She could barely find the opportunity to be alone and he could barely be convinced to try not to be alone. One more way they were opposites.

"Maria told me when I got here that you'd taken Serrano out. Long drive out here. Next time we should carpool." She smiled at him before checking out the landscape that stretched below them for miles.

"They ought to open a place on the island. On the north end. All that undeveloped area would make an ideal place to ride."

"You should mention it to her. Maybe she and her husband are looking to expand."

"Maybe." He'd be gone soon anyway. It wasn't his concern beyond selfish reasons, though the drive all the way out here had been therapeutic in its own way.

"Was Gemma awake when you left?"

"Not that I know of. Why?"

"She's been having trouble sleeping. She says she's getting uncomfortable, but I think it's stress."

"With good reason. She's got guts, I'll give her that."

He felt Mercedes staring at him but refused to acknowledge it.

"You almost sound like she's become more than a roommate."

"Decent housekeeper, too."

"Nice." She whacked him on the arm.

One of the horses nickered softly, but other than that, silence stretched out between them and around them. An expectant silence. He knew it was a matter of time before she broke it, likely with pesky questions he wouldn't care to answer, so he ended it himself.

"So what gives? Thought you only came out every other weekend."

"If I didn't know better, I'd suspect avoiding me was the reason you did decide to ride today."

He took another drink and watched a small, rabbit-size animal tear across the dirt into the trees in the distance below.

"Stressful week," Mercedes said eventually. "Riding helps me forget about it for a couple hours. Same for you?"

Looking more closely at her, he noticed her milk-chocolate eyes lacked their usual sparkle. Faint shadows darkened the skin beneath, and now that he thought about it, her smile earlier had been thin somehow. Hollow.

"What's bugging you?" he asked, in large part to avoid her inquiry. He had zero desire to discuss his dad.

She absently plucked the dried grass out of the ground as she continued to stare off into the distance. "My sister."

"Charlotte?"

The half smile she gave him was almost gratifying, but he had the fleeting thought that he wanted to hear her laugh. Odd. Her laugh couldn't fix any of his problems and he'd never been one for fixing someone else's, unless they happened to be of the emergency-medical type.

"I did tell you she hates that name, right?" she asked.

"Must've slipped my mind. What's up with Sister Charlie? You said she just moved back to town?"

"Not back. She's never lived on the island before. The longest she's been here was eight days and, come to think of it, that was probably the previous longest eight days of my life. Or definitely in the running." She picked more grass. "She's living with Gram and me until fall."

"Looked like you got along okay the other night."

"You were with us during the magical fifteen minutes she and I were on good terms."

"Why don't you get along?"

Mercedes tossed her pile of grass down and cradled her knees to her. "It's a sibling thing. You know how it—oh. I guess you don't know how it is."

"Sibling is a taboo subject in my house."

"It's becoming one in mine. Living in the same house as adults… We were never very good at it when we were kids. We're worse now. I'd like to get along better with her, but every time I try to do something nice for Charlie, it backfires."

"Maybe you're going about it all wrong," he suggested.

"Yeah? What would you suggest, oh sibling expert?"

"Don't try to do nice things for her."

She smiled sadly. "Kind of my flaw. I can't help myself. I've always been the one that handles things. I like handling things."

"Things?"

"Okay. Everything." She glanced down at the sunscreen. "Are you going to put that stuff on or are you going to make me do it for you?"

"You try to take care of everybody, don't you?"

"There are worse afflictions," she said stubbornly, as if she'd had this argument more than once.

"Worse than caring too much?" He picked up the tube and unscrewed the cap. Squirting a modest amount into his hands, he slathered it onto his cheeks and nose. "I suppose so." He had a handful of worse afflictions himself. Matter of fact, his "afflictions" made her overhelpfulness seem an awful lot like a virtue.

She rested her chin on her arms and looked as if her dog had died. The desire to give her a hard time for being a better person than he'd ever be suddenly disappeared.

Without thought, Scott reached out and touched her shoulder. Squeezed it briefly.

Mercedes turned her head and met his eyes with a steady intense gaze he found himself unable to break at first. In that moment of connection, he wanted to do more to make her feel better than just brush her shoulder, and for once it wasn't a sexual urge. Not entirely, anyway.

Averting his eyes, he rose. "Time for me to head back."

He wasted no time in striding the dozen feet to where Serrano stood switching his tail. Scott stuck his empty water bottle into his saddlebag and took out the other he'd bought on the drive in. Then he climbed up and swung his leg over till he was settled in the saddle.

"Mercedes," he said to her back.

She turned around and he tossed the water to her before gently jabbing his feet into Serrano's sides and retreating.

CHAPTER THIRTEEN

IF SCOTT WAS GOING TO MISS anything about San Amaro, it'd be the people he worked with. Though he tended to be one of the least social in the department, there was no way to do this job without feeling part of the brotherhood.

Outside of the station, the EMS staff and the firefighters acted as a single unit. They worked together as one department, volunteered together for events, played on the same intramural teams, particularly when the opposition was the police department.

But at the station, all bets were off. Especially when any sports or competitions, spontaneous or otherwise, were involved.

Penn Griffin had found a football outside the station this morning. After lunch, he and Cale Jackson, a fire lieutenant, had challenged Scott and Rafe to a scrimmage out back in the sand.

Rafe had the ball and Penn was putting pressure on him as he tried to pass. He finally got one off and Scott ran toward their makeshift end zone, where the ball was headed. Cale was on him hard. They both went up for the ball and Scott managed to come down with it.

"Touchdown!" Rafe yelled, his hands in the air.

Joe Mendoza, the fire captain on duty, opened the patio door and came outside. "Who's winning?"

"We are, of course," Rafe said. "Twenty-one to seven. My boy Scott has some skills."

"You paramedic types just have more free time to goof off at work and practice." Penn stole the football from Scott, tossed it straight up and caught it.

"When's the last time you had a big fire?" Scott said, having overheard them complaining about a lack of action earlier today.

Penn ignored the question. "You play in high school?" he asked Scott.

"Wide receiver. You?"

"Same."

"Someone's here to see the short-timer," Joe said.

It wasn't until everyone looked at him that it clicked with Scott. He was the short-timer.

"Who is it?"

Joe shrugged. "Some kid. He's in the reception area."

Scott headed through the station's living area and down the hall to the public door. The "kid" was as tall as he was. Thin as a pole with black hair. He was checking out the memorial plaque on the far wall, his back to Scott.

"Can I help you?" Scott said as he approached the guy.

He wasn't really a kid, Scott saw as the guy faced him. A few years younger, but by Joe's forty-something standards, he might as well be an adolescent.

"Hi," he said, holding his hand out to Scott. "Greg Wolf."

"Hi, Greg. Scott Pataki. Good to meet you." They shook hands. "What can I do for you?"

Greg glanced around nervously. "Is there somewhere we could talk? It'll only take a couple of minutes."

Scott nodded to the main door. "Looks like the courtyard's empty. That work?"

Greg nodded and they walked outside. Scott followed him toward the back of the long, curved wall that held the fire-service mural painted by Evan Drake's wife. When Greg leaned his forearms on the top of the wall, Scott followed suit, curiosity jabbing at him.

"I just wanted to thank you," Greg said, looking out across the street toward the department training facility. "For saving my life eighteen months ago."

Scott didn't know what to say. He didn't remember seeing this guy before, didn't remember saving him. "You're welcome," he finally said hesitantly.

The guy studied him then looked away. "I tried to kill myself. Took a bottle of pills. Came damn close, from what the doctors said. They also said one of the reasons I was alive was because of you. My heart stopped beating. You got it started right away. Got meds in me to counteract what I'd taken."

Scott still didn't remember—he'd worked too many overdoses in his time. "No problem. I was just doing my job."

"My outlook is totally different now. I like my life."

"How old are you?" Scott asked.

"Nineteen. I've got a lot of years left."

Greg took out his wallet from his back jeans pocket and opened it, then held out a photo of himself with a petite girl with arresting brown eyes. Her whole face was lit up with happiness—and so was Greg's in the picture, for that matter.

"This is Elena," Greg said. "I married her five weeks ago." He was grinning widely, his eyes coming alive. "She's the love of my life, man."

"Congratulations," Scott said, meaning it. Something about this guy's happiness was contagious.

"Thanks. But that's not all." Greg turned toward him. "We found out today we're going to have a baby."

Scott laughed and shook Greg's hand again. "Double congrats, then. Awesome news."

Greg nodded, still grinning. Then he sobered and looked Scott in the eye. "I was messed up before. She's helped me turn my life around." Emotion made his voice thick. "I wouldn't have this chance if you hadn't, you know. Done your thing."

A knot formed in Scott's chest and all he could do was nod.

"This baby that we're going to have, it wouldn't even exist..." Tears filled Greg's eyes and his Adam's apple rose and lowered as he swallowed. He burst into an embarrassed laugh. "Sorry."

"No. Nothing to be sorry about. I'm happy you're doing so well."

Looking down, obviously still a little embarrassed, Greg nodded. "I just wanted to let you know, man. It's because of you. Thanks again." He shook Scott's hand one more time, nodded awkwardly and walked off toward the visitor's parking lot, smiling the whole way.

Scott stared after him and belatedly realized he wore a goofy grin himself. He sniffed, glad the lump-in-the-throat sensation was fading. Blinking several times, he told himself the moisture in his eyes was because of the wind. He again leaned on the wall, his back to the station, and worked to collect himself, to suppress the emotions that had blindsided him.

FOR THE FIRST TIME, Mercedes was starting to believe that maybe Gemma had a chance of making it on her own with her baby. She didn't doubt the teenager's devotion and ability to be a mom—it was the money angle that made Mercedes, and probably Gemma herself, lose sleep.

The second job could make all the difference. Claudia Winn, one of Mercedes's favorite clients, was as desperate for a weekend babysitter as Gemma was for more income. It would be long hours, between Claudia's kids and the other thirty-hours-a-week babysitting gig, but Gemma's relief this evening was tangible. After one more congratulatory hug, Mercedes had said a quick goodbye and let herself out.

While she'd been inside, the downpour had stopped, at least for a temporary reprieve. She eyed the heavy clouds as she took the wet stairs slowly down to the parking lot.

She was about to get in her car when Scott's sports car two spots over caught her eye. Gemma had mentioned she hadn't seen him at all since two nights ago before she'd gone to bed. Though he came and went as he pleased and didn't report in to Gemma, forty-eight hours was longer than his usual.

When Mercedes looked closer, she realized he was sitting in the driver's seat of his car. The engine was off. His head was reclined and he didn't move. She kept watching as she got into her own car, waiting for him to get out and go inside. Or even stir.

She stuck her key in the ignition absently but didn't start the car. Waited some more, still keeping an eye out for a sign of…anything. The rain started to pick up again, which blurred her vision, but she could see enough to know he hadn't moved.

What in the world? Was he drunk? Dead?

A knot in her stomach tightened as she yanked her key out, opened her door and hurried through the rain to his window.

His eyes were closed, face drawn, and when she tapped on the glass, he didn't respond. A second panicked tap with her keys made him slowly turn his head toward her. He stared at her with disconcertingly flat eyes, unseeing.

"Scott, what are you doing?" she said loudly enough to be heard through the door and over the weather.

Instead of answering, he turned his head forward again. Closed his eyes. Her hair and clothes were getting increasingly wet and she shivered, though it had nothing to do with the rain and wind.

"Scott!" She hit the window hard again in frustration, and when he didn't react at all, she ran around to the passenger side, mumbling to herself about how she was going to kill him if he was drunk. Double kill him for driving his car.

She whipped open the passenger door, thankful it was unlocked, and dropped into the bucket seat. Pushing her wet hair out of her face, she turned to him, ready to rail. And froze.

His eyes were open now, staring in front of him, and his face was noticeably pale. He wore jeans and an EMS T-shirt, wrinkled and filthy. It looked as if he'd lived in it for a week.

"Scott?" She touched his arm, gently at first, then she grasped it, panicked. "What is wrong?"

His lids lowered and she shook his arm.

"Have you been drinking?"

Finally he shook his head. "Not yet."

She was so relieved that he wasn't tanked that it took several seconds for the implications of his reply to sink in.

"Not yet? You're not drinking anything. Tell me what's going on, Scott. Please."

He opened his eyes. Swallowed hard. The silence stretched with her tension and she forced herself to loosen her grip on him. He opened his mouth as if in slow motion and she noticed his lips were abnormally dry.

"I lost him."

"Lost who?" Mercedes slid her fingers down his arm and took his hand in hers. He didn't grasp hers, but he didn't pull away, either. "Did something happen at work, Scott?"

Again, he opened his mouth, but no words came out. He closed it, shook his head slowly, with so much pain etched on his face. Emotional, gut-wrenching pain.

"Why aren't you at work now?" she continued as all kinds of possibilities shuffled through her mind. Was he hurt? Sick?

"Shift ended this morning—7:00 a.m."

"Then what...where have you been for twelve and a half hours? Scott, please talk to me. You're scaring me."

"I've been...walking. Along the shore." He checked the dashboard clock. "Didn't know I was gone so long."

"Who's lost, Scott? Talk to me."

"He died in my arms. Two years old." His voice seemed to short out and became a whisper. "I couldn't bring him back. Couldn't save him."

Oh, God. She couldn't imagine. Actually, she kind of could—her mother had died as Mercedes held her hand. But...a child so young. With the added weight of feeling responsible, of being the person who was supposed to be able to give that boy a chance to live…

She brought his hand to her lips, squeezed her eyes shut. Her instinct was to throw her arms around him and pull him close, but the front seat of a sports car made that a challenge.

"That's terrible. I'm so sorry." Inadequate, useless words. She wove her fingers with his, his hand unresisting, unmoving. "This was at work?"

She took his nonresponse as an affirmative.

"I'm sure you did everything you possibly could, right? But such a little one…that's extra hard to swallow."

He didn't give any indication that he heard her. Mercedes searched her mind for something to say, some way to soothe this hurting man.

"You're one of the very best at your job, Scott. Faith told me this." She waited for him to nod, urged him to acknowledge that truth, but he just sat there.

"Medicine can't fix every single thing. You of all people know that. It can't save every life." She rubbed her hand up and down his arm. "You can only do so much."

"It was Brad Gilbert's son. Elliott. Cutest little man. Big blue eyes…"

A sick feeling rolled through Mercedes's gut. He'd known the boy? "Who is Brad Gilbert?"

"Firefighter. My colleague." He squeezed his eyes tightly shut as if fighting off a powerful emotion. "I couldn't save my friend's boy."

CHAPTER FOURTEEN

OH GOD, OH GOD, OH GOD. How could she ever make him feel okay?

Mercedes looked around frantically, as if there was any kind of answer out there for how he could handle this. How she could help him. The clock on the dashboard reminded her she needed to get food to Gram, who was probably alone by now as Charlie was on an overnight trip to Austin, and Yoli's shift was over. She was almost an hour late with Gram's dinner, and she needed to take some of her pills with food.

She made a split-second decision and jumped out of the car, back into the heavy rain. She ran around to Scott's door and opened it. Ducked her head inside.

"Move over," she told him. "Climb to the other seat, Scott. Hurry, I'm getting soaked."

He looked at her as if she'd lost her mind.

"I'm not leaving you, but I have to get to Gram. You're coming with me."

Seconds ticked by and her shirt became so wet

she could wring it out. "Just do it." She pushed at his upper arm.

Without his expression changing, he hoisted himself over the small console between seats, moving like a half-dead man, then dragged his legs over. She wasn't sure he could fit until he pushed the passenger seat back all the way. She wasted no time in climbing in and slamming the door on the storm.

Scott's keys were in the ignition and Mercedes turned them till the engine started up smoothly. She reached for the gearshift and realized the car was a manual. Of course. What overgrown boy would buy an automatic sports car? She'd learned to drive a stick-shift car—sort of—years ago, when Nadia had had one for about six months before she totaled it. Saying a little prayer, Mercedes put one foot on the brake and shifted into Reverse.

The start wasn't smooth, but she didn't stall it. Glancing at Scott sideways, she figured if he didn't notice, she hadn't done too badly.

The two-mile drive was on the adventurous side, but Scott didn't comment. She pulled into the carport to get the car out of the rain.

"Come on in," she said, grabbing her purse.

He didn't move. "You live here?"

It didn't seem the right time for a smart-aleck

response. "I need to get my grandma's dinner and pills, but then we can talk."

"I don't need to talk." He said the words with a hint of venom. At least that was a sign of something besides numbness.

"Then you can come in and we won't talk. You can eat if you want to, or stare at the wall, but you're coming inside."

"Not really up for meeting your family."

"I get that. Charlie's gone. Gram is most likely in her bed waiting for me to bring her some food. She won't know you're here if you don't want her to. Please, can we go? She needs to take her medications."

He deliberated silently for a moment then went for the door handle. Thank God. Though she didn't have the faintest clue what she was going to do with him.

She hurried through the rain to the front door, with Scott trailing more slowly behind her. Gram was in her room, as Mercedes had guessed.

"You can wait on the back porch if you don't want to meet Gram. There's a refrigerator out there. Help yourself to a drink, whatever you want." She caught her mistake too late. "Not whatever you want. There's pop." *Leave the beer alone,* she willed him.

She pointed toward the kitchen as they entered the house and he headed in that direction. Mercedes followed him and flipped the oven on to reheat leftover casserole for Gram.

Scott hesitated at the table. Watching him from behind, she wanted to wrap her arms around him. He looked like a lost boy. Without a word, he walked to the back door and went out on the porch.

Realizing her wet clothes were dripping all over the tile floor, Mercedes hollered out a hello to Gram, then clambered up the stairs and changed into dry jeans and a shirt in record time. She took a towel to her hair, knowing it was a lost cause but not wanting it to soak her dry shirt. She twisted it into a sloppy bun, off her shoulders. Then she headed to Gram's bedroom.

"I was worried about you," Gram said as Mercedes bent down to hug her.

"I was worried about you."

"You got wet?"

"Little bit." Mercedes smiled. "Sorry I took longer than I expected. How long ago did Yoli leave?"

"She stayed about fifteen minutes later than usual. We got to talking."

"I'll have dinner ready in twenty minutes for you. I've got some stuff to take care of. Do you want to stay in here to eat?"

"That's just fine, sweetie. I've just been reading away."

She held up a paperback book and Mercedes did a double take. Gram had the same book she'd seen on Scott's stack in his bedroom.

"Good book?" Mercedes asked as she headed for pill central in the bathroom.

"I enjoy the travel descriptions, but this guy is full of baloney when he gets to going about his philosophy."

Mercedes grinned to herself, expertly doling out the right medications into her hand.

As soon as Gram had downed her pills, Mercedes put the casserole in the oven and set the timer on her cell phone. She went out to the porch, relieved to see Scott sitting there in the near darkness, though she didn't know what she'd expected. The steady rain outside the screens insulated them from the world. Normally she'd find the sound soothing, but tonight the air was too tense. Though there'd been no thunder or lightning all day, the atmosphere seemed full of danger. Tragedy.

Scott sat stiffly on the wicker love seat, one hand on the arm of it, the other in his lap. Staring straight ahead, out at the pool. It seemed too much for her to sit right next to him, so she pulled one of the chairs closer to the love seat.

Scott frowned and watched Mercedes settle into her chair, propping her feet up on an ottoman. It was the first time he'd really looked at her today. He'd only been half aware of her when she'd climbed into his car uninvited. Now she was shadows and shades of gray, as she'd had the sense not to turn the overhead light on. Though he couldn't say what she'd been wearing before, her clothes were now dry, so he guessed she'd changed them.

"Why am I here, Mercedes?"

She'd been fluffing a throw pillow and stopped, setting it in her lap, and touched his forearm. "You're upset. I didn't want you to be alone."

He looked at her hand on his arm, registered the hot-pink shade of her nails. Alone was how he got through things. Alone with a bottle.

He didn't know why the hell he'd let her strong-arm him and force him to come with her. Actually, he hadn't let her do anything. Hadn't realized what was going on, he'd been so absorbed in the horror of the evening before. Seeing Elliott's blue eyes filled with terror, seeing his lifeless body. Hearing Brad's inconsolable cries when he'd arrived at the hospital.

"What can I do, Scott?" she asked, placing her hand on the arm of her chair. "Will you tell me what happened?"

What could she do? He strained his mind, aching to come up with something that would give him relief from the nightmare. The search was futile. Struggling to swallow around the lump in his throat, he shook his head slowly.

He leaned forward, elbows on his thighs, giving thought to getting the hell out of here.

Mercedes's phone beeped and she stood. "Gram's dinner. Want something?"

The thought of food made him sick to his stomach. He shook his head again.

"Don't go anywhere," she said as if his thoughts were written on his face. "You're better off here than having Gemma throw Twenty Questions at you. Besides, I have your keys." She put her hands in the front pocket of her jeans and jingled them as proof, then walked past him and back into the house.

Trying to convince her to give him his keys sounded like a gargantuan task. The idea of walking all the way home was unfathomable. He hadn't slept, hadn't even tried to close his eyes and pass out, since two nights ago. His arms and legs felt as if they'd tripled in weight and he ached all over. Besides, if he did go home, he'd immediately give in to a drink.

He wasn't going anywhere.

Neither, it seemed, were the incessant images, the memories, even the sounds of the fourteen-minute call last night.

Fourteen minutes. Fourteen crucial, unchange-

able minutes that altered so many lives forever
and ended one.

Scott jumped up. Unmindful of the downpour,
he stormed out the porch door to the backyard.
Without considering, he whipped his shirt over
his head, kicked off his shoes and shed his pants.
His boxers were soaked from the rain before he
even jumped into the pool, but he didn't care. He
dived into the warm water, surfaced and broke
into freestyle. It took him only four strokes to
reach the opposite end but that didn't slow his
pace.

He didn't give any credence to the soreness or
the heaviness of ten minutes before. The water
took some of the weight away, gave him something else to focus on. If he could make his
muscles hurt from swimming, that was power.
Control. He'd much prefer causing his own pain
than having it inflicted upon him by something,
anything else. Especially some kind of cruel fate
that he wanted no part of.

Lap after lap, he pushed himself. Gloried in the
fire in his lungs when it hit. The rain splattering
on the surface of the water gave the pool an oth-
erworldly, surreal feel and he became gradually
distanced from the horror of the past twenty-four
hours.

More time passed. Maybe fifteen minutes?
Twenty? It didn't matter. He ceased the laps

abruptly and pushed off the side of the pool, floating on his back, letting the rain pound down on
him. Wash it away.

He opened his eyes at the same time the porch
door flew open. Mercedes rushed into his line of
vision and stood at the edge of the pool, hands on
her hips, rain pelting her. She raised one hand,
palm up, as if to question what in the world he
was doing. Or maybe when he'd lost his mind.
He didn't respond.

She looked toward the house, then turned back
to him and stared. Crossing the ten feet or so to
the patio table, she took her phone and his keys
out of her pockets and stuck them under the table
out of the rain. When she straightened, she peeled
her now-wet jeans down her legs, folded them in
quarters and placed them on top of her phone.
The alternate-reality feel of the moment intensified as, her back still to him, she unbuttoned her
shirt, tugged it off and threw it on top of the pile.

The image of her when she finally faced him
was burned into his memory permanently. The
curve of her breasts were partially covered by
ivory-and-black lace. Her body narrowed at her
waist, then curved out again into sexy, feminine
hips. Skimpily cut panties matched her bra. Her
breasts rose with her arms as she unclasped whatever was securing her hair and let her long mane
cascade down over her shoulders.

An hour ago, he'd felt dead, but now his body had a faint glimmer of life. Very faint. That said a lot about how messed up in the head he was, because that body of hers warranted full-out flames.

Mercedes walked to the side of the pool and jumped in without hesitation. Perfect time to close his eyes and shut out the world again, to prevent her questions or at least postpone them.

She let him get away with it. He felt her swimming around him, skimming along the bottom beneath him, pausing at the side of the pool to rest.

As the rain slowed to a sprinkle, he started to come out of the numbness he'd managed to attain by swimming. He took in a slow, deep breath and pushed himself to the bottom of the pool, letting the silence and the isolation wash over him. He sat there until his lungs were empty, then pushed off to the surface.

Mercedes was at the edge of the pool, her elbows hitched on the concrete deck, her back to him. Steeling himself, he joined her, standing on the ledge that ran around the perimeter about four feet down. She glanced at him but didn't say anything. They rested there for several minutes, watching the raindrops splatter in the puddles. Scott continued to fight off images of Elliott Gilbert.

"It was a peanut," he said eventually.

Mercedes turned her attention to him expectantly.

"Smaller than my little fingernail. One chocolate-covered peanut that the little guy didn't even like." His voice was rough, raw. "An undiagnosed peanut allergy."

He heard Mercedes suck in air and expel it loudly.

"I asked what he'd eaten when we arrived on the scene. All his mom could tell me in her hysterical state was that he'd had chocolate. No known food allergies. It wasn't until later, much later, that they figured out the culprit."

He closed his eyes, tried to let the sound of the gentle rain soothe him, but there was no comfort.

"Not that it mattered what it was. Knowing that wouldn't have changed anything Rafe and I did. It wouldn't have reversed the outcome."

Mercedes moved her arm toward him and touched his. Squeezed his upper arm and didn't take her hand away. For some reason, that little gesture gave him the strength to continue.

"Brad was on duty, too. Any other time, he would've been there on the call with us, but by random bad luck, the engine had another call at the same time we did. He wasn't there when his boy…"

The lump in his throat pulsed painfully and he fought the emotion threatening to drown him.

"That's terrible, Scott. I'm so sorry."

"I don't know how I'll ever look Brad in the face."

"He of all people should understand. He faces the same kinds of things himself, right?"

Scott didn't answer. There was no "same kinds of things" for losing your child. He couldn't really begin to imagine what Brad and his wife were going through right now, although hearing them from the hallway in the minutes after the doctor had called the boy's death gave him a sample of the soul-deep pain.

"I don't know how you do the job you do," Mercedes said quietly. "You guys are heroes, Scott. Think about the lives you save."

Greg Wolf, the newlywed and father-to-be, came to mind, but Scott pushed him away. No life they'd managed to rescue canceled out the one they hadn't saved last night.

"Nineteen more days," he said, more to himself than her. "Six more shifts. I don't know if I can do it."

"You have to. You don't want to let that one be your last shift, the one that stays with you."

He considered that. Nodded vaguely. Then his thoughts returned to Elliott. "He was still conscious when we got there," he said hoarsely. "His mom called 911 pretty quickly. I got the IV in on the first try, pushed epinephrine through his little body. Rafe got the oxygen going right away. We might as well have been putting water through him for all the effect it had." He shook his head helplessly.

Scott recited every procedure he and Rafe had done. The results—or lack thereof—of each. He remembered every detail as if some kind of hypersensitive memory had kicked in. Forgetting Mercedes was there, he poured it all out.

"The second ambulance got there as we were loading him in the back. One of the other guys drove our rig to the hospital while Rafe and I kept working on Elliott in the back." He'd actually been kneeling on the gurney, still trying to get a heartbeat, as Rafe wheeled them into the emergency department.

"There was nothing else you could have done," Mercedes said when he stopped talking.

He finally looked at her straight on. "That's what makes it so damn hard to swallow."

Scott pulled himself out of the pool with his arms and sat on the side, his legs dangling in the water. He leaned on his hands behind him and angled his face to the darkening sky. The light sprinkle of rain intensified at that moment and he let the drops wash over him, as if it could cleanse him. The wind had picked up and the rain was now cooler than the water in the pool.

He pulled the night air into his lungs, relishing the crispness of it. As the minutes passed, he began to feel marginally better. Less heavy-hearted. Deep, even breaths became almost therapeutic, as had, apparently, pouring it all out, putting it out to the universe.

Mercedes moved sideways in the pool so she was directly in front of him. She lifted her arms to his thighs, just above his knees, and braced herself there instead of on the pool wall. Her touch seemed to center him.

Maybe he could get through this night. Maybe, eventually, he could let himself sleep.

The sky was almost entirely dark now and the heavy clouds covered the moon. When he looked down at her, black-and-ivory lace commanded his attention. He could make out the tops of her breasts spilling out of her soaked bra.

He slid back into the pool, slipped his arms around Mercedes to keep her close and allowed himself to let the woman awaken something inside him besides pain.

CHAPTER FIFTEEN

MERCEDES WOUND HER ARMS around Scott's neck, as she'd been longing to do ever since she'd found him in his car. He braced his feet on the under-water ledge, knees bent, creating room for her between his legs.

She'd been struggling for the right things to say for the past hour. She reached out with her eyes instead, attempting to convey her concern for him, her empathy for the tragedy he'd been through, without words.

They were so close their breaths mingled. Scott's gaze lowered to her lips and the energy between them heated in a single heartbeat. She inhaled shakily, shallowly, drawn to him. Fighting it. It wasn't the right time....

He moved the final inch, pressing his lips to hers, tightening his arms and kissing her with so much urgency and pent-up need she didn't care if it was the right time. Didn't care if she breathed. As long as he didn't stop.

They had to stop.

"Scott," she managed to get out. "No."

It took him several seconds to break the contact, and she had just as hard a time allowing the cool air to come between them. He didn't loosen his grip on her at all.

"This isn't right. Not now," she whispered. "Not after what you've been through—"

"Shh, Mercedes." His voice was a low, sexy growl that made her shiver. He trailed his knuckles gently along her jaw from her ear to her chin. "Please. I don't want to think anymore."

She managed to look into his eyes for a good second and a half before giving him what he needed, what she wanted. Closing the space between them, she gave in to the need that pulsed through her. Tried to kiss his pain away.

Scott held her with both arms, pulling her body flush against his, letting her feel the physical effect she had on him. His tongue demanded entry into her mouth. She matched his desire wholeheartedly, answering the moan that came from deep in his throat with needy sounds of her own.

As he kissed her, he slid his hands to her rear, on top of her underwear. She ached to have him slide them beneath the material, to touch her everywhere. One hand trailed along the back of her thighs to where they met. Dipped between her legs. He gently lifted her legs, one at a time, and hooked them over his so she straddled him. The shift not only made it easier for her to hold on, it fit their bodies together intimately. With nothing but cotton and lace between them.

His fingers inched under her panties and kneaded her bare skin as he continued to devour her mouth. He slid his fingers lower to the most intimate part of her, teased her opening. She angled into his hand, aching for him, and gasped when his finger entered her. Throwing her head back, she arched toward him.

He kissed her neck, running his tongue along the length of it. Continuing to tease her with his finger, he withdrew till she nearly begged, reentering her, sending fire to every one of her nerve endings. Her climax came quickly, and her control broke, shattering to pieces around him. She tried to catch her breath, curling into his arms. He drew her chin up so he could kiss her again.

Before she could regain any semblance of mental functioning, Scott broke the contact of their lips, angling his head to the side. "Do you hear that?" he whispered into her ear.

"What?" She kissed the side of his neck. "What's wrong?"

"That," he said, pulling slightly away from her.

It took her several seconds to register what he was talking about, but when she did, she snapped out of her lust-induced trance instantly. "My phone. Gram."

How long had she been out here? What was

she thinking, completely forgetting about her grandma?

Scratch that question. She hadn't been thinking at all. Hot shame burned her cheeks and her conscience.

She untangled her body from his and popped out of the pool, jogging around it toward the table. The ringtone stopped just before she uncovered her phone. As soon as she did, the display confirmed what she'd been afraid of.

"I need to go inside," she said, guilt washing through her and making it impossible to think.

She was in nothing but her underwear and bra. Soaked. And Gram needed her.

God.

Scott was at her side before she could figure out what to do.

"Towels," he said. "You need to dry off."

Towels. Duh. "We have some in here." She entered the porch, rushed over to the utility cabinet in the corner and grabbed two thick towels. She handed him one and as soon as she had the water out of her face, she reached for one of the terry-cloth robes on the top shelf.

"I can't believe I forgot about her," she said in a low voice as she toweled herself off. Dropping the towel, she pulled the robe around her and knotted the belt. "I have to—"

"Go," he said, pressing a quick kiss to the side of her head. "I'll find my keys and let myself out."

She nodded, leaning over to wring her hair out, wondering what Gram needed. She'd left her with her dinner in her bedroom, the TV tuned to her Monday-night shows. She was no doubt long finished eating, but she wouldn't track Mercedes down with the phone for that.

One last squeeze of her hair and she hurried inside, leaving Scott to fend for himself.

"Gram?" she called out as soon as she opened the door.

"Sadie?" Gram's voice was unsteady, as if she was upset. Mercedes hurried to her room.

"I'm sorry, Gram. I was swimming…" She hadn't told Gram that Scott was here, first because Scott hadn't been in the right mind-set to meet her—and Gram definitely would want to be introduced to him. Now she still couldn't do it. Couldn't fess up to him being the reason she'd lost all track of time and forgotten to check on Gram.

Her grandma squeezed her eyes shut and her lip trembled. When she opened her eyes, she didn't look at Mercedes. "I'm so sorry, Sadie," she said, distressed. "I…" She shook her head.

Mercedes frantically tried to figure out what was wrong. She lowered herself to the bed, holding Gram's hand. "What is it, Gram?"

Her grandma shook her head, again closing her

eyes. "I hollered for you several times. I didn't know you were outside. I couldn't hold it..."

Understanding hit Mercedes. Gram had needed her to help with her bedpan. They'd put off adult diapers because Gram could use the bathroom or a bedpan...as long as she had help. She'd let her down big-time.

"It's okay," Mercedes said, hugging her, her heart breaking. "Everything's going to be okay. I'm so, so sorry, Gram."

"No, I'm sorry. Such a bother—" Gram broke off and shook her head.

"We'll get it cleaned up and then I'll whoop you in a game of Scrabble, okay?" She brushed a tear out of the corner of her eye.

Gram was humiliated and it was completely Mercedes's fault. Her grandma had needed her and she'd been all over Scott in the pool, oblivious to her responsibilities.

Mercedes kissed her grandma's forehead, barely able to breathe. Gram was paying the price for her selfishness.

BEING NICE WASN'T Scott's thing.

So when the idea struck him, when he was two people away from the front of the bagel line, he shot it down. There was no reason to pick up a bagel and take it to Mercedes. Didn't matter how much out of her way she'd gone for him the other night, or how distressed she'd been when she ran inside to her grandmother. He didn't need to take her breakfast.

He hadn't seen her since she'd rushed off and, truth be told, he wanted to see her. He needed to convince himself she was as amazing as the woman who had taunted him in his dreams since he'd sneaked out of her backyard.

And yet, he didn't want to give her the wrong idea and make her think there was something between them more than there was.

Another person ahead of him got her order, paid and left, moving Scott one spot closer.

Oh, hell, he was being an idiot. Buy the damn bagels, deliver them and forget about it. It was breakfast, not an engagement ring.

"Can I help you?" the teenager with two braids in her hair and a small hoop in one side of her nose asked from behind the counter.

Scott realized he didn't have the first notion of what kind of bagel Mercedes Stone preferred. Or if she even liked bagels. "I'll take one of each flavor."

"All eighteen of them?" the girl said, eyebrows raised.

"How about six. You pick." She could share with her grandmother and sister, but even the three of them probably wouldn't know what to do with a dozen and a half.

"Cream cheese?" the girl asked.

So much for a simple nice gesture. Selfish and antisocial were easier by far.

"Add a couple tubs. Your favorites."

The girl shrugged and filled a paper bag for him. He ordered a breakfast sandwich for himself, plus a large coffee, paid for everything and left. He got in his car and headed toward Mercedes's house before he thought too damn hard about it.

MERCEDES WAS GOING TO seriously harm her sister.

The nonchalant "it's for you" Charlie had hollered up the stairs after the doorbell rang had done nothing to prepare her for the sight of Scott standing in her living room just inside the front door. In broad daylight.

She watched from the top of the stairway, unseen, as Charlie chatted with him. Even after working for the past twenty-four hours straight—according to Gemma—he looked good enough to make Mercedes's stomach do some Olympic-worthy flips. And that was without smiling. Flashes of the other night hit her and the stairway grew suddenly warm.

She shut down that line of thinking immediately, still upset with herself. Normally, she didn't hide things from Gram, but she still felt so guilty for forgetting her that she hadn't said anything except that she'd been swimming. Keeping the truth from Gram only compounded the guilt—okay, not the whole truth. She didn't want her grandma to have a heart attack. But she should have admitted Scott had been there. If she'd explained how upset he was about what had happened at work, Gram would have understood.

Why on earth was he here now? Scott wasn't exactly the drop-by-and-chat type. Trying to pull off nonchalance, Mercedes headed downstairs.

"Hey," she said, as if it was no big deal to see him. As if she hadn't been nearly naked with him in the pool, with him touching parts of her very few had touched. Her face reddened at the memory.

"Hi," Scott said. "Brought you ladies some breakfast." He held up a bag from Bagel Zone.

When she glanced at her sister, Charlie shot her a knowing, irritated look that said, *You've been holding out on me.*

"Thank you," Mercedes said to Scott, feeling oddly shy. She ignored her sister. "That's… really nice of you. Are you staying for breakfast?"

"Grabbed myself a sandwich and ate it on the way here. Busy shift last night. I didn't have much time to eat."

Relieved, Mercedes took the bag from him and peeked inside, breathing in the aroma of fresh-baked bread. "Dibs on the everything bagel," she said to Charlie, and handed her the bag. "See if

Gram wants one. I haven't gotten her breakfast yet."

"You should introduce Scott to her. She loves meeting people." She gave Mercedes a smug look as she took the food to the kitchen.

Bad idea. The sooner Scott left, the better.

"How was work?" Mercedes asked him once they were alone. She crossed her arms over her chest, trying for a middle ground between unfriendly and too happy to see him.

"Tolerable." He stepped closer to her and dropped his voice. Averted his eyes. "I, uh, just wanted to tell you thanks for listening to me Monday night."

"I wish I could've helped you more."

"You helped a lot." He met her gaze, then her hair seemed to snare his attention. He reached out and captured a lock, ran a section of it between his index and middle finger, from her shoulder to the ends.

The gesture was somewhat intimate. Distracting. She fought to ignore it.

"When is the little boy's funeral?"

"It was yesterday. While I was working. I'm still trying to figure out if that was a coincidence or not."

"I'm sure it was." The urge to touch him was overwhelming. She kept her arms tightly clenched. "Thank you for cleaning up the porch and the backyard."

He'd folded the towels and left them on one of the chairs on the porch, and had done the same with her wet clothes. Once she'd gotten Gram taken care of for the night, she'd rushed out in a panic, intending to hide the evidence only to find he'd already handled everything.

"No problem."

There was something in the way he watched her so intently, almost hungrily, that made it hard to think straight.

"Glad you made it out in one piece. I realized later I forgot about the padlock on the gate," she said.

He shrugged. "I climbed the fence. No big deal."

"Sorry I kind of freaked out on you when the phone rang."

"Hey, you owed me a freak-out."

"Guess we're even."

A tense silence fell over them and she wondered why he still made no move to leave.

"So, are you going to introduce me to your grandma?"

"You really want to meet her?"

"I like talking to older people. Particularly when they're fully conscious and not having a medical emergency," he said.

She led him down the hall reluctantly, though she wasn't sure the reason for her hesitation. Charlie was right. Their grandma liked to meet people they brought to the house. It made her feel more involved. Less "stuck inside."

"Gram?" she said as they approached the bedroom. "You up for a visitor?"

"Of course I am."

Charlie was standing next to Gram's bed, two plates with toasted bagels and cream cheese in her hands. Mercedes grabbed the bed tray she'd propped up against the wall and set it across Gram's lap.

"I was getting there," Charlie said, setting down the plate with the sesame bagel.

"Gram, this is Scott Pataki. He's Gemma's half brother I told you about. My grandma, Ruby Herman."

"Very nice to meet you." Gram extended a bony, shaky arm to him and Scott stepped forward to take it.

"It's an honor to meet you. You're the Ruby Herman the women's shelter is named for?"

"Yes, sir." Gram nodded proudly.

"Mercedes talks about you a lot, but she never told me you had ties to the shelter. And she never mentioned you were a heartbreaker."

Mercedes's eyes widened. Scott was flirting? With her eighty-four-year-old grandma? That, more than just about anything, put her in serious danger of falling for him.

"Mercedes didn't mention you were a charmer, either." Gram smiled, eating up the attention and the flattery. She really didn't get to see people besides her granddaughters often enough, let alone a hot twenty-something man. "She did tell me you're a paramedic."

"Yes, ma'am."

"Guess I better be nice to you, then. I might need a ride someday."

"I always drive faster for you pretty ladies."

Her grandma's laughter was musical. Scott seemed genuine, proving his earlier claim that he had a soft spot for the elderly. He looked relaxed, too. More comfortable than he usually was. Who'd have guessed the unfriendly, self-absorbed man Gemma had first introduced Mercedes to had such a heartwarming side to him?

While Mercedes appreciated that he was brightening Gram's day, she absolutely didn't need further reason to care about him. The other night had been a lot of physical attraction. That was problematic enough. Real feelings…

She hurried out of the room, mumbling that Gram needed her morning tea.

"I could've gotten the tea," Charlie said, following her to the kitchen. "Then you could stay and talk to your boyfriend."

"I don't have a boyfriend. Why didn't you stay in there with them?"

"Breakfast delivery?" Charlie raised her brows in doubt. "I've had boyfriends who didn't go that far out of their way for me."

"Maybe you've just had the wrong boyfriends." Mercedes stuck a mug of water in the microwave and heated it, then dropped a tea bag of Earl Grey, Gram's morning favorite, over the edge.

"You might have a point. I'll be on the patio," Charlie said curtly, and strode out the door.

Mercedes stirred in a spoonful of sugar the way Gram preferred, braced herself against Mr. Paramedic's charms and went back into the bedroom.

When she walked in, Gram and Scott barely noticed. He'd made himself comfortable in the chair by the head of the bed. They were deep into a debate about the travel book they'd both read, apparently on opposite sides of the argument—whatever it was—going back and forth good-naturedly.

"I'll give you that," Scott said. "You may have a point."

Gram raised her chin a notch and smirked.

"I better get going," he said after checking his watch. "Before you beat me on another point." He stood and faced Gram.

She smiled at him, her eyes lit up like Mercedes hadn't seen them in some time.

"It was nice to meet you, Mrs. Herman. I'll bring the sequel by when I'm done with it."

"Then we can argue some more," Gram said.

"I'll look forward to it," Scott said.

Mercedes would cling to the hope that he'd forget. She'd already affected Gram once because of her being too distracted by Scott. She had no intention of letting it happen again.

CHAPTER SIXTEEN

MERCEDES SWORE OUT LOUD as she jabbed her cell phone to end the call.

"What's wrong, sweetie?" Gram said from her bed behind her. They'd just gotten her settled after a Scrabble doubleheader at the kitchen table.

"It's Gemma." Mercedes rushed from the window she'd been gazing out as she'd listened to Gemma, to Gram's bathroom. She counted out Gram's nighttime pills even though she wasn't due to take them for another three hours. "She's having abdominal pains. I'm worried they might be contractions."

"She's not full-term yet, is she?"

"Not even close. She has two months left. Maybe a little more than that."

She set the pills on the nightstand and made sure the TV remote was there, as well. "Do you need the bedpan?"

"Not right now. Charlie's here, isn't she?"

"Charlie!" Mercedes took out a clean nightgown for Gram and laid it on the dresser as her sister strolled in.

"What's up? We're on for our show, right?" Charlie asked their grandma.

"I have to take Gemma to the hospital," Mercedes said. "I might be gone for a while—"

"We'll be fine." Charlie sat down in the chair on Gram's left side and reached over to the bowl of candy corn on the bed tray.

"You don't have anywhere to go?" Mercedes asked, hurrying in and out of the bathroom, setting on the dresser Gram's toothbrush, toothpaste, water cup, washcloth and anything else she might need.

"I'll be here all night. Go. Everything's fine."

Mercedes surveyed the dresser, trying to think of anything she might have missed. "Everything Gram'll need is right here," she said. "Her pills are over there." She pointed at the nightstand. "Ten o'clock for those—"

"Mercedes." Charlie rose and walked over to the dresser, looking at everything. "Really? I've been here for almost three weeks now. I know the drill."

"Just trying to make it easier for you."

"Gram and I will be fine. Now, go."

Mercedes looked at Gram.

"She's right, Sadie. We can handle it without you."

"Call me if you need anything," Mercedes said, addressing both of them. She realized she was

worrying too much, but after the other night...
She reminded herself that guilt was making her act irrationally, then bent down and kissed Gram before jogging out to her car.

When she turned into the apartment parking lot, she automatically scanned it for Scott's car. Still not here. Gemma didn't know where he was.

Mercedes pulled up at the foot of the stairs and left her CRV parked there illegally. She didn't bother to knock on the apartment door when she got there. "Gemma?" she called out as she entered.

The lack of response freaked her out. The living room and kitchen were empty, so she ran to Gemma's room.

Gemma was sitting on her bed doubled over. "It hurts," she said as Mercedes went to her.

"Where does it hurt? Still in your back?"

Squeezing her eyes shut against the pain, Gemma nodded. "And front." She let out a loud breath and a curse. "Okay. Little better now."

"Can you walk?"

The teenager took in a long, deep breath and straightened the rest of the way. She stood slowly, warily. Nodded.

"Let's go."

"Don't I need a bag or something?" Gemma asked, her voice shaky.

"That's only when you go in to have the baby.

You're not having the baby tonight." Maybe if she said it emphatically enough, she'd be right.

Gemma nodded, looked around then picked up her purse from the bed.

"That thing is so big, you might strain yourself carrying it," Mercedes said. "I'll take it."

"I've got it," Gemma said. "I'm okay right now."

Not sparing time to argue, Mercedes took Gemma's arm and ushered her to the door.

They made it all the way to the hospital without another spell, which Mercedes considered a good sign. If they were contractions, they weren't coming very close together. Immediately after they were ushered into a room in Labor and Delivery, a nurse came in to assess Gemma. As she worked, she asked questions.

"How long have you been having pain?" the nurse asked Gemma.

"Since…this morning sometime."

"What?" Mercedes had been trying to stay out of the way, but now she hurried back to the side of the bed. "Gemma. This morning?"

"What time this morning, hon?" the nurse asked, counteracting Mercedes's franticness with a calm, patient voice.

"I don't know. Not long after I got up. Maybe seven-thirty?"

"Why didn't you call me, Gemma?"

The nurse made notes and then set aside the clipboard and washed her hands.

"I thought it was just normal pregnancy discomfort," Gemma said.

"And you went ahead and went to work?"

"I had to. It's not like they can find another babysitter if I don't show."

The nurse approached Gemma and started a physical exam. Mercedes stopped her scolding and took Gemma's hand.

"I think they're going to have to find another babysitter, hon," the nurse said. "You've started dilating."

"What does that mean?" Gemma asked, paling.

Before the nurse could answer, Gemma's grip on Mercedes's hand intensified. Times one hundred. The nurse came around to her other side and calmly, softly talked her through the contraction.

Mercedes continued to hold her hand, but her mind went into overdrive, trying to process the possibility that Gemma's baby could come tonight. They weren't ready yet. She hadn't saved up enough money to support herself and her baby, hadn't been able to buy anything for the baby, and Mercedes wasn't sure Gemma was ready mentally yet, if she ever would be.

And the baby…would it even survive at this point? She knew doctors could work miracles these days, but she didn't know enough about fetal development to have any idea what they could expect.

And money…what if she wasn't insured by her mom's policy? What if her baby needed weeks of hospitalization? How would she ever handle that?

"Over?" the nurse asked, and Gemma exhaled and nodded.

"I'm going to call in the doctor and get you something for the contractions. I want you to try to relax. No panicking," the nurse said. She looked at Mercedes. "You neither."

Mercedes laughed nervously. Guiltily. She was freaking out more than Gemma and she should be the one keeping Gemma calm. "No panicking. Got it. She's going to be okay?"

"She'll be fine and so will the baby."

"She's having the baby?" Mercedes and Gemma exchanged a look of fear.

"No, no. We should be able to get things stopped. I'll be back with the doctor."

Gemma's shoulders sagged with relief at the nurse's answer. Mercedes spoke the words out loud—repeatedly. "Everything's okay."

Just over an hour later, the medication had done its job. Most of the frenzy in the room had been reduced to silent worry on Mercedes's part. She'd been doing her best to hide it from Gemma, but the longer she sat there, with the exhausted teenager drifting in and out of sleep, the more distraught she became.

According to the doctor's optimistic report, the baby seemed to be healthy. But one thing he'd said had stuck with Mercedes—Gemma would be restricted to bed rest, possibly for the rest of her pregnancy. How in the world would she make it on her own if she had to lie flat for the next two months and not work?

Mercedes was sitting in the easy chair in the nearly dark room when she heard a soft knock on the closed door. She hopped up and hurried to the door, her bare feet soundless on the tile floor. She was so wrapped up in her thoughts that the sight of Scott leaning against the wall surprised her, even though she'd left him a voice mail asking him to come. In her defense, it seemed like half a lifetime ago.

"You got my message."

"All three of them," he said with a ghost of a smile. "How is she? What's going on?"

She stepped out into the hallway, pulled the door closed and updated him, spilling everything out in a long, run-on sentence.

"So, she's okay?" he asked when she paused.

"Yes. For now."

"Mercedes, breathe." He gently grasped her upper arm. "Let's go with that 'for now.'"

Mercedes took his advice and inhaled, her

eyes closed. He let go of her arm. She sagged against the other side of the doorjamb, fighting hard against the desire to lean into him instead. "You act like you counsel people through medical emergencies all the time or something."

"Usually only necessary when the patient takes a turn for the worse. Not when she's doing 'okay.'"

She acknowledged that with a slight, noncommittal nod. "I wondered if you were working tonight."

"I was on the mainland picking up some equipment for my new job."

"You leave in how many days?"

"Sixteen."

Another reinforcement of how pressing Gemma's newest challenge was. Her mind immediately returned to searching for options.

"Hello?" Scott said. "Are we going in or are you her watchdog?"

"Sorry."

"You need to relax." His voice, barely more than a whisper, had a soothing effect on her. "I'll say hi to her and then I'm getting you out of here."

"No," Mercedes said, straightening. "I'm not leaving."

"There's nothing you can do here. She'll sleep better if she knows you're not squashed into a chair. That's not comfortable for anyone."

Mercedes opened the door, stubbornly ignoring his rationale. Even if he might have a point.

Gemma barely stirred when they came in. Scott stared at her stiffly for a couple of minutes, until Mercedes nudged him. "Let her know you're here."

Earlier, Gemma had been sure he wouldn't come, that he couldn't care less that she was in the hospital. She didn't often show that it mattered to her what Scott thought. Though he did his best not to get Gemma's hopes up that they could be close, hearing that he'd gone to the doctor with her last week led Mercedes to believe he cared more than he let on.

Scott sat on the side of her bed and cleared his throat. "Hey, Gem."

The girl opened her eyes. "You made it," she said with a drowsy smile.

"I made it. Just wanted to say hi and I'm glad you're okay. We're going to let you sleep now."

Gemma nodded and glanced at Mercedes, who'd returned to the easy chair on the other side. "Night." She closed her eyes again, still smiling.

Mercedes thought, not for the first time tonight, how young Gemma was. It was easy to forget because she didn't act like most seventeen-year-old girls.

They sat in silence for several minutes, ensuring that Gemma was out for the night. Scott eventually stood and went around the bed to Mercedes's side.

"Let's go," he whispered.

Mercedes scanned the room, ignoring him.

"Mercedes." He touched her shoulder and she looked up at him. "She's down for the count. Come on."

"I hate to leave her," she whispered back.

"She's fine. You're not staying."

She checked to see that Gemma hadn't stirred, knowing he was right. Gemma just needed to sleep, and holding a vigil in her room wouldn't do anyone any good.

"You can come back first thing in the morning."

Wishing she could do something to help Gemma overall, she had sense enough to know there was nothing to be accomplished tonight. She nodded reluctantly, picked up her purse and stood.

He put his arm around her shoulders and ushered her out into the hallway. He didn't let go until they were outside on the sidewalk, heading to the parking lot. She didn't want to like it but she did.

"Come with me," he said, his voice still hushed.

"What? Where are you going?"

"On a drive."

"I should get home."

"How come?"

"Gram might need me." She knew it wasn't a valid excuse even as the words tumbled out of her mouth.

"Your sister's there, isn't she?" he said. "She can handle anything that comes up."

Mercedes stopped walking. "Let me call them to make sure everything's okay."

"If that'll convince you to say yes, call away."

She pressed a button on her phone, remotely curious where he wanted to drive. And why. When she asked her sister if everything was okay, Charlie was insulted that Mercedes felt the need to check in.

"We're fine, Mercedes. She's ready for her ten-o'clock pills. Relax."

"Okay, okay," Mercedes said. "Just be sure to listen for Gram even after she falls asleep. Sometimes she—"

Her sister cut her off and insisted she had everything under control.

"Okay," Mercedes relented, aware that Scott was listening intently. "Fine. I'll be home later."

She ended the call and tried to come up with another reason not to go with him.

"Come on," Scott said. "I can tell by looking at you that you're about to implode."

Defeated, she started walking again.

"Where are we going?" she asked.

"You'll see when we get there."

CHAPTER SEVENTEEN

"IT'S MY FAULT SHE'S IN the hospital."

Mercedes blurted the words out after ten minutes of silence in Scott's car.

He'd driven north out of San Amaro proper. The old road stretched several miles through the part of the island that was too narrow for development. He'd hoped the peacefulness out here would help her calm down—her agitation had been tangible from the moment he'd arrived at the hospital. To think that was after the worst of Gemma's ordeal was over. She wasn't doing anyone any good in her state.

"What?" He darted a glance of disbelief her way, but it was too dark to see much now that no streetlights illuminated the road. "How do you figure?"

"I'm the one who got her the second job."

He pulled the car over along the side of the otherwise deserted road and the two right wheels hit sand. "That's not even rational, Mercedes," he said, turning off the engine.

"It's completely rational. She's been working

nonstop for the past week, pushing herself too hard. Not sleeping enough."

"Listen to what you're saying. She has been working too hard. She has been pushing herself. Gemma made those decisions, not you."

"She's desperate and seventeen."

"Yes. All you did was try to help her. The preterm labor is nobody's fault."

She threw her head back against the headrest, drummed her fingers on the armrest of the door. "You're probably right, I guess. I can't help feeling responsible, though."

He shook his head in amazement. Mercedes was the best thing that could have happened to Gemma and here she was, beating herself up. "You've done nothing but good things for her. Helped her get jobs so she can save money for her baby, given her rides, taken her out for food, strong-armed me to give her a place to stay…"

Mercedes finally looked at him and he thought he could see the beginnings of a smile tugging at her lips. "We didn't strong-arm you. Much."

"I'm sure tonight was upsetting, but she's okay now. You need to look ahead instead of back."

"That's just as stressful. What is she going to do, Scott?"

He reached across the console and took her hand. "Do you ever try to just live in the present?"

Mercedes frowned at him. "Do you?"

He chuckled. "Some days that's easier than others." Like now. This moment was decent. Just him and Mercedes and a never-ending stretch of sand and water. If he could just get her to shut out her worries, for her own sake. "There's not a thing we can do for Gemma tonight, is there?"

Mercedes thought about it for several seconds—stubbornly looking for a way to contradict him, if the set of her jaw was any indication. "I suppose not."

"Okay, then." He reached across her and dug through the glove compartment for a flashlight. "Come on."

"Where are we?" She looked around as if just noticing they weren't in the city anymore.

"Middle of nowhere." He got out and walked around the car. Opened her door and took his shoes off then threw them in the backseat. "Leave your shoes here and come on." He held out his hand. She slid her flip-flops off easily and accepted his help but let go as they started walking toward the shore.

"I never pegged you for the romantic-walk-on-the-beach type," Mercedes said.

"You'd be correct."

They climbed over the dunes, around the dark patches of sea grass. The rustle of the grass in

the light breeze was drowned out by the perpet-
ual roar of the waves.

"Okay, you're not romantic, so are you a serial
killer leading me to my death?"

He responded with a halfhearted chuckle and
flipped on the flashlight. As they made their way
along the waterline, he swept the sand in front of
them with the light, searching.

Mercedes looked from him to the light beam
and back.

"There!" He hurried forward, tracking a ghost
crab as it sped across the sand as if leading them
ahead.

"A crab?" Mercedes followed him, sounding
unsure.

"Ghost crabs. Scared of them?"

"You brought me all the way out here for
creepy crawlies?" she asked, sounding intrigued
and unsure at once.

"You've never been ghost-crab hunting?"

The one he'd spotted scurried into the water,
out of sight.

"No. Sheltered life. I grew up in Austin. No
sand."

"I used to do it when I was a kid, but back then
I caught them and put them in a bucket to see how
many I could catch in a night."

"Do people eat them?" she asked, frowning and

scanning the illuminated sand in front of them with some trepidation.

"You'd have to eat about a hundred to make a meal. I let them go at the end of the night."

"Don't they pinch?"

"They can. That's why we're just looking."

She exhaled and her shoulders relaxed noticeably.

"Come on," he said, letting her catch up. "Let's find more."

After the second crab, he offered her the flashlight. She hesitated before taking it.

They walked for several minutes before she spotted one and let out a little-girl scream. She tracked it with the light for a few feet then lost it.

"Fast little buggers," she said.

"They can run up to ten miles per hour."

"They're kind of nasty, aren't they?"

Scott laughed and challenged her to find another. "I'm ahead, two to one."

She pushed her hair back behind her shoulders as if getting down to business. "Of course you are. I didn't have a flashlight till now."

"There's also the issue of your fear of ghost crabs."

"I'm not afraid."

"If you say so." Her sudden bravado amused him.

"There's one!" Mercedes stopped and shined

the light on a crab a half-dozen feet in front of them. It took off at full speed, heading right toward them. Directly toward her feet.

She screamed, dropped the flashlight and leaped toward Scott, grabbing on to him and lifting her feet so he had no choice but to hold on to her. She screamed again and Scott laughed. Hard. And held on to her, not at all disappointed with the turn of events.

"It touched me!" Mercedes said, craning her neck to look for the crab below her.

"You scared it away. You have ghost-crab cooties now."

"You planned that." Mercedes tried to act upset, but she tightened her arms around his neck and curled into him.

"I've never been hunting with someone scared of harmless little ghost crabs."

"You paid the little creepy crawly off," she accused, grinning, looking into his eyes.

"If I knew it'd end up like this, I would have tried."

Mercedes inhaled Scott's masculine scent as the mood between them changed from playfulness to…a different kind of play entirely. She'd honestly not meant to jump into his arms like a preteen in a haunted house, but now that she was here, she couldn't make herself slide down to her feet.

Scott's gaze dipped to her lips momentarily. She was so close she could practically count his eyelashes. Unable to resist, she drew her hand from the back of his neck around to his jaw. She ran her fingers over the shadow of stubble, thrilling in the roughness, in the intimacy of touching a part of him most people didn't.

Scott shifted her in his arms. His eyes lowered again as he closed the inches between them and touched her lips with his. Lightly. More tenderly than she'd ever expect from such a hard-living man, especially after the urgency of the last time they'd kissed. It sent shivers up her arms and she tightened her hold on him, every inch of her body reveling in the heat of their contact even though the air around them was still hot and humid.

He kissed her slowly, thoroughly, drinking her in at his leisure, as if time ceased to exist. Her tongue danced to the tempo he set, letting him lead yet taking for herself as well, exploring his mouth, memorizing every part of him.

He growled deeply as they each tried to pull the other closer, relished every inch of contact along their bodies.

"Hang on," he whispered, the brush of his breath on her ear eliciting a moan from her. Still holding her, he dropped to his knees, then maneuvered himself to sit on the sand with her draped across him. Before either one of them could settle or get comfortable, their lips met again, more insistent, desperate for contact.

He laid back and Mercedes followed, feeling his hardness at her center. Her hair was everywhere, draping over him, and he ran his fingers through it.

"Been dying to touch this again. You have amazing hair."

Mercedes laughed and swallowed a protest. "I'm sprawled all over you and you just want my hair. I might be insulted."

"Uh, no. I don't just want your hair. I have every intention of touching as much of you as you'll let me."

She pulled away for a heartbeat. "Is there a question in there?"

"There might be."

He nipped at her lips affectionately, making it difficult to concentrate on anything else. His fingers still played in her hair, making her smile and think maybe her curls weren't as bad as she'd always thought.

While she was flattered that he liked her hair, she made a point of distracting him from it by finding the hem of his tee and pushing it up, treating her hands to the ridges and valleys of his solid chest. She skimmed her fingers over his nipples, back to his abdomen, exploring his upper body as if to sculpt it later.

He intensified the kiss, plunging his tongue into her mouth more deeply. Their bodies aligned and his hands dropped to her rear, molding her into him. Mercedes let conscious thought slip away, surrendered to sensation: the texture of his short hair, his periodic moans, the heat of his hands gliding over her bare skin. The gulf roar became background noise, an insulator, closing them off from the rest of the world as their desire turned more insistent.

"So?" he whispered in her ear, again giving her chills.

"So?" She blinked her eyes open reluctantly, as if being yanked from a really good dream.

He brushed her hair to the side, cradled her jaw in his palm. "I want you. All of you, right here, now. The hair's nice, but…" His grin was filled with wicked intent, his eyes with a powerful need. "You have to say."

The pounding of her blood to the center of her said an unequivocal yes. Her brain wasn't quite there yet.

"I told myself I wasn't even going to kiss you again," she said, her voice lower than normal.

"I'm irresistible that way."

She laughed huskily. "Maybe I should move over so your ego has enough room."

"Don't you dare go away." It was practically a growl, and the low vibration of his voice did something to her. "I'm not asking for anything besides right now, Mercedes. You know I'm leaving."

As he kissed her again, she let his words sink in. The need pulsing through her made right here and now seem like a very good idea. She longed to have his hands all over her, to let him quell the burning ache at her core. As long as they both understood this was a temporary thing, a physical thing and nothing else, right now was enough. It was perfect.

Except...

"Scott?"

He answered with a hungry sound as he continued to kiss her senseless.

"I don't want to end up like Gemma," she managed to say, sounding breathless.

He didn't seem to hear her at first. After a couple seconds, he opened his eyes. "Like Gemma? Pregnant?"

Mercedes nodded as she trailed her finger over his chin, jaw, cheek.

"I think I have something."

"You think you do?"

"Ninety-five percent sure I do." He held her to him at the waist and shifted so he could dig out his wallet from his back pocket.

Mercedes occupied herself by kissing up and

down his jawline, his earlobe, his neck, following the path her fingers had taken.

"Hundred percent," Scott said, his voice strained.

"Then what are we waiting for?"

Scott dropped his wallet and the condom package on the sand beside them and put all his focus into making Mercedes crazy with wanting him. The gentle, unrushed tempo was long gone, giving way to their urgent need. He lifted her T-shirt over her head and tossed it to the side.

Mercedes grinned when she saw it and considered how unprepared for this she'd been. She hadn't thought twice about the old, comfortable clothes she was wearing when she'd rushed out of the house to Gemma. "I normally dress nicer on first dates."

"I'm terribly concerned about what you're wearing," Scott said. "Only because you're still wearing it."

Mercedes sat up and removed her bra. "Better for you?"

His hands were sliding up her sides to her breasts before she got the words out. He positioned her so he could tease her nipple with his tongue, swirling it around, taking it into his mouth, intensifying the ache inside her for more. She gasped his name. Tried to remember how to breathe.

Without pausing the wonderful torture on her breasts, he moved his hands back down her sides and under her exercise shorts. Hooking his fingers inside the waistband of her panties, he slid everything down in one easy motion.

"I've reconsidered," he said as he moved his mouth to her other nipple. "I like the easy-access feature."

"Whatever it takes to make you happy." She sucked in her breath as his hands roved over her flesh.

Holding her on his lap, he sat up and pulled his shirt completely off. He shook it out and spread it at his side, smoothing the edges out. "Here," he whispered. "I left the instant-romance props at home, so this will have to do as a blanket."

She crawled onto the shirt, grateful for some barrier between her backside and the sand. She didn't dwell on that gratitude for long, though, because Scott sidetracked her. He unsnapped his jeans and removed them and his boxer briefs. The sight of his naked body leaning over her in the moonlight had her reaching out, pulling him down impatiently so she could touch and taste him again.

He kissed her lips briefly, tenderly, then kissed and suckled his way down to her collarbone, her breasts, her navel. Mercedes cradled him between her legs, the friction between their bodies burning her up. His erection brushed along her inner thigh and she arched into him. When she grasped him, he moaned and moved into her hand, then eased himself up her body so he could devour her mouth. She raised her knees and opened herself to him as she reached out blindly to the side to find the condom packet. Scott teased her entrance with his tip. It was all she could do to rip open the packet and put the condom into his hand.

Scott lifted his body to sheath himself. When he finally entered her, she cried out. He stilled to let her body get used to his. Mercedes angled toward him even closer, wrapped her legs around his and moved her hips.

He whispered in her ear, telling her what she did to him and how she was driving him mad. Sweat slicked their bodies as their urgency increased. She held on to his backside, urging him deeper, climbing, burning from the inside out. She pressed her mouth into his shoulder to muffle the sounds she couldn't hold back as he carried her higher and finally to the edge. He plunged over with her, calling her name out and making sexy primal sounds with no concern for where they were.

Gradually, their surroundings came back into her consciousness. She held Scott to her, savoring the weight of him so fully centered on her. He buried his face in her hair and nuzzled her cheek.

An appreciative, satisfied sound from him whispered over her ear, and goose bumps popped up on her arms.

Scott eventually moved to her side, breaking the intimate connection of their bodies. He kissed her slowly, reverently, pulling her toward him.

"That was worth every grain of sand embedded in my body," he said.

"That'll teach you to leave the instant-romance props at home." Mercedes grinned and traced a line on his chest. "Thank you for the T-shirt. You're sweet."

He laughed, a lazy, sexy, satisfied sound. "Sweet isn't something I've been accused of before."

"I think you're just misunderstood."

"I think you're temporarily blinded by postlust bliss."

"There's that ego again. What happened here?" she said, barely touching a long, semihealed scrape on his upper arm.

Scott looked embarrassed. "Nothing."

"That's a big nothing. Come on, tell me. How'd you cut your arm?"

He looked away and shook his head dismissively. "It happened during my gallant escape from your backyard."

Mercedes tried not to laugh. "The fence?"

"Been a long time since I've scaled a six-foot privacy fence. I was in a hurry."

"My hero," she said, unable to hold back a big grin. She propped her chin on his chest. "I hope this is as out in the middle of nowhere as it feels, otherwise someone probably got an eyeful. And an earful."

"They might still be getting a very pleasant eyeful now." Scott ran his hand over her rear affectionately and Mercedes lifted her head to scan the area around them.

"We parked four miles north of town and probably walked another half mile after that," he said. "There's no one around to see your perfect ass shining in the moonlight."

She smiled but sat up to hide her perfect ass from the world. "I'm never going to get all the sand off."

"And you had my shirt," he said, acting injured. He got to his feet and held his hands out to her. "Come on."

"Come on what?"

"Sand-removal services."

She let him help her. Before she could even get her balance, he scooped her up. He jogged to the water and splashed in, still holding her. When they reached water up to her waist, he put her down and pulled her to him. The sensation of being naked in the gulf, the pull of the waves over her skin, gave her an overload of naughty thoughts. Scott kissed her, tasting of salt. She wound her arms around him until their bodies met and heat shot through her again. One night with him wasn't enough. She wanted more.

Unfortunately, what she wanted wasn't the only thing she had to consider in her life.

CHAPTER EIGHTEEN

GOOD SEX MADE A MAN DO stupid things. Like sniffing a T-shirt, for instance.

Scott sat in the driver's seat of his car, the engine running. Gemma needed a ride home from the hospital. Apparently Mercedes had to stay with her grandmother because the afternoon caretaker had canceled at the last minute, so he'd agreed to pick up Gemma. Except he'd gotten waylaid by a blasted piece of clothing.

It was his shirt, the one he'd been wearing last night, and it smelled like Mercedes. Like her floral-scented shampoo and whatever else it was that made the scent of her so feminine and...erotic.

Stupider than smelling around for a sample of Mercedes's sweetness was, well, where to start? Maybe the very act of inviting her to get into his car last night would be considered unwise by some. Getting naked on the beach, yeah, he could imagine arguments against that, but he wouldn't concur. It was impossible to consider the most amazing sex of his life to be a negative.

There was a suspicion nagging at him that it

wasn't just that the physical act had been so superior. That maybe there was more to it than body parts and sensations.

Hell, there was no *maybe* about it.

Dumbest thing he could do was to develop some kind of feelings for Mercedes. So what had he done?

Mercedes wasn't his typical roll in the sack to meet his needs. There was the flickering of more there.

Scott winged the shirt into the backseat and swore at himself.

"WHAT'S EATING YOU?" Gemma's voice sounded loud in the front seat of his car. Particularly so since they hadn't said more than a couple words since leaving the hospital.

"Hmm?" Scott put his turn signal on and waited for two cars to pass before pulling into the lot of their apartment building.

"You've been in your own little world since you got to the hospital," Gemma said. "What's up?"

"Did you need me to stop and get you anything before we get home?"

"Little late to ask that now, isn't it?" There was teasing in her tone. Amazing, considering the past twenty-four hours and the deepening of her predicament. She definitely wasn't fainthearted or easily deterred. He found himself respecting that about her.

"Want some movies? Books?"

"Maybe," she said noncommittally. "I'll borrow some books from you, if that's okay."

"It's fine." That reminded him he'd promised Mercedes's grandmother a book. Another dumb move on his part.

He pulled into the handicapped spot that he'd never in his three years in this dump seen anyone use.

"Rebel," Gemma said.

"Anything for the patient." He got out and went around to her door. "I'll move it later. You don't need to walk half a mile."

"It wouldn't even be a quarter of a mile. but thank you." She took the hand he offered and pulled herself awkwardly out of the low-to-the-ground car. "This must be what it feels like to be sixty." She started to reach for her purse in the front seat.

"I'll get it," Scott said forcefully. The last thing he wanted was for her to pop that baby out now. For his sake and hers. And the baby's, come to think of it.

Gemma stood back and let him get it for her. They didn't speak all the way to the apartment door.

As he used his key on the lock, he could feel

her staring at him from the side. He ignored her and went inside.

"Bed or couch?" he asked.

"Couch. I'll just get a couple of—"

"I'll get them. What do you need?"

"Pillows. Blanket. Book. Winning lottery ticket."

He nodded. "I can do all but one. You. Couch. Now."

"Yes, sir."

Scott shook his head as he rounded the corner into the hallway. When he returned, he helped her get settled by piling the pillows up on one end and spreading the blanket on top of her.

"You really think you need that thing?" he asked. "It's pushing a hundred out."

"I need comfort. I hate hospitals." As soon as she'd reclined, she sat up again and swung her feet to the floor.

"What are you doing?" Scott asked.

"I need a drink."

"I've got it."

"You make kind of a cute nursemaid."

"Don't push your luck." He went into the kitchen and tracked down the largest cup he could find. Filled it with water and ice and was about to take it to the living room, when he stopped. Gemma went through cheese popcorn like crazy. He got the unopened bag of it from the cupboard, plus a box of cookies, an orange and some sesame crackers.

Back in the living room, Scott arranged all the snacks on the coffee table where Gemma could easily reach them.

"Wow." She sat up, inspected the food stash like a toddler in a toy store. "For me?"

"You can get up to pee. That's all. This should tide you over for a while."

She went for the popcorn bag right away. Scott sat on the coffee table, waiting for her to settle again. Then he held out the water to her.

"Thanks," she said, and took a drink.

He was about to stand, when she stopped him.

"So." She opened the bag as she spoke. "Something happen between you and Mercedes again?"

Again? What had Mercedes told her? The denial that had been on the tip of his tongue disappeared. Instead, he said, "What makes you think that's any of your business?"

She shrugged, took a handful of popcorn and held the bag out to him. He refused. "I can get the story from Mercedes."

"I'm not telling you anything," he said, knowing she probably spoke the truth.

"But I'm right. You two are involved."

"No." At least they shouldn't be. And what was "involved" anyway? Gray area. Not that he needed to define it, because it wasn't going to continue.

"I think it could work," Gemma carried on. "Kind of a light-and-dark type of thing."

"Light and dark. Let me guess. I'm the dark?"

"You sure as heck are not light."

That made him smile. "Don't waste your time on romantic notions. I'm leaving soon."

She sobered and set the popcorn bag aside.

"Has…Dad tried to contact you again after that first time?" he asked. Part of him wondered if some kind of confrontation had added to her stress level.

"I don't know. Somebody knocked on the door a few nights ago when you were at work. I didn't answer."

"He showed up once when you weren't here."

"What'd he say?"

"He wanted to apologize."

"And you let him in?"

"I figured he'd keep coming back till I heard him out."

"Probably. When was this?"

"Last Friday."

"It was Sunday when he came looking for me. If it was him."

"I'm guessing he had to head back to Houston or wherever he's living now for the workweek."

"Houston," she confirmed. "What did you say

to him? Are you best buddies now?" The anger in her voice took Scott by surprise.

"He wanted me to convince you to move in with him."

Her shoulders tensed. "What'd you say?"

"Told him you don't listen to a thing anyone tells you."

"Nice. What a creep." She met his eyes. "Him. Not you."

"Better be him. I brought you cheese popcorn," Scott teased. He stood. "You better keep your butt on that couch."

"Yeah, yeah."

He headed toward his bedroom, seriously talked out. As he reached the hallway, Gemma's words stopped him.

"You know, I was worried at first," she said. "About you being a jerk." He faced her, sensing there was more. "You're not so bad, though. Especially considering the jackass you have for a father."

Scott battled a grin. "You're not so bad yourself, kid. All things considered."

He immediately regretted his overfriendliness and retreated down the hallway, out of sight.

CHAPTER NINETEEN

"SHE'S IN THERE FUSSING over Gram," Charlie said to whoever had just knocked on the front door. Mercedes glanced at her watch as she headed to the living room to intercede, Higgans weaving his way between her feet with every step. It was past 10:30 p.m. and she wondered who…

Scott. His words weren't discernible from here, but just the sound of his voice affected her. Her stomach dropped and she couldn't hold back a smile.

"Hi," she said as she approached them. "I'm not fussing. Gram needed a drink. What's going on?"

He hadn't shaved and she became fixated on the thought of running her fingers over his rough chin again. Kissing him. More.

"Could we go outside?" he asked curtly, indicating the front of the house instead of the back, where they'd be more comfortable.

Obviously he wasn't as happy to see her as she was to see him. No day-after-sex haze of contentment for him.

"Sure." She smiled again for Charlie's benefit.

"I'm going to put this in Gram's room," Charlie said, holding up a paperback.

Mercedes nodded absently and followed Scott outside.

He sat stiffly on the edge of one of the two rarely used chairs to the left of the front door. Mercedes took the other one, curiosity and confusion making her fidget.

"Hi," she said awkwardly, harboring a futile hope that getting away from her sister would re-establish some semblance of the connection from last night.

"I picked up Gemma earlier—"

"Yes, thank you for doing that. Charlie was gone, Yoli called last-minute and I had no idea how long it would take to get Gemma settled."

"Wasn't a problem." He drummed his fingers on his knee. "This isn't going to work."

The words hit her like a sock in the gut. She didn't know what "this" was, exactly. Them? Gemma? Something else? Still, her insides knotted up.

"What isn't going to work?"

"You need to convince her to go home."

It took her a moment to process what he meant. "Gemma? She doesn't have a home to go to. Her mom—"

"She's not supposed to get up except to go to the bathroom," he said. "Not to get herself food, a drink, to switch a movie. She's stuck on the couch. I can't be there with her every second. I told you guys, I'm not a babysitter. Besides, I leave in fifteen days."

She stared at him, taken aback as if he'd struck her. The warm, tender Scott from last night was long gone. This version was cold. Distant. His jaw was locked stubbornly and he didn't look directly at her.

"Okay," she said, not bothering to hide her surprise. "I can stop by—"

He laughed coldly. "Mercedes, you can't take care of two people in different places, not to mention work a full-time job. Be realistic."

"I was going to say I could stop by a couple times a day. Maybe Charlie could help."

He shook his head and looked at her as if she was crazy.

"She goes back to the doctor in a week, right?" Mercedes said. "He might release her from bed rest, or at least modify it a bit."

"He might. Or he might not."

"What do you want me to do, Scott?"

"I already told you. Make her understand this is no longer working out. She gave it a go and might even have made it work, but preterm labor changes the whole game."

"Are you…kicking her out?"

"Where did you think Gemma was going to

live when I'm gone?" He leaned his elbows on his thighs and rubbed his hands over his face. "Give me a little credit, Mercedes. I'm not going to put her out on the street. But it's time for all of us to figure out the very near future. No matter how you look at it, Gemma needs help."

"Her mom kicked her out. That won't work. I'd take her in in an instant if she wasn't allergic to my cats."

Several seconds ticked by and the wind rustled the palm tree at the side of the porch. Mercedes barely registered it as she again racked her brain for a solution for Gemma.

"She needs to stay with our father," Scott finally said. He said it like it was a prison sentence, and yet there wasn't an ounce of hesitancy in his voice.

"I don't think that's going to fly, Scott."

"It's the only option."

It was Mercedes's turn to laugh in disbelief. "Do you think that little of her? You hate the man."

"He wants her to live with him. He's driven down here twice to talk to her. That's…more than her mother's done. She hasn't even heard from the woman. Besides, he's not hurting financially."

Points in Mr. Pataki's favor, but…

"Do you know what that would do to her emotionally? Her stress level?" Mercedes shook her head. "That's the last thing she needs."

Scott's shoulders sagged a bit, as if he'd lost momentum for his argument. "Got any other ideas? Is there a bed available at the shelter yet? Can she stay there?"

"A couple have opened since she was there, but they're full again. We can't offer that kind of full-time help anyway. We can't handle people with medical needs."

He stood. "Well, let me know if you come up with anything. If you won't talk to her, I will."

"Then why'd you ask me in the first place?" Mercedes said, her volume rising as she also stood. This was so not the man she'd been with on the beach last night.

"Because she'll listen to you more than she'll listen to me."

There wasn't much space for him to walk past her, but he did so without touching her. Without looking at her.

"Scott."

Once he was past her, he stopped, looked up at the starry sky.

"This is how you're going to handle it? Really?"

"I never asked to handle anything to do with Gemma."

"I'm not talking about her now," Mercedes said quietly. "We had an agreement. No expectations.

No strings attached. That's what we both want. So why are you acting like this?"

"How am I acting?" Sounding bored, he watched a car turn in to a driveway down the street.

"Like you're scared I'm going to try to put some claim on you."

"Claim if you want. It won't get you anywhere."

"I don't want, Scott! All I want is to be treated, I don't know, like...someone who matters."

"I never hid from you, from the day I met you, that this is the person I am. I need to go back to Gemma. Good night."

Mercedes stared after him, speechless, as he strode purposefully toward his car. On some level, she understood his worry about Gemma, but that didn't make it okay for him to treat her so coldly. As tough as the pregnant teenager's problems were to solve, they seemed a lot less impossible than whatever was perpetually bugging Scott.

Scott wasn't proud of being an asshole.

He hadn't planned to act like one to Mercedes. He had a lot of things eating at him, but he'd thought he'd worked through most of it. After leaving Gemma on the couch with her snacks and a book, he'd burst into what he figured was maybe a bit of rage or panic. Who knew? Who cared? Whatever it was, it'd propelled him into packing everything he didn't use on a daily basis and then emailing his new boss to let him know he could start anytime. Of course he hadn't heard back right away and probably wouldn't. And he realized there was little chance of starting early. But what the hell…he'd put it out there anyway.

All because he'd let himself get too involved. With Gemma. With Mercedes.

He shouldn't have taken it out on her. Even if it would be easier to make her hate him now, that was the coward's way out. He needed to apologize, treat her well until he left town—even if he did keep her at arm's length—and get the hell gone.

MERCEDES HAD BEEN sidetracked by her thoughts, absorbed by worrying about Gemma and, yes, the way Scott had acted last night. But that was no excuse.

There was no excuse.

When she turned the corner toward home, the sight of the ambulance in their driveway still made her heart lodge in her throat, even though Charlie had called to warn her. She'd had to call the landline at the shelter—because Mercedes had forgotten to charge her cell phone. Hadn't even thought about checking it that afternoon when she'd hurried out the door, nearly late for her shelter-volunteer shift.

She called herself another round of a dozen different names as she parked the car in the street and ran into the house. Charlie had said Gram seemed okay, but an eighty-four-year-old woman didn't fall out of bed, lose consciousness and not suffer any consequences.

"Gram!"

Mercedes hurried toward the bed and barely registered that one of the paramedics was Scott. She barely registered anything except Gram's weak smile and forced cheer when she said, "There's my Sadie."

Charlie was on the opposite side of the bed, at the head of it, out of the paramedics' way. She held Gram's hand.

"Her vitals are looking good," Scott said with a glance at Mercedes. "Seems to be no worse for wear, with the exception of a nasty bruise-to-be on her arm."

Mercedes nodded, unable to speak, and took Gram's other hand.

"Your grandmother's a hearty one," the other paramedic, a female with thin brown hair pulled back in a ponytail, said.

"Gram…" Mercedes's throat clogged up with so much guilt she couldn't get another word out.

"Shh," Gram said. "I'm okay, honey." She squeezed Mercedes's hand.

That her grandma was comforting her when it should have been the other way around only made Mercedes feel worse.

"I'm so sorry I didn't answer my phone." Again, that was all she could manage before being overcome. She fought to hold it together in front of everyone, and the only way she had a chance of doing that was to shut up. She bent over and kissed her grandma's forehead, lingering there for several heartbeats.

"Mrs. Herman, are you sure you don't want us to take you in?" the female paramedic asked.

Alarm made Mercedes straighten quickly and implore Scott with wide, questioning, probably tearful eyes. She didn't think twice about how they'd left things last night.

He shook his head and touched her arm. "She looks okay, but it wouldn't hurt for her to have a doctor check her out."

"I'm not going to the hospital." Gram was insistent, her voice stronger than it had been since Mercedes had come in. "As long as I have a say, I'm choosing to stay put." She grinned at Scott. "Though I do recognize I would have a very nice escort."

"We could do it your way, however you want, Mrs. H.," Scott said, making Mercedes again

wonder if they should be pressing Gram harde
to get checked out. "Full lights and sirens if yo
want to arrive in style."

Gram pursed her lips and shook her head stub
bornly. Mercedes looked at Charlie to gauge he
opinion.

"She said no," Charlie reiterated. "If she ha
any problems, we can take her in ourselves."

"As long as we can recognize the problems,
Mercedes said, not convinced.

Scott and his partner, Paige, according to he
name tag, had been putting equipment away. I
seemed they were now done, as they both re
turned their attention to the patient.

"Mrs. Herman, if you're sure, I'll just have yo
sign my form here saying you decided not to hav
us take you to the hospital." Paige fiddled with a
clipboard and multiple pieces of paper, stickin
a pen in her mouth to free her hands.

Gram nodded and attempted to prop herself up

"I'll raise your bed," Charlie said.

Normally, Mercedes would have been all ove
helping her, but she was still agonizing ove
whether they needed to take Gram in. What if she
was bleeding internally or had some other issue
that wasn't readily apparent? She caught Scot
watching her and nodded toward the hallway.

"Stop beating yourself up, Mercedes," he sai

in a quiet voice the second they hit the hall. "You couldn't have done anything."

"If I'd been here in the first place, she wouldn't have had to reach for her remote control. Wouldn't have stretched too far and fallen."

"No way to know that. The important thing is she's okay."

"Is she?"

"If I could see a reason for her to receive further medical attention, I would tell you."

"If she was your grandma," Mercedes said, "would you push her to go?"

He considered, then shook his head. "If she was my grandma, I'd watch her carefully for the next few hours. If she has any nausea or vomiting or seems disoriented at all, I'd advise having her examined."

Mercedes stared into his eyes for a moment and understood he meant what he said. "Okay." She nodded. "I trust your opinion."

As he and Paige collected their equipment and headed to the door, Mercedes recognized that she trusted more than his medical training. Regardless of how much he'd upset her last night, she was glad he was the one to answer Gram's call for help. What that signified…well, she chose not to ponder it. She returned to Gram's side, where she should have been in the first place.

CHAPTER TWENTY

MERCEDES WAS OUT OF HER CAR practically before it came to a stop in the carport. If Charlie wasn't here—and Mercedes couldn't tell if she was or not since her sister still didn't have a car—Gram would be starving. Seemed as if Mercedes was leaving her in the lurch more often than not lately. She had to do better.

She knew better than to schedule an appointment with talkaholic Morgan Billings, one of her most important clients, so late in the day. But truly, when Morgan called, she came running. He contributed to a significant part of her income.

"Hello?" she called out when she opened the front door. "Gram?"

"Hey," Charlie hollered from Gram's room. "We're back here."

"Let me help." Mercedes rushed into the bedroom as Charlie got Gram from her wheelchair to her bed.

"We're doing just fine." Charlie began tucking the blanket around their grandma.

"Sorry I'm so late," Mercedes said as she bent to kiss Gram's cheek. "Morgan Billings."

"I expected it, sweetie," Gram said. She kept up on a lot of Mercedes's clients and was plenty familiar with Morgan's tendencies.

"I can go out and pick up some food if you two haven't—"

"Of course we've eaten," Charlie said. "You missed out on my specialty."

Mercedes frowned absently as she did an inventory of Gram's potential needs—pills, drink, TV remote, pajamas. "And that would be?"

"Pizza delivery." Charlie grinned and continued tucking the blanket around Gram's thin body.

Mercedes walked to the dresser and pulled out a nightgown. "Gram's due for clean pajamas."

Charlie took the gown and set it aside. "Thanks."

Mercedes stood there waiting to help with the change, but Charlie flopped into the chair.

"It's easiest to change her now before she gets too comfortable," Mercedes said, picking up the garment.

"We'll get her taken care of before she goes to sleep. Don't worry."

Mercedes frowned, about to explain why it was much easier to do it now, when Gram spoke up.

"I'm just fine, Sadie. If I fall asleep in this for one more night, it's not the end of the world. Relax, sweetie."

Mercedes put the nightgown on top of the dresser and left the room, curbing her frustration. She hated that Charlie had had to cover dinner. It was one thing if it was planned, but Mercedes had run out for her last-minute meeting without having the chance to touch base and make plans with her sister, who'd been at the beach sketching. She didn't want Gram to have to fret about anything. Adding one to their small family had thrown their rhythm off.

Though Mercedes usually watched Gram's favorite sitcom rerun with her, she headed out to the back porch instead. It seemed Charlie and Gram were just fine. She felt like the intruder and she didn't care for that at all.

She missed the way it used to be. Just her and Gram.

It wasn't five minutes later that Charlie joined her.

"I thought you were going to watch Gram's show with her," Mercedes said.

"I was until you got your panties in a wad. What's wrong with you?"

"Nothing's wrong."

Charlie took the wicker chair next to Mercedes, propped her feet on the ottoman and crossed her arms. "I'm not incompetent, you know."

"I never said you were."

"Maybe not in words, but you continually insinuate it by correcting everything I do. I'm just trying to help. To be part of the family."

Mercedes leaned her head on the back of the chair, thinking of all the times since Gram's stroke when she really could have used help. It'd taken time and a lot of effort to rearrange her life to be able to work from home. During that period she would have loved to have had someone to share duties with. She'd even asked Charlie to come down at one point, but her sister had brushed off the suggestion and claimed she had to work. "Guess I'm just not used to having help."

"Looks like it's time to get used to it."

"For how long?" Mercedes asked. "You're staying until, what, fall? Earlier? When boredom strikes? And then Gram and I have to readjust when you get tired of bunking with us?"

Tense seconds ticked by. Mercedes ran her fingers up and down her opposite hand and avoided looking at her sister in the dimness of dusk.

"I came here," Charlie started in a quiet, controlled voice, "to try to get closer to you and Gram. To get to know you both better. To be more of a family. I've had some good moments with Gram."

"Better late than never," Mercedes snapped, the resentment that had been bubbling for years finally coming out. The aloneness, the me-against-the-world feelings that had swarmed her after their mother's funeral returned in full force, as if no time had passed.

"With you, there's no chance," Charlie went on. "It's like you have this inner circle with Gram and you won't let anyone mess with that. Won't let anyone in. Not even your sister."

Renewed grief nearly choked Mercedes. She forced words out past the ball in her throat. "Maybe if you were here when I needed you, that wouldn't have happened."

"That's not fair."

"That's completely fair! Gram's all I have. All I've ever had since Mom died and you ran back to New York the second the funeral was over. I'd do anything for her."

"You do everything for her, Mercedes. So much…to a compulsive extent." Charlie bolted up and went to the other side of the porch. She gazed through the screen at nothing, one hand on her hip. "It was hard enough to lose Dad. Crushing to lose Mom after that." She paused and raised her chin, eyes closed, as if fighting off the pain. "Maybe it was wrong of me to go back to New York instead of stay with you, but…we all grieve in our own way."

"Yours was always running away," Mercedes said to Charlie's back.

"But I'm here now."

"So I'm just supposed to drop everything and... take you while I can get you?"

"I've never given you any reason not to trust me," Charlie said quietly.

"You've never given me any reason to trust you, either."

Mercedes would love nothing more than to have a sister she could rely on, who she knew would always be there to help with Gram and, yes, to be a family.

And yet, Charlie had shown too many times that her heart wasn't in the whole *family* thing. It was easier in the long run for Mercedes to continue as she had been—taking full responsibility for Gram and expecting nothing from her sister. "What is it you want from me, Charlie?"

"Let me in." Her sister spun around and sat on the ottoman facing Mercedes. "And if you can't let me in, let someone in. You're using Gram as an excuse, but I don't buy it."

"Oh, you don't?" Mercedes's voice climbed in volume. "You don't think I could just be that dedicated to caring for the one person who was there for me? You can't imagine someone who truly puts their family first?"

"Of course I can. I just think there's more to it than that. I think you're scared. And I think that's sad."

"Good thing I don't care what you think."

Her sister studied her. "You know, until recently, I never really thought about how losing both our parents affected us so deeply. I may have run away physically, but you've built up mile-high emotional walls."

Blood pounded in Mercedes's head and she clenched her fists so hard her nails dug into her palms. "Gram's waiting for you."

When Charlie didn't move, Mercedes shot up from her chair. "I'm out of here. Don't wait up."

CHAPTER TWENTY-ONE

MERCEDES HADN'T PLANNED to end up at Scott's when she stormed out. She hadn't set out to go anywhere specific, just away for a few hours. And yet she found herself in the parking lot of his apartment building.

Scott's. Not Gemma's. She'd be happy to see Gemma, but the teenager wasn't what had drawn Mercedes here. As much as she would have liked to lean on Gemma as an excuse, there was no sense in lying to herself.

She wanted to see Scott tonight.

Would've been nice if she'd thought to change into something besides the business clothes she'd worn to meet her client. The thigh-length skirt and button-down blouse looked as if she'd been wearing them for two days and weren't exactly comfortable, but…who knew, maybe she wouldn't be wearing them for long. That would suit her fine. Maybe what she needed was a heavy dose of no strings attached. Something to cure the emptiness inside of her.

Mercedes got out and headed for 6A, hurrying

across the unlit lot uneasily and thinking again how this wasn't the ideal place for a teenage girl. But then, Gemma wasn't going to be here for long, no matter what solution she found.

She knocked quietly, realizing she didn't even know if Scott worked tonight.

Footsteps sounded on the other side—Scott's, she'd bet, based on the heaviness of them. There was a pause, and she sensed he was looking out at her through the peephole. The door opened and he appeared perplexed.

"Is your grandmother okay?" he asked right away.

"She's doing well. Shouldn't she be?"

"She seemed good when we left last night. You just look upset."

"I'm fine. Hello, by the way."

"Hi." He stepped back and let her in. "Gemma crashed over an hour ago. Said she's got her days and nights mixed up because all she does is lay around."

"Scott." Mercedes studied his now-familiar face—the blue eyes that were less wary around her but never fully unguarded, the strong line of his jaw darkened with stubble. She longed to reach out and run her fingers over it, the memory of his rough chin almost tangible. He closed the door, muffling the usual noise of his neighbors.

She glanced around to verify that they were

alone. A video game was suspended on the screen at the other end of the living room and one of the floor-level gaming chairs was surrounded by evidence that he'd been camped out there for some time—a box of crackers, a plastic convenience-store cup with a lid and straw, a crumpled paper sack from a burger joint. The TV and a light in the kitchen offered the only illumination. "I'm here to see you, not Gemma."

"Oh." He stuck a hand into the pocket of his cargo shorts and looked at his feet.

"I can…go if you're busy."

He snapped out of whatever awkwardness had overcome him. Shook his head and gestured toward the kitchen. "No. Come on in. Want something to drink?"

"No, thanks." She didn't know how to say what she wanted. Didn't exactly know what she wanted, really. Comfort she couldn't ask for. Distraction. Reprieve. Instead of going to the kitchen, she walked to the other gaming chair and fell into it. "Didn't mean to interrupt your game. Which level are you on?"

He stood at the other end of the room for several seconds staring at her, then joined her. "What's going on? Why are you here?"

She shrugged. "Wanted to get out of the house. Charlie's staying with Gram. This is right before the ambush area, isn't it?" she asked, pointing at the screen.

He stared at her another moment then turned to the TV. "Yeah." He picked up the controller. "Want to play?"

"I'm better at watching."

He pushed a button to restart the action and got through the virtual ambush with no trouble.

Some time later, he spoke again. "You must have played before."

"Gemma was playing when I was here the other day."

"She's supposed to be lying down. Low stress."

"She stretched out on the floor here. I tried to tell her a combat game wasn't good for her blood pressure, but she gave me a look like I'm being overprotective."

"I know that look."

He turned the game off abruptly.

What am *I doing here?* She tried to come up with a way to bow out.

Scott cleared his throat. "Wasn't sure you were still talking to me after I dropped off that book for your grandmother the other night."

"I talked to you last night."

"You didn't have much choice," he said.

Mercedes ran her finger around the lid of the sweating cup. "Should I not be talking to you?"

"I was an asshole."

She pretended to consider that. "A little bit."

"I shouldn't have treated you like that."

"No."

"You sure you don't need a drink?"

When Mercedes met his gaze, he nodded toward her finger, still tracing circles on his cup. She retracted her arm. "I'm fine."

Muffled yelling came from another apartment followed by the sound of a door slamming. She waited for him to say more.

"Was that your way of apologizing?" she finally asked.

He let out his breath. "I think I've apologized to you more than I have to anyone in the past ten years. Don't want to wear out the word *sorry*. But I am."

She'd been over the whole thing since last night, the drama of Gram's accident making her realize there were more pressing issues than him being less than nice to her. She shrugged. "I know you were worried about Gemma."

Scott closed his eyes for a moment, knowing it was pointless to deny that. Hating it still that anyone had started to worm their way into his life. The truth was he'd been damn glad to see Mercedes at the door tonight. A gut reaction. The wrong one.

And yet, he bridged the space between them by putting his hand on her shoulder. She stared into space, seeming not to notice the touch. She radiated sadness, from the droop of her shoulders to the lack of the usual spark in her eyes. He couldn't force himself to turn her away. Though she hadn't admitted to anything when he'd said she looked upset, there was no question something was bothering her. He might be an insensitive male, but he wasn't stupid.

He waited for her to explain herself. She still hadn't even said why she'd come over. Apparently she wasn't going to volunteer anything.

"Mercedes."

He wasn't sure why he spoke her name, but it turned out to be the coup de grâce. When she met his gaze, her eyes were glassy with moisture.

Damn.

He stood and held his hands out to her, unable to deny the unfamiliar urge to comfort her. "Come here."

That she took his hands and came so willingly only proved further how upset she was.

"What?" she asked once they stood face-to-face. It killed him that she looked at him as if maybe he could make everything okay. He was the last person capable of that, but he was powerless to keep from trying.

"Sit on the couch. Tell me what's bothering you."

She seemed to gauge his sincerity and apparently he passed the test. Still holding one of his hands, she went to the couch and sat down. Once he was seated, she moved up flush against his side. Without thought, he put his arm around her, drawing her into his chest. She reached across him and held on to him, burying her face. Her lilac scent reached him and he closed his eyes. He had no idea how long they sat like that. Didn't care. Didn't pay heed to any lingering doubts or warnings. He just tried to be what she needed.

"My turn to apologize," she finally said, loosening her hold on him. "I didn't mean to squeeze the life out of you."

"I'll let it go if you tell me what's wrong," he whispered into her hair, twisting his fingers through the long strands. He would never tire of touching her hair.

"It seems dumb to say it out loud. Just a fight with my sister."

She shifted until her head rested in his lap, her body stretched out toward the opposite end of the couch. She faced away from him, her hand resting on his bare leg at the hem of his shorts. Her fingers moved lightly back and forth over his skin. Distracted him. He wove his fingers through hers to keep his mind from veering in the wrong direction.

"Why did you fight with your sister?"

Mercedes rolled to her back so he could see her

face. "I don't even know. I was late getting home and was worried about Gram. Charlie says I don't trust her. That I won't let her get close to me."

He tried to follow that. "Do you trust her?"

She was quiet for a long while, her brow furrowing as she considered. "Mostly," she finally said.

"How do you mostly trust somebody? Isn't it all or nothing?"

"Whose side are you on?"

"Neutral sounding board. Needed clarification."

She frowned. "I trust her intentions with Gram. Charlie would never do anything to hurt her."

"Okay. But?" This was fast becoming one of those discussions he wasn't wired to fully understand, but he strived to do his best.

"I guess I don't trust her to stay. She didn't before."

"Before when?"

"Ever, really. She left home as soon as she finished high school. Didn't even stay the summer before she started art school in New York. I was fourteen when she took off."

He didn't speak. Figured it was better for her to just keep talking until she got through everything.

"Do you want me to shut up or do you want my life story?" she asked, and he couldn't help being a little amused.

"Is there a middle ground?" he asked as he caressed her cheek with the back of his finger.

"All or nothing." She mimicked his phrase completely seriously and he recognized there was a right answer in this situation.

"Tell me it all."

Again, she measured him with her eyes before continuing. "My parents were in a motorcycle wreck when I was ten." Her voice went hoarse with emotion. "My dad died at the scene."

He took her hand as she closed her eyes and swallowed hard.

"My mom was paralyzed from the waist down."

He'd worked wrecks like that. They were some of the worst. But he'd never known any of the victims or their families. Though motorcycle collisions got to him anyway, he'd never been exposed to this side of them. "That's awful, Mercedes." He tightened his grip on her hand.

She nodded as she squeezed her eyes shut and tears spilled over, down the sides of her face. He used his other hand to brush them away. She let out a noisy breath and said, "Sorry."

"No reason to be. So who took care of you and your sister after the accident?"

"We did. Gram came to stay with us for a few weeks. We had nurses and therapists to help once Mom came home."

"You were only ten years old."

"My mom always said I was old for my age." Mercedes smiled sadly. "I think I was that way even before the accident."

"She must have needed a lot of help."

"I was glad to do whatever I could for her. I actually liked doing things for my family."

"And Charlie?"

"I tried to take care of stuff so she didn't have to."

"Seems like she should've been doing that for you," Scott said, beginning to understand Mercedes on a different level.

Mercedes shook her head. "Role reversal, I guess. Maybe we were born in the wrong order. I was the one who tried to protect Charlie from… I don't know what. Everything. I liked being Mom's go-to girl."

He couldn't imagine losing a parent so young. When he was ten, he'd had it pretty easy. When his own family life had combusted, he'd been eighteen years old. Though no one had died, technically, he supposed it had been similar in that his family was lost to him suddenly. He'd been years older and his parents had still been living. And yet, Mercedes seemed to have handled her tragedy so much better.

"Seven years later, my mom suffered a massive heart attack." She kept control of her composure, but he could see it was a fight. "Charlie came back for the funeral. She stayed for a week then went back to New York."

It all clicked into place for him at that moment. "She left you then, at an awful time. So you're worried she would do the same again."

Mercedes pressed her lips together. Nodded. "It's stupid, I know. I'm an adult. It's been just Gram and me for years."

"It's not stupid. What about the rest of what she said? That you don't let Charlie get close to you. Where'd that come from?"

Mercedes became pensive. "Maybe she's right about that. Kind of goes together with expecting her to leave, I guess. Why put myself out there if she's going to leave again? I'd love for our family of three to be tighter, but I'm not the one who moved thousands of miles away."

She seemed to have run out of steam and he lost track of how long they sat there in the near dark, not speaking, his fingers gently playing in her hair. Her breathing deepened, evened out. That she trusted him enough to first open up about her past and then to fall asleep on him had an inexplicably profound effect on him. On several levels. The first was a sort of awed humility. Though he'd been with plenty of women in his life, he'd never let himself experience this. Beyond that, well…he was a male. She was a beautiful woman with a sexy body, one that he'd been lucky enough to explore in detail. One that had been etched into his consciousness.

One that was stretched out across him so that he could feel every breath and see the subtle shifts—the rise of her breasts with each inhale, the vague shifting of her abdomen as she exhaled.

His own body responded to the sight of hers. The need to show her what she did to him pounded through his veins. But he wouldn't let himself go there. Not only was she upset and in need of something besides a lover tonight, but he'd promised himself. He wasn't going to get any closer. He could listen, but he couldn't touch.

Scott leaned his head back on the top of the couch cushion and forced his brain to other things. Baseball had never worked for him as a distraction because he had a hard time giving a damn about the game. Instead, he systematically went through the procedures for every emergency-medical situation he could think of, mentally listing every painstaking step.

Aeons later, when he heard Gemma make a bathroom run and return to her bedroom, his body and thoughts were under control. Maybe he'd dozed off himself. He checked his watch. Ten after one. Mercedes seemed to have settled in and, though he loved the idea of her on top of him, his neck was stiff from his position.

He slid out from under her without waking her,

then bent to pick her up in a cradle hold. If she was going to stay overnight, she was going to be in his bed. No matter how hard it would be to keep his hands and other parts to himself.

Once he had her settled under his blankets, he crawled in beside her and put his arm around her possessively. He settled in to watch the minutes on the digital clock change.

Though he had to get up for work at six, it was going to be one hell of a long night.

CHAPTER TWENTY-TWO

MERCEDES AWOKE TO the sound of a door closing. It took a few moments for her to realize where she was—Scott's bedroom. By herself. It must have been the front door, because this one was slightly ajar. The clock said it was just after six-thirty in the morning. He probably had to work today.

But back to Scott's bedroom. She relaxed into the pillow and breathed in the scent of him, smiling. She'd spent the night in his arms.

Glancing down at her body, she verified her next realization—fully clothed. Her work clothes from yesterday were twisted around her and extra wrinkled, but fully intact.

She drowsily hugged his pillow to her and something in her gut did a light little spin move. That she'd spent the night without things getting physical…for some reason that seemed meaningful. Significant.

She sat up, a little alarmed, not wanting to think too hard about it.

The sound of the shower turning on in the hall bathroom brought her still closer to reality.

Gemma was here and awake. She wasn't ready to face Gemma or anyone. She definitely didn't want to explain what was between Scott and herself, not when she was still sorting through it.

Mercedes hopped out of Scott's bed and left the covers as they were, then hurried to his bathroom. Searching for a pick for her hair, she swore quietly, finding only a fine-toothed comb. Of course. He wouldn't have use for a pick, but that little comb would never get through her hair. She finger-combed it briefly before giving up, then rushed to the living room, thankful the shower was still running. Grabbing her shoes and purse, she sneaked out.

The complex was uncharacteristically quiet, almost peaceful, but she knew that was deceiving. As was the calmness she'd felt upon waking up in Scott's bed. Shaking her head to rid it of that line of thought, she walked to her car and got in.

Instead of turning right off Miller Street, she took a left. Gram would only just be waking up, and for once she was content to let that be Charlie's responsibility. She needed time to herself. A chance to think.

She took the road that went north out of the San Amaro city limits. She drove several hundred feet beyond the last large beach house, out of sight of it, then pulled over, left the car on the side of the road and headed for the dunes. The wind was whipping today and the gulf was fighting back, throwing turbulent, rough waves at the shore. The sun was barely visible through a blanket of clouds, leaving the air on the shore chilly, especially for the middle of summer. Mercedes welcomed it as she sat on the sand.

Sex with Scott had been one thing. One glorious, toe-curling thing. Last night had been entirely different.

Being held by him when she was reeling from the argument with Charlie, when she'd been forced to ruminate on some of the hardest times of her life to understand what had happened between her and her sister… Just thinking about it warmed her from the inside out.

But old habits died hard.

Instinctively, she slammed down on that warm fuzzy feeling sneaking in as she always had in the past.

Gram was her first responsibility. As she'd said so many times—and meant it in her heart every single one—she'd have a chance for love and her own family later.

She pounded the sand with her fist in frustration, propelling the fine grains several feet in front of her.

The truth stared her in the face.

Scott was the kind of man that she could fall in love with.

Her chest tightened with fear and she knew at that moment what it must feel like to be floating in outer space with no tether and little hope of landing somewhere safely. She knew what it was to have no sense of direction, no idea if she was going forward or back. Only that she couldn't get her feet under her.

Mercedes rolled onto her stomach in a near panic. She crossed her arms under her forehead and came as close as she dared to literally burying her head in the sand. Her feelings scared the life out of her.

She wasn't supposed to care so much about Scott.

Countless gut-deep breaths later, the anxiety started to recede. And along with the easing of the choke hold on her chest came a return to rational thinking.

Which led her to a realization she didn't want to face: Charlie might have been right about her. Okay, not might have been. Charlie was right. Caring about someone scared the crap out of Mercedes...in part because she was terrified of being left by yet another person. Just the thought that she could fall in love with Scott had freaked her out—with good reason. She already knew he was leaving.

The squeezing on her chest came back for a moment, but she fought it off.

She wasn't in love. She wasn't stuck wondering when he was going to take off. Everything was okay.

Because she had her eyes open, she could protect herself from getting hurt. Even if Charlie hadn't been right, Mercedes knew what she was up against. That brought a certain calmness to her. If the fear was not knowing if or when someone would leave her, then she was going to be okay. Yes, she would absolutely miss Scott when he was gone, but she'd deal with that when the time came.

For now, she vowed to enjoy every minute she got with him.

"So," GEMMA SAID as Scott sat on the living room floor in front of the couch. He opened the pizza box on the coffee table and cut a piece of Carnivore's Delight for each of them.

"So?" He handed her a plate and dug in to his pizza.

"Was it my imagination or did you have a girl in your room the other night?" The normally somewhat sullen Gemma had been overcome by a smug version.

He didn't share her amusement. He and Mercedes hadn't made much noise at all and by the time he'd taken her to his bed, she was asleep. He finished chewing. "Nosy much?"

"Work with me. I'm marooned on the couch, I'm as big as an elephant and my social life consists of one-sided get-to-know-you-intimately dates with an assortment of doctors." She popped a pepperoni into her mouth. "Let me live vicariously through you."

"You can get up from the couch," he said. He'd never been so relieved as when her doctor had decided earlier today that a little bit of movement was okay for Gemma. She was still on bed rest but not quite as strict.

"Big excitement to make my own toast," Gemma said, wrapping a string of melted cheese around her finger. "So, was it Mercedes?"

Scott couldn't say why he was so annoyed by her persistence, but he was. The other night had been no big deal. He'd kept his word to himself by keeping his hands to himself. No one needed to make it into more than it was. "I'm leaving in a little over a week, you know." Maybe distraction would work.

"How much are you going to miss me?"

"Loads," he said absently. "Gemma, have you figured out where you're going to go yet? What you're going to do?"

Turning to make eye contact, he couldn't believe how nonchalant she looked, sitting there eating pizza. Gemma shrugged halfheartedly.

"I hope by then I'll be off bed rest completely and able to work."

Scott stopped eating. Stared at her. Did she have no concept of how up a creek she was? Gemma wasn't a dumb girl—that much he was sure of. Was she in denial? "The chances of your doctor lifting all forms of bed rest are slim to none. You need to face up to that."

She was quiet for some time. Thoughtful. Her plate was empty but she didn't reach for more. "You're not a doctor." The accusation in her tone was something he'd never heard from her.

"I don't have to be. I heard what yours said."

"This is called positive thinking."

"Gemma, look, I know you're stressed, but you don't have to take it out on me. I'm trying to help."

"How are you trying to help?" She sat up straight and her voice rose in volume. "Raining on my parade does me no good. But then what do you care? You'll be out of here." Now she sounded like a petulant little girl and he was reminded of her actual age.

"You knew from the beginning that I was leaving," Scott said, keeping his voice measured and a lot calmer than he felt. He moved up to the edge of the couch, on the opposite end from her. "There's an option here, Gemma. One that would see you through the baby's birth. Help you get started on positive ground."

In spite of her anger, he saw an uncharacteristic flash of hope on her face. "What option?"

"You're not going to like it," he warned. "But I think you need to move in with Dad. He's offered—"

"Unbelievable." She pushed herself awkwardly off the couch faster than he'd seen her move since her hospital stay. "That's so not going to happen."

Gemma hurried out of the living room and slammed the door to her bedroom. Getting this upset wasn't good for her or the baby, Scott knew. She needed to calm down, but she also needed to see reason. Face reality.

He swore and walked to her door, wondering how he'd ended up in this role of trying to steer her to do what needed to be done, against her will. The role of a parent or…a big brother.

He'd never signed up for this. Didn't know the first thing about advising or being a good influence. There was a fine line between trying to force Gemma to move in with their dad and helping her decide it was the best thing for her. He just hoped his approach put him on the right side of the line.

CHAPTER TWENTY-THREE

MERCEDES JUMPED UP FROM Gemma's bed at the sound of the front door closing. She glanced at the girl to make sure she still slept. It'd taken more than an hour to calm her down, plus Gemma's favorite band playing over and over on Mercedes's smartphone to get her to finally drift asleep after her argument with Scott.

Now, judging by the slam of the door and his hard footsteps down the hallway, he was seconds from waking her up.

When he went into his room, Mercedes left Gemma's, quietly shutting her door, turning off the music that would be stuck in her head for days. She headed without hesitation to Scott.

When she entered his room, he stood near the bathroom, his back to her, and he'd just taken a T-shirt off. All that remained were wet knee-length swim trunks. Mercedes allowed herself a moment to appreciate the muscles on his back, rippling with his movements like smooth waves in the bay. Gone was the panic from the morning after she'd spent the night. Looking at him now, with so much of him bared, the concepts of just-for-fun and here-and-now were easy to embrace.

"You were swimming," she said in a hushed voice to his back as she eased the door shut behind her.

He whipped around, obviously startled. "When the urge for a drink gets overpowering I have to do something. What are you doing here?"

"Gemma called me. Really upset. She's asleep now."

He scowled and disappeared into the bathroom with his wet shirt. When he walked back into the bedroom, he no longer carried it.

"I'm not going to apologize." He leaned against the doorjamb, set his jaw stubbornly and crossed his arms over his lickable chest, not that she was checking it out or anything.

"I never said you should." Mercedes sat on his perpetually unmade bed.

"Moving in with her dad is the only thing she can do. She's living in some kind of dreamworld if she thinks her doctor is going to release her completely from bed rest."

"I know that, Scott."

He looked at her in surprise but didn't relax. "Then what the hell is she thinking?" His voice climbed.

"Shh. Let her sleep. Come here."

"I need to shower."

That presented all kinds of interesting possi
bilities. She got up, walked over to him and said
as much.

"Why aren't you yelling at me?" he asked
peering down at her.

She stifled a grin. "When have I ever yelled
at you?"

"You think moving in with her dad—"

"Your dad," she corrected, but he ignored her

"—will stress her out too much. Last I knew
you were pretty loudly against the idea."

"I was wrong." She ran her index finger over
his tanned forearm, still crossed in front of him

"Say that again?"

"You were right. Moving in with your dad is
the best thing for Gemma to do, at least until she
has the baby and can work again."

He ignored her touch, though she continued it
admiring the taut muscle, the coarse hair.

"You're admitting you're wrong?" There was
the faintest hint of a smile in his voice. "You must
want something from me."

"You're more astute than you look," she said,
moving her hand from his arm to his chest as she
started at him.

He swallowed hard, as if she was getting to
him and he was trying like crazy to fight it. She
allowed herself a self-satisfied grin, his barely
discernible reaction empowering her.

"What did you tell Gemma?"

"I listened to her, let her rant for a bit and then I told her I agree with you."

His brows furrowed. "Is she pissed at you, too?"

"No. She didn't say much at all because I think she realizes we're right."

"You don't make an ounce of sense."

"Remember, she's only seventeen years old, no matter how mature she usually acts. Seventeen and her body's running rampant with pregnancy hormones. She's scared."

"She should be."

"You have to realize what she's going through today. You forced her to face up to the fact that her big plan to make it on her own, to forge her way for her baby and herself, has failed. I know and you know it's because of fate throwing her a cruel twist with the preterm labor. She might have been okay if not for that. But she's not thinking about that. She's just thinking *epic fail.*"

"Was I supposed to let her go on in denial?"

"No. You did the right thing."

"So we're all in agreement then? She goes to live with him?"

"She's swallowing that. She'll get there." She pried his arms away from his chest. "I do think it's extremely sweet and a little bit sexy that you've started to care about her."

"Who said I care?"

"It's okay to care, big gruff guy." She pressed her lips to his chest as she'd been dying to do. He sucked in a quiet, quick breath. "You've been swimming in the gulf."

"When I leave, I don't plan to keep in touch," he said, his voice going rough as she whisked her tongue over his nipple. "With anyone."

"You've mentioned that before. Kind of tough to check in much when you're in the middle of the ocean anyway." She forced herself to sound indifferent. Refused to consider how much she was going to miss him. Later. There'd be time later to cry her eyes out, get over it and move on. "Keep trying to fight it, Scott."

"I'm not fighting anything," he said, even as he closed his eyes, as if bracing himself against what she was doing.

The more he fought, the more determined she became to get to him, to push him past the limits of his control.

Mercedes teased his other nipple with her tongue then kissed her way lower, to his navel. To the trail of hair below it that disappeared beneath the waistline of his swim trunks.

"If you would just let yourself care about people," she said in between kisses, "stop working so hard to prevent it, you might find out it's not so bad."

"Not so bad, huh?" he said, his abdomen muscles tensing.

"Can even be good. You really need to get out of your wet clothes." Without waiting for a response, she circled her hands around to his back, dipped her fingers into his shorts and drew them down his legs.

He was no longer able to hide his arousal—it was there in plain sight, his hardness jutting toward her in invitation. When she touched the tip of him with her tongue, he groaned. Surrendered.

She looked up at him, his half-closed, lust-filled eyes watching her with unveiled need. Running her hands up the front of him, she allowed herself a moment to drink in the full beauty of his sculpted, naked body. He gently threaded his fingers through her hair as his lids lowered. When he opened his eyes again, there was a plea in them—the acquiescence Mercedes had been working for. She didn't take time to enjoy her victory.

When she took him fully in her mouth, a sound of pleasure rumbled from his chest. She suckled him, teased him, caressed him, endeavored to make him crazy, and if the things he said were any indication, she'd hit her mark. She ran a hand up the back of his leg and over his tight, muscled butt.

Scott's fingers tightened in her hair, and the

other hand cradled her cheek. With another groan, he gently pulled her upward, forcing her to take her mouth from him.

"Come here," he said in a husky voice. He grasped her elbows and helped her to stand.

Even though Mercedes was fully clothed and Scott had yet to touch her anywhere besides her face and hair, desire pounded to her middle, made her ache.

"You're sure Gemma's asleep?" he whispered into her ear, his breath making her shiver.

"Out cold." She ran her hands up his chest again as he pulled her close, his gentleness giving way to urgency.

His lips sought hers and his hands roved from her waist upward, beneath her baby-doll tank, burning up her flesh. When he reached the elastic beneath her breasts that substituted for a bra, he made quick work of the shirt, pulling it over her head and tossing it to the side. Baring her. He palmed her breasts, brushed his thumbs over her sensitive nipples, circling them, teasing them, and she arched her lower body into him. He leaned down to take one breast in his mouth at the same time his hands dropped to the zipper of her shorts. Her lower half was bare before she could catch her breath, and she pushed her body into him, from shoulder to knee, craving his heat. Needing him inside her.

Scott grasped her rear and picked her up, drawing her knees up on either side of him, his hardness pressing into her abdomen. He carried her into the bathroom and set her on the edge of the counter, kissing her, touching her till she didn't remember or care where they were.

She heard a drawer open, heard him fumble around, but until he pulled away, putting inches between them in order to sheath himself, she didn't register what he was doing. When she was desperate for him to close the space between them, he paused.

"Mercedes."

He only spoke one word, in a whisper, but as their eyes met, time halted and she lost herself in the intensity of his gaze. Before she could absorb the significance of that look, he was pulling her closer to the edge of the cold countertop and entering her.

Their bodies came together with so much raw need, as if they were making up for the chaste night they'd spent together, and Mercedes thought she would die if he attempted either slow or gentle. He matched her urgency with every thrust, driving her higher until her body became nothing but warm, tingling nerve endings. Her orgasm was quick and sudden and it was all she could do not to cry out and give them away. Scott paid no heed to the fact they weren't alone in the apartment and called out her name, then whispered to her exactly what she did to him.

Mercedes smiled into his chest, grasping on to him, breathing hard. "So much for discretion."

He growled in reply and picked her up, their sweat-slicked bodies still connected. He touched his forehead to hers then kissed her slowly, tenderly, in complete contradiction to the pace of their lovemaking. The kiss was so slow and loving her eyes filled with tears.

"My turn to say you were right," he whispered.

She opened her eyes and tried to shake the remaining lust-induced fuzziness from her brain. "About what?"

"That was definitely 'not so bad.'" He trailed kisses along her jaw and drew his fingers through her hair, down past her shoulder, pushing it behind her.

"Not so bad, huh? Thank goodness. I would hate to inflict anything horrible or unbearable upon you."

He let his hands roam over her again, slowly, reverently studying each part of her he touched. "There's not a cell in your body that's unbearable." Again, he kissed her, a simple, lingering touch of his lips to hers. "You're amazing. Fantastic. Beautiful. And damn good at…that."

She laughed, an uncharacteristically husky sound. "You're not so bad yourself, gruff man."

Scott pulled away from her and turned on the water in the shower. Sated or not, she couldn't help appreciating the view as he bent over to test the temperature. When he straightened and turned around, he caught her getting an eyeful. The heat in his eyes told her he liked the attention, and when he took her into the shower with him, he returned the favor and then some. Mercedes might never again be able to look at a bar of soap without thinking of him.

When the water finally went cold on them, they hurried out. Scott wrapped a towel around her and grabbed one for himself. As he was drying himself off, his phone, sitting on the back corner of the counter, buzzed. He picked it up and read the screen, and just like that, his entire mood blackened before Mercedes's eyes.

"What's wrong?" she asked, pausing as she was about to take the towel to her hair.

Scott shook his head and grumbled. He leaned against the wall, crossing his arms. "Voice mail from…my father."

Ah. That explained it. "Wonder what he wants."

"He's calling me back. I left him a message about Gemma. Knee-jerk reaction to seeing his name."

They went into the bedroom to get their clothes. Scott's mood was ruined, and though Mercedes didn't like that the closeness between them was altered, it bothered her more that his dad had such an effect on him. Especially when Scott had initiated the contact.

"Do you think you'll ever forgive him?" she asked as she pulled her shorts on.

Scott scowled and grabbed a pair of jeans. "Would you?" He spit the question out.

"I don't know. It must have been pretty ugly when you learned his secrets."

Scott sat heavily on his bed, his jeans still unfastened. He tossed aside the shirt he'd been about to put on. His dad's message had jolted him from one extreme to another in a split second. "*Ugly* doesn't begin to describe it."

Mercedes adjusted her tank top and lowered herself to the edge of his bed. On the one hand, he knew snapping at her wasn't the right thing to do. And yet, when it came to his father, Scott didn't spend a lot of time worrying about what was right and wrong. He just…reacted.

He allowed himself to do something he rarely did—to think about the past. "I had a good childhood," he said eventually. "Only child, cool parents who showed up at my games, cared how I did in school, knew my friends. The three of us were pretty tight." He leaned his head back against the headboard. "We had our battles from time to time. I pushed them about curfews and other things, but we were…a normal family. Or so I thought."

His pulse pounded in his head but he continued, refusing to let the emotions get the best of him. He'd never told anyone the whole story. Maybe it was time to air it out. "My mom found out somehow, I don't even remember the details of how anymore. She learned he had a longtime girlfriend in Fort Worth. And a seven-year-old daughter." Scott shook his head in disgust. "He traveled there every week for work. Had for as long as I could remember. He acted so damn devoted—always made it back for any game I was in, even if he had to turn right around and go back to Fort Worth right after. I never once suspected…"

Mercedes stretched out on her side, pulling herself closer to him, propping herself up on one elbow and putting her other hand over his. He didn't acknowledge it.

"I left," he continued, his voice thick. "I had two weeks till graduation and I moved in with a buddy of mine and his family. My mom…I still don't know what the hell she was thinking, but she stuck around for a while, telling herself they could work through it. I was so pissed, I wouldn't have anything to do with her, either."

"Were they able to reconcile?"

"She finally kicked him out sometime that

summer. I was on my own by then, working toward becoming an EMT. She and I made peace but it was never the same."

"Where is she now?" Mercedes asked.

He laced his fingers with hers, realizing he was glad for the contact. "She died about five years ago." He swallowed hard. "She had a fast-spreading cancer, but she never told me. Not until the last days."

Mercedes wrapped her arm around his middle. "I'm sorry," she whispered. He held on to her arm and nodded but didn't say anything else. Wasn't sure he could get anything else out. Something about her sympathy made this harder.

"Scott?"

"Yeah?"

"I don't blame you for being so upset with your dad. What he did was…well, awful. I can't imagine."

"He ruined our family," Scott said. "That's one thing. Bad enough. But what I struggle with even more is that for years, he looked us in the eye and told us he loved us. And then he drove off to his other family."

Mercedes nodded and he noticed there were tears in her eyes.

"It's on the tip of my tongue to say what he did was unforgivable," she finally said.

"Understatement."

She pulled herself up to sit next to him, leaning against the headboard. "I wish you could, though."

"Could what? Forgive him?"

"Yeah. What if you did it for you? So you could move on."

He scoffed. "Not going to happen."

"I can't pretend to know how you feel or what you've been through, but what I can see from here is that your anger is still affecting your life."

"You don't just get over something like what he did."

"Are forgiving him and 'getting over it' the same thing?" she asked. "I don't know. But I watched your mood do a one-eighty just from seeing his name on your phone. All that stress and anger can't be good."

"Just let it go?" he asked, disbelieving.

Mercedes studied him for a long time, then took his hand in hers. "Wish I knew how to, so I could tell you." She kissed his fingers, then crawled on top of his lap and kissed his lips until he forgot what they'd been talking about.

SCOTT WAS ONE WEAK son of a bitch.

Mercedes had gotten a call that her sister had to run an errand, so she'd gone home to her grandma. If she hadn't…how long would he have let her stay?

Too damn long.

One little overture from her and he was a goner. A pushover. Okay, maybe the overture wasn't so little—what man could have turned her down? But still.

Pathetic.

Apparently his promises to himself didn't hold much water. On his own behalf, he'd never expected Mercedes to turn into an aggressive sex kitten and strip him down. But he'd acknowledged that getting any closer to her was a bad idea when he was leaving, and yet he'd given in to her anyway.

Not only had he gotten naked with her, but he'd, hell, told her about things he didn't tell anyone.

Five more days. One more work shift.

CHAPTER TWENTY-FOUR

SO THIS WAS IT. SCOTT'S last shift of the job he'd thought he would never live through. As he walked out onto the apparatus floor toward the ambulance, a wave of nostalgia took him by surprise.

Crazy. Not going there.

Shift change was about to take place but he'd arrived early. Eager to start his last day? Eager to get it over with, more likely.

He started going over the ambulance, checking every piece of equipment, restocking the supplies that were low, though there wasn't much to refill. Paige and Cale had worked the shift before him and they were good about having things ready to go. Next, he touched up their cleaning job, unnecessarily scrubbing down any spot he could find. Inside and out.

Hiding out, much?

He snorted derisively to himself and shook his head in disgust. Damn coward.

Today was Brad Gilbert's first day back on the job since his boy had died.

Scott stood, hands on his hips, helplessly surveying the spotless, well-stocked ambulance, nodding. Yep, he was a big-time coward. He'd be content to avoid his colleague for the entire shift and then slip out of town without ever having to face up to him.

Since the ambulance was ready to go and then some, Scott excused himself while the others did their daily roll call and job assignments. Call it short-timer's syndrome, call it being a chicken-shit, whatever. Rafe could tell him what chores he was assigned to do.

Scott skirted behind the group that had gathered at one end of the garage where they met at the start of each shift. He spotted Brad, standing to one side, his shoulders sagging like a beaten-down man. Scott was just about knocked on his ass with regret and grief on behalf of his colleague.

He wandered aimlessly into the workout room with no intention of working out. It was quiet in here, the sound of the air-conditioner fan blowing on High calming in a way. If anything could be calming today. No one would happen in here until this afternoon at the earliest.

He found himself at the punching bags and popped one of them once, halfheartedly. Unsatisfied, he swung at it again, this time putting everything he was worth into it. The connection with the bag, the smacking sound of his fist on vinyl, was gratifying. Addicting. He hit it again. And then another dozen times, beating the living hell out of it.

"Hey." Rafe came in behind him and didn't say a word about his battle with the bag or his absence from the mandatory meeting. He'd been on the call when the boy died, too. He likely knew exactly what was going through Scott's mind. Maybe even felt the same way, though they hadn't spoken about it since the end of the shift the tragedy had happened on and even then they'd barely said anything. Wasn't much they could say.

Scott nodded at him and socked the bag one last time.

"You're on outdoors," Rafe said. "They're going easy on you for your last day."

"Thanks. Might as well get on it." He walked out of the workout room and Rafe followed him, but when Scott turned right at the end of the hall toward the sliding glass door that led to the patio, Rafe went left.

He was grateful for the outdoor-chore assignment, not only because it was mindless and easy but because it was solitary. He picked up litter that had blown against the building from the beach, straightened the patio furniture, watered the few plants that someone had decided added to the atmosphere. Then he tended to the minimal landscaping. He was sweeping the sand off the patio with a heavy-duty broom when he heard the glass door slide shut behind him.

"You're going to break that thing if you don't ease up on it." Brad's voice reached him from just behind his right shoulder.

A knot twisted Scott's gut and he ceased sweeping. "Hey."

Brad took a step so they stood even, side by side, and they both gazed out at the testy gulf, the wind forming tumultuous waves and blowing the gulls off their flight paths.

Every second that ticked by became more awkward. Strained. Scott scoured his brain for the right thing to say—for anything worth saying. What did you say to a man who'd lost his son?

What did you say to a man whose son died in your arms?

Bone-deep regret balled in Scott's throat, pulsed at his temples. He closed his eyes, wishing for a way to excuse himself without earning the clod-of-the-century award. Straightening his shoulders, hating his helplessness, he faced Brad.

"I wake up thinking about him. Seeing his face." Scott's voice cracked and he swore to himself. "Wishing like hell I could have—"

"Stop."

Scott lowered his gaze, unable to take the sorrow in the other man's eyes for another second… berating himself for saying the wrong thing.

"There's something I need to say to you," Brad started. He paused to swallow.

"Go ahead. Get it out," Scott said, anticipating harsh words, almost needing to hear Brad's anger and sadness directed at him. Anything was better than that horrible weighted silence.

"I've gone over Elliott's last day so many times in my mind," his colleague began. He spoke haltingly, as if too many words at once intensified the pain. "From every angle. What if I could've been there instead of on a gas-leak call? What if my wife and I had had him checked for a peanut allergy before then? What if we'd been the kind of parents who don't allow their kids to eat sugar? What the hell if?" He stopped again, stared at his work boots. "The questions are driving me up the goddamn wall."

Scott nodded. Waited.

"The one thing that I don't question," Brad continued, his voice thick with pain, "is whether or not anything else could have been done for my son in that moment. During that call." He stopped again and closed his eyes, then took a shaky breath. "I hate every horrible thing about that day, but the one thing I am thankful for is that you were the man who answered. You were the guy in charge."

Scott jerked his gaze back to Brad in confusion.

"Because if I had to choose one single person whose hands I would put the life of my son, my wife, anyone important to me in…hands down, that person would be you."

Unable to speak, Scott cleared his throat.

"You're the best guy at the job."

"I don't know—"

"I do."

Scott watched as Brad gathered his composure, as if making a decision to close out the choking emotions for right now.

Brad swore, a single impassioned word, stared out toward the water as he shook his head, looked up to the sky. When he spoke again, his voice was closer to normal. "So, thanks, man, for being there for my boy."

HE SHOULD'VE BOUGHT the damn bottle of whiskey after all.

The rest of Scott's final shift was just about as tough as facing Brad Gilbert had been.

He'd actually gotten in his RX8 at the end of his shift, driven to the liquor store—the only one on the island that was open so early—and pulled up right in front. Stared at the window where all the neon beer and liquor signs hung. Somehow, he'd convinced himself that alcohol would only dull his senses for so long and that it wasn't what he needed.

That'd been before he'd driven up and found Mercedes's car in his parking lot.

He didn't want to see her. Didn't want to be attracted to her or remember what it'd been like to hold her two days ago. He didn't want to remember what her soft skin had felt like beneath his fingers or how her hair had smelled like lilacs. And he didn't want to act as if everything was fine between them when really there could be nothing.

He leaned against the headrest, eyes closed, he wasn't sure for how long. Not long enough, because when he opened them again, her car was still there.

Shouldn't she be working? Tending to her grandmother? Volunteering at the shelter?

Then he spotted a newer-model pickup truck he'd never seen before with three Dallas Cowboys stickers plus a Cowboys license-plate holder. If that wasn't his Cowboys-crazed father's truck, he'd go abstinent for the rest of his life.

He'd called the old man back and explained Gemma's situation to him. His dad hadn't committed to any particular plan, and Gemma hadn't spoken a word to Scott since he'd brought up the idea of her moving to Houston, so Scott had no idea what was going on. He found it hard to believe that Gemma had accepted her fate, even after what Mercedes had told him. If she had, wouldn't she have broken her silence toward him before now? And why did he care that she still wasn't talking to him? Maybe that was a more pressing question.

Could be an ugly scene in there. Just what he was in the mood for.

He propelled himself out of the car and toward the apartment of fun. If he hadn't promised Rafe he'd go out for one last night tomorrow, Scott would have walked in, picked up his belongings and headed right on out the door and off the island without looking back. Next best thing would be for everyone to be holed up in Gemma's room so he could get to his and lock the door.

The first person he ran into was his dad, who stood in the hallway outside Gemma's room, leaning against the opposite wall. Scott could hear noise coming from inside the room.

"There he is," his dad said, putting on a jolly act that Scott couldn't stomach, today or ever.

He gave his dad a look of warning and went into the kitchen to avoid everyone. He stood at the counter trying to decide what to do next. Leaving was damn tempting, but he was bone-tired, having not slept a wink all night, and just wanted his bed. Besides, he'd like to part with Gemma on positive terms. It remained to be seen if she was of the same opinion.

"Scott, I wanted to thank you for calling me." His dad had come up behind him and stood in the kitchen doorway.

"Don't," Scott said tersely. He turned to face him. "Don't think you and I are buddy-buddy or even okay. The only reason I called you is because Gemma needs…someone and she doesn't have a lot of choices at the present moment."

His dad's features fell and he tilted his head first one way then the other. *Win some, lose some.* "You did the right thing, at any rate."

"You don't get it. I did the only thing. I couldn't walk out of here leaving her to fend for herself." He looked pointedly at his dad.

It had the effect he'd hoped for. His old man's shoulders drooped farther and he averted his eyes. Best of all, he dropped the subject. Scott left the kitchen and headed down the hall toward his bedroom.

Gemma was sitting on the floor of the hall bathroom, an open box at her side and a scowl on her face. He braced himself as he paused at the doorway.

"Hey," he said, keeping his tone friendly. "You leaving today?"

"What does it look like?" Her words were laced with venom.

"Looks like you're packing up."

"You should know, since you called him."

"I had to, Gemma. Because I didn't figure you would and I didn't want to leave you by yourself."

She haphazardly reached into the cabinet under the sink and threw whatever she drew out into the box. Hard. Brushes. Hair things. A hand mirror. Makeup. "It'd be better if you called the cops or social services."

"No, it wouldn't."

"I trusted you, Scott." Her voice dripped with accusation. "When I moved in, you told me you weren't going to call my parents."

"And I didn't. Everything changed when you went into preterm labor."

"I told you things I haven't told anyone else," she said so he could barely hear.

He racked his brain and remembered her confession about the baby's father. "I kept them to myself."

Her scowl deepened but she said nothing else, just kept tossing things into the box. From the racket some of them made on impact, not everything was remaining intact.

Scott stood there as seconds ticked by, not knowing what else to say but not wanting to leave things like this. Finally, he shook his head and turned toward his room.

"Scott." Mercedes spoke from Gemma's room as he passed the doorway.

He stopped and closed his eyes against the reaction just her voice caused in him.

Weak, weak, weak.

As soon as he could blank his face, he stepped into the room and looked at her.

Holding a conversation with his eyes closed would be much wiser and easier.

Her hair was pushed back with a thin white band. Her brown eyes sparkled flirtatiously and her cheeks held a hint of pink. Her tanned legs were stretched out in front of her, left mostly bare by her short shorts. She wore a snug tee with Yankees scrawled across the chest and stripes on the short sleeves—a boyish style that ramped up his heart as much as any silky pink something would do.

She couldn't have shown up in a flour sack today. Hell, who was he kidding? She could wear a Coleman tent and he'd still want to jump her.

"Didn't know you were a Yankees fan," he said, forcing his eyes from her chest.

"I'm not a baseball fan of any kind. I just liked the shirt."

He just liked the shirt on her.

"Did Gemma talk to you?" she asked as she folded a blanket.

"If you can call it that. She's still pissed."

"Your dad apparently called last night and told her to have her things packed. She didn't tell me till this morning. We've got a ways to go." She gestured at the mess around her.

He wanted to touch her so badly and stuffed his hands in his pockets to refrain from doing so.

"Want to help?" she asked, smiling up at him.

"No." He spit it out before he did something stupid. "I... No."

Her smile disappeared. "Is something wrong?"

Wrong? Was anything not wrong? He stared at her, tried to memorize every inch of her so he'd have that image later. "Nothing you can fix."

He walked out of the room, into his. Managed to shut the door calmly instead of slamming it the way he was itching to do. Collapsing on his bed, he found no peace.

He stubbornly laid there for over an hour trying to sleep, or at least relax. When he could no longer stand it, he sat up. Swung his feet to the floor, threw his pillow and swore.

He was the adult here. Making peace with Gemma was the right thing to do. Though she was currently acting like a petulant twelve-year-old, he reminded himself what Mercedes had said. The teenager was stressed to the hilt and her moods were all over the place.

When he got to the open doorway of her bedroom, he was surprised that the room was mostly cleared out, including the twin-size mattress she'd had on the floor. The truth was that Gemma traveled light, just like him.

She stood in front of the beat-up dresser his previous roommate had left. Her backpack was on the floor next to her, the large pocket unzipped, and Gemma was packing the final few things.

"Almost ready?" he asked.

Sullen silence met him. She tossed a couple items into the bag without looking at him.

"Gemma." Scott walked across the room and leaned on the wall next to her. As he stared at her, willing her to talk, he noticed again how pretty she was, in spite of the weariness that remained in her eyes. Their father's eyes, he remembered, though he no longer saw Dale Pataki when he looked at her. "I didn't betray you. I did the only thing I could think of to make sure you'd be okay."

She didn't look at him or stop tossing things into her bag. Scott leaned his head back against the wall in frustration. He might be the adult, but he sure as hell didn't know how to handle this situation like one.

The dresser was finally clear. Gemma bent down to zip up the backpack.

"I'm sorry," he said, surprised to realize the apology was genuine. "This isn't how I wanted to leave things."

"Whatever."

He'd never heard so much emotion forced into a single word. Sadness. Hurt. Anger.

Gemma hoisted her bag up on one shoulder and he stepped toward her.

"You're not supposed to lift anything."

She took a step away, ignoring him and ensuring that he couldn't grab the backpack. When he thought she was going to walk out without another word, she paused and met his gaze. There was so much pain reflected in her eyes he flinched.

"You know what? You're just as bad as he is. You run away from your family and anyone else who needs you. I thought you were bigger than that, but I was so wrong about you."

He felt the blow in his gut as if she'd actually punched him.

"Have a nice life on your boat." Gemma turned on her heel and marched out of the room.

"I'll be out in a minute." Mercedes spoke quietly to Gemma as she passed her in the doorway, and Scott realized she'd probably been standing there listening to the whole exchange.

Nausea erupted inside him like lava shooting upward to become a volcano as Mercedes came into the room. She touched his upper arm in concern, but he turned away.

"She didn't mean it," she said.

He clamped his jaw down hard and didn't look

at her. She'd meant it because it was true. He was doing exactly what his dad had done ten years ago and again to Gemma in the years since.

"Scott." There was a hint of pleading in her voice. "Remember, she's—"

"Go," he said firmly.

Mercedes stared at him, her hand still on him. He shook it off and stepped away.

"Just go."

Another five seconds ticked by before she shifted and blew out a discouraged breath. "Can we talk later?"

"Goodbye, Mercedes."

TWENTY MINUTES LATER, Scott jogged up the stairs to his apartment, bottle in hand. He needed a drink of whiskey so badly he was sweating. It'd been a considerable feat not to open it and take a swig the second he'd gotten to his car, right there in the liquor store parking lot.

He burst into his unlocked apartment, planted himself on the couch. His hands shook as he broke the seal. Once he had the cap off, he didn't stop to savor the aroma. He lifted the bottle with barely a thought, touched it to his lips and savored the warmth all the way down his throat.

CHAPTER TWENTY-FIVE

GOODBYE, MERCEDES.

Even more than the actual words, the tone Scott had used for them echoed through Mercedes's mind. Over and over, more than an hour after he'd spoken.

She knew somehow that he'd intended those two words to be final. The way he'd acted today—again—was chilly and distant. On some level, she understood he was pushing her away now to prevent an emotional goodbye scene, and there was even a little part of her that was in favor of it. But it was a very small part.

The rest of her ached. Not with physical pain. Gemma's belongings were sparse, the heaviest thing being the mattress Faith's parents had given Gemma that she and Mr. Pataki had carried out to the back of his truck. Moving her had been remarkably quick and simple.

The ache was centered in her chest and throat and made her pulse pound at her temples. Tears threatened as she drove down her street toward home, finally, after appeasing Mr. Pataki and joining him and Gemma for a quick brunch before they left town. Mercedes had left her house only three hours ago, but now, strangely, everything felt different. Off, somehow.

Parking in the carport, she went in the front door and directly up the stairs to her room, not wanting to talk to Gram or face Charlie right now. Not that Charlie would speak to her—they hadn't exchanged more than necessary information about Gram since their blow-up.

She was going to miss Gemma even though they'd promised to touch base daily. But that wasn't what was causing the feeling that someone had drilled a hole in her heart.

The cause was no great mystery. She might have been able to fool herself for the past two weeks, but now that Scott's departure was imminent, there was no hiding from it.

She shut her door and kept the lights off and the curtains closed. Fell onto her bed, her head at the foot of it.

It wasn't that she could love Scott. It was that she did.

How she'd managed to fall in love with the man who had started out being such a hard, cold person, she couldn't quite say. It was as Gemma had said from the beginning—there was a good person, a special man, beneath the surface. A man who cared so much about every call he went on that he had trouble handling the ones he couldn't win. A man who fought hard not to care about someone in his personal life because, she was learning, when he did, he cared with every fiber of his being. She'd seen a flash of it in his eyes the other day when they'd been together.

The tears overflowed and fell down the sides of her face, dampening her ears, her hair, her quilt. A feeling of helplessness and dread pressed down on her chest. The weight of it made it difficult to breathe and she rolled to her side and squeezed her eyes tight against the pain. Her heart was racing out of control and it felt as if the room was closing in on her. Nothing she did helped. Nothing made the blackness ease up on her. She wanted to crawl out of her skin and escape from whatever was happening to her. She bolted upright, desperate to rid herself of the suffocating feelings.

What was wrong with her?

She tried to coach herself through breathing slowly. Inhale. Exhale. It helped a little, but when she heard Charlie bumping around in the room next to hers, she hesitated for only a second before hurrying out into the hall. She knocked on the mostly shut door.

"Yeah?"

There was no warmth in her sister's voice, but Mercedes didn't care. She barged in and sat on

Charlie's bed, pulling her legs up to her chest and hugging them.

"Sadie?" Charlie rushed to her side. "What's wrong, honey?"

When her sister's arms went around her without pause, the tears ran and Mercedes cried without restraint. Charlie didn't ask any more questions, just held her, brushed her hair back repeatedly in soothing motion. When Mercedes felt as if there was nothing left inside her, she slowly caught her breath. Wiped her eyes.

"I'm sorry," she said, her voice higher than normal and thready.

"No… Shh." Charlie took her hand as Mercedes straightened. "Tell me what's wrong. It's okay."

Still drawing in air cautiously, as though she'd been in the fight of her life and was afraid it wasn't over, Mercedes reached for a tissue from the nightstand. Dabbing her eyes, she shook her head. "I don't know. I freaked out. I thought I was going to have a heart attack. Room was closing in on me. Hard to breathe."

"You're better now?" Concern shone in Charlie's eyes as she handed Mercedes another tissue. "Your mascara is everywhere."

"Better than I was." The panicked feeling was gone, but the other stuff was still there.

"What happened this morning, Sadie?"

Mercedes swallowed hard. "It's Scott. He'
leaving in two days."

"You love him."

Mercedes's head popped up in surprise.

"I could tell you cared about him." Charli
smiled sympathetically. "He's leaving anyway?"

The pressure on her chest, as if a fist wa
squeezing it, returned. Mercedes took in a slow
drag of oxygen to fight it off.

"He doesn't know how you feel." Charlie state
instead of asked it.

She shook her head. "There's no point in tell
ing him. He's going. Plans to break all ties. That'
the whole point of his leaving."

Charlie watched her knowingly. Patiently.

The only sound in the room was an obnox
ious ticking. Mercedes glanced at the nightstand
"That alarm clock is older than Gram."

"The ticking helps me sleep. Don't change th
subject."

Mercedes blew out a breath and closed he
eyes. "I think maybe…you were right." The word
pained her, but not as much as the facts. "I'r
scared. Of loving someone." She dared to loo
her sister in the eye. "Happy now?"

Charlie brushed the back of Mercedes's hand
"I'm not as evil as you think."

"That's why I haven't told him," she said. "Wh

I didn't want to face up to it myself. If you love someone and they go away, it hurts too much."

"Like Mom and Dad," Charlie whispered sadly, leaving no doubt now that she had suffered as much as Mercedes had. Mercedes had sometimes wondered, because Charlie had never let it show.

Mercedes nodded and tears filled her eyes again. "And you."

Charlie studied her, her brows furrowed as if she was deep in thought. She pursed her lips and looked away. "I'm sorry, Sadie. I never realized I was making it worse for you. I was just trying to handle my own pain, I guess."

"When you went off to college so far away, I was..." She bobbed her head, trying to find the right word. "Devastated." A sad laugh burst from her. "I know I usually took care of Mom the most, but somehow having you around made it easier. It gave me even more of a reason to want to help. So that you wouldn't have to. I know that doesn't make sense."

Though Charlie was in profile now, Mercedes saw a tear fall down her cheek.

"I couldn't handle it. You were so good to her and I felt useless."

"What?" Mercedes stretched out on her side, closer to her sister. "You weren't useless."

"That's what it felt like. You were the one Mom turned to. She asked me for help only when you were gone. I should have tried harder, but caring for people…it doesn't come naturally to me the way it does to you."

Understanding clicked into place like two magnets coming together. "And now here we are in the same place. With Gram. I try to do everything and you feel like crap when I get pissed that you don't do things my way."

"Bingo."

Mercedes opened her mouth and closed it as she absorbed that. All the while, she'd told herself she wanted to make Charlie's life easier, make her stay more enjoyable, but she'd been making her sister miserable. "Why didn't you ever say something?"

"Because it was my problem."

"Not entirely," Mercedes admitted. "If we're laying everything on the line, I have to confess I get jealous of you and Gram. I know it's dumb. She's always so happy to see you."

"Mercedes, what you and Gram have…I want in on that. I'd give anything to be that close to you two."

"Grass is always greener, right?"

They both breathed, sized each other up pensively.

"I'm sorry about our fight," Mercedes finally said.

Charlie took her hand. "Me, too."

"I'm still kind of worried you're going to defect once I get used to having you around."

"I'm not. I loved the city, but I meant what I said about family. I need mine. I want to be here for you and Gram and I want you to be here for me. But you know? Anytime you care for somebody, there's a risk."

"I don't like that risk."

"But you have friends, right? And lots of people in your life."

"I have Faith and Nadia. They were the ones who embraced the new girl when I thought I was going to die of sadness. Everyone else, besides you and Gram, I try not to get attached."

"What about Gemma? You didn't hesitate with her."

"She needed me," Mercedes said without thought.

"Who else? You're a social girl. I know there are others in your life."

"My clients. The people at the shelter." Mercedes shrugged. Then she grinned sheepishly. "All people who need me in some way. I'm messed up, huh?"

"Maybe," Charlie said. "I love you anyway."

It'd been years since Charlie had said that to her. She couldn't remember the last time, but it felt good to hear it, to feel the peace it brought. "Love you, too. Even if you wait too long to get Gram into her pj's."

CHAPTER TWENTY-SIX

FRIDAY NIGHT, THE NIGHT before Scott's departure, Mercedes followed Faith and Nadia from their parking spot down the street to the patio at the Shell Shack. Faith had invited them to Scott's surprise going-away party several days ago, reasoning that even though they didn't work with him, the party was in a public place and the more people who showed up, the merrier. *Merry* wasn't quite what Mercedes was feeling right now. She was more...nauseated. Shaky with anticipation and, yep, fear like nothing before.

She had yet to tell her girlfriends anything about her and Scott. The three of them hadn't gotten together for a couple of weeks, true, but they'd been in frequent contact via text and email. And still, she'd remained mum on the subject. While Nadia went out frequently, Mercedes having a date, let alone a sleepover or two, was hardly the kind of news to be shared through electronic devices.

As they made their way to the corner of the busy patio nearest the beach, Faith was greeted by more muscled men than should be legal. Some of them were accompanied by women and Mercedes recognized several faces. Her senses were on hyperdrive as she covertly ascertained that the guest of honor hadn't yet arrived. Though she couldn't wait to see him, she was also terrified.

Nadia disappeared to the bar for drinks for all of them. Mercedes stood back a little as two other firefighters she'd met before, Clay and Evan, razzed Faith good-naturedly for who knew what.

"You're Charlie's sister, right?" A dark-haired, gorgeous woman sidled up to her, leaning close to be heard over the cacophony of rambunctious firefighters and EMS people.

"I am." It took Mercedes a moment to recognize the woman. "And you're Selena." The artist.

"Selena, Evan's wife, Christian's mom...I answer to all of them." She smiled warmly. "I adore your sister."

"So she introduced herself to you after all," Mercedes said. "I'd hoped she would. She doesn't know many people here."

"Her work is amazing. I love it," Selena said. "I'm really excited about our plans."

Mercedes racked her brain, trying to figure out what plans she referred to. Her confusion must have shown on her face—or her lack of a response gave her away.

"Didn't she tell you?" Selena asked, her eyes disbelieving.

Mercedes chuckled. "Until the last couple of days, we've been involved in a high-stakes sisterly feud. But I'm happy to report, we're over it." *Happy* didn't begin to describe it. She hadn't realized how much the cold war had been weighing on her. "What kind of plans do the two of you have?"

"We're going to open our own gallery and studio. It'll have a shop for locally made items, as well, and we hope to offer classes."

"I've seen your paintings. The two of you together will be a big draw." Mercedes caught herself pulling one of Nadia's favorite moves—talking to one person while keeping an eye on the rest of the place. She forced herself to tune in completely to Selena.

Selena tilted her head and raised one shoulder modestly. "I don't know about that, but we hope we can make a little money while doing what we love." She continued, explaining where the building they were interested in was located and how they hoped to use the space.

Mercedes was genuinely thrilled for her sister's opportunity, and if she was honest with herself, the idea that Charlie would have something else besides her and Gram tying her to the island comforted her. She chastised herself momentarily for needing that extra security.

Nadia returned with a drink for Mercedes, and Clay's wife, Andie, joined them. Their conversation turned to other topics—their children, Mercedes's job, being married to a firefighter.

"You're the one who went out with Penn Griffin, aren't you?" Selena asked Nadia when Penn wandered near their group to talk to some of his coworkers.

"Um…" Nadia took a drink of her Sandblaster through her straw. "Depends on your definition of *went out with*."

"What?" Mercedes had only been about sixty percent tuned in as she'd returned to scanning for Scott, but Nadia captured her full attention now. "What do you mean by that?"

"Long story. How did you know we went out?" she asked Selena.

"Evan is like the gossip columnist of the station, I swear. He and Penn work a lot of shifts together."

"So what happened?" Mercedes asked. "This is different from the time you had to cancel last-minute?"

Nadia nodded, her brows raised as if she couldn't believe it—whatever it was. "It seems he and I were just not meant to be. We rescheduled after last time—I had to bail really late because of work. Totally uncool, I know," she explained to the others, "and this time it was even worse. We made it out to a restaurant—Bay City Grille— and were in the middle of dinner when I had another emergency for work."

"What do you do?" Andie asked, frowning.

"I oversee sales, events and marketing for Silver Sands. My family owns it."

The other two nodded with understanding. The hotel was one of the biggest on the island and, honestly, just from what Mercedes knew, Nadia's job was huge. Too huge for one person.

"So…it was bad," Nadia continued. "We'd made a gigantic scheduling mistake at work and booked the same room for two different large groups. I had to run out right after Penn and I got our food."

"That *is* bad," Selena said sympathetically.

"So are you going to try one more time?" Andie asked. "'Third time's a charm' kind of thing?"

"Uh-uh," Nadia said, emphasizing with a shake of her head. "I'm pretty sure Penn hates me. It's okay. Lots of fish, you know. Although he is an extremely good-looking fish." She stole a quick look at him.

Mercedes had become engrossed in Nadia's drama for the few minutes it'd taken her to tell it, but now she checked the patio yet again. Consulted her watch, her heart hammering. It was a few minutes after he was supposed to arrive. A wave of light-headedness rolled over her. She set her drink down on the nearest table, the thought of another sip nauseating. If she made it through this evening, it'd be nothing short of amazing.

When word spread that Scott and Rafe were on their way down the street, she considered taking a walk on the beach that ended up anywhere but back here.

She spotted him before anyone else did. The second he appeared on foot from the north, even before he and Rafe were illuminated by the bright lights in the hotel parking lot next door, she recognized his gait. His physique. It took several seconds before he was close enough for anyone else to say with certainty that it was Scott. Mercedes's mouth went dry and she edged toward the bathroom. By the time everyone yelled "Surprise!" she was only halfway to her objective. The noise level seemed to triple and her nerves stretched tauter.

Once she reached the restrooms, set off to the side between the bar and the hotel in a separate building, she calmed herself, soaking in the relative quiet. One other stall was in use and by the time Mercedes emerged from her stall, she was alone.

Gazing at herself in the mirror, she reapplied lip color and tried to make her hair behave. It was particularly rebellious tonight thanks to even-higher-than-normal humidity, and she swore at it.

It was crazy and counterproductive for her to get so worked up about talking to Scott. She realized this but that didn't help her calm down at all. "Nothing to lose," she said to her reflection as she blotted moisture off her cheeks. "Worst-case scenario, he leaves just like he planned."

"Who leaves?" Faith walked in and Mercedes was both mortified that anyone had heard her and relieved it was only Faith. "You talking to yourself a lot these days?"

Mercedes turned and leaned her butt against one of the porcelain sinks jutting out from the wall. She was too strung out on nerves to even make a joke.

"You okay?" Faith washed what looked like a spilled drink from her hands.

Mercedes nodded. "Just feel a little off. I need more sleep." And tranquilizers. And a side of steel nerves.

"Thought I saw you come in here. Scott just arrived."

"I know."

Faith furrowed her brow and stared at her, suspicious.

Mercedes wished she could uncross her arms, smile and lead her friend out the door confidently, as if nothing was scaring the life out of her.

"Mercedes? Do you need me to take you home?"

Tempting. Oh, so tempting. "No."

"Is it your stomach? Head? What's going on?"

She met her friend's concerned gaze head-on. "Scott."

Faith's eyes widened in understanding. "You and him?" She smiled and raised her brows. "Really?"

"It's complicated."

"Hold on just a second. I'm texting Nadia to get in here."

"How about not in here?" Mercedes said, imagining all the interruptions. As much as she didn't want to discuss Scott in public, she needed big-time moral support. "Beach?"

"Good plan." Her overeager friend typed in another message on her phone. "Let's go." Faith put her arm through Mercedes's and they skirted the patio to the sand.

They took their shoes off and set them in the shadows against the concrete-block seawall and waited near the stairs for Nadia. She was still hollering comments over her shoulder to whomever she'd been talking to when she descended toward them.

"What's up, y'all?"

The three of them started walking toward the water.

"Mercedes hooked up with Scott." Faith kept her voice low.

Unfortunately Nadia didn't. "You and Scott? The guy who's leaving?"

"That's the one," Mercedes said. "Gemma's half brother."

"He's also the one who came to your grandma's rescue, right?"

"Aw, that's so romantic," Nadia said. "So you and he hooked up for a night? Was it after Gram's fall?"

"It was before. And it's more than a night."

She felt Faith watching her quietly from the side, while Nadia's reaction was less subtle.

"You guys didn't warn me I'd need to bring a bottle of champagne for this conversation. All I have is wine." She opened up the oversize purse on her shoulder and took out a full-size bottle of cabernet. A little more digging and she produced a corkscrew.

Faith laughed. "That's what I love about you, Nadia. Always thinking."

"I can go get some champagne—"

"No." Mercedes held her back. "There's not a happy ending."

The three of them walked several yards and found a dry spot in the sand to sit. Nadia busied herself opening the wine bottle. "The bartender only gave me this." She took out a single plastic wineglass. "We'll have to share, girls."

Mercedes held her hand out for the first sip.

"We're going to need details, Mercedes," Faith said patiently.

As Mercedes filled them in on the whirlwind since she and Scott had first kissed out at the stables, they passed the glass around in a rotation, refilling it more than once. When she got to the scene the day before that ended with Scott telling her goodbye, Nadia put a hand on her shoulder. "Why'd he have to act like such a jerk?"

"Easy," Faith said. "I'd venture a guess that he cares about Mercedes and is too much of a wimp to handle any kind of goodbye besides an angry one."

That was similar to Mercedes's thoughts, but it was reassuring to hear someone else say it.

They were all quiet for some time, looking out at the white edges of the waves barely visible in the moonless night, passing the wine around.

Nadia swished the dark liquid around then took a swallow. "So. Is that the end? A fun fling while it lasted?"

Both of her friends' gazes sought out Mercedes and she shook her head resolutely. "Not if I can help it. I'm going to ask him to stay. Tonight."

CHAPTER TWENTY-SEVEN

MAYBE HE'D HELD ON TO Mercedes for an instant longer than "casual" when he'd said hello and hugged her. Or maybe it had been wishful thinking on her part.

She, Nadia and Faith had spent a little over an hour on the beach before returning to the party. Then they'd played it cool, waiting for Scott to make his way around the fifty or so people who'd come out to wish him well. As they'd waited, Mercedes had held conversations with several different people and she couldn't remember a thing she'd discussed with any of them. Not because of the wine.

Scott had been surprised to see her there, and though she'd gauged his reaction thoroughly, she wasn't sure if he was happy about it or not. He'd kept a neutral expression the whole ten minutes he'd talked to her and her friends, and avoided saying anything personal to her.

Mercedes was driving herself crazy trying to analyze every little thing, when none of it mattered except for his reaction when she spoke to him alone later tonight.

Now it was nearing one and people were starting to clear out. Nadia had snagged a table as others left it and the three women sat by themselves, talking about inconsequential subjects. Or rather, Nadia and Faith talked. Mercedes sweated on the inside. She watched Scott closely for signs that he was getting ready to call it a night and tried to work through what she was going to say to even get him to hear her out.

Nadia placed her hand on Mercedes's, making her realize she'd been fidgeting with a folded-up beer label someone had peeled and left on the table. "It's going to work out however it's meant to work out," her friend said.

"Not much longer." Faith lifted her hair from her neck and fanned herself off. "I know waiting is torture."

"Understatement."

"How could he not want you?" Nadia said, well-meaning but more than a little tipsy. "I mean, you're fantastically amazing and I bet you're good in bed, too."

Faith giggled and lightly slapped her. "Shh. Even if you're right. He'd be lucky to have you, Mercedes."

"If he doesn't go for it, it's because he's not worthy."

Mercedes had to crack a grin at her nutty friends, even though she'd stopped drinking hours ago and was sober.

Scott said goodbye to Selena, Evan, Clay and Andie as they departed a couple of tables away and Mercedes's heart sped up. He looked in their direction and met her eyes. Held her gaze for long enough to boost her confidence a little. Then he walked toward them.

"This is it," Faith said under her breath.

"Fantastically amazing," Nadia repeated as she stood.

"Hey, ladies." Scott came up between Mercedes and Faith and put a hand on each of their waists. "Thank you for coming tonight. I'm blown away that so many people were here." He didn't look at Mercedes. This close, she noticed his eyes were slightly red and there was a sheen of sweat on his forehead.

"Wouldn't miss it," Faith said. "Are you calling it a night?"

He glanced around. "Just about. Couple more people to say goodbye to."

"Scott." Mercedes had no idea how she found her voice.

He finally looked at her, dropping his hand from her side.

"I'd like to talk to you…afterward. When you're done."

She saw him swallow and hesitate for a split second and then nod. "Give me a few." Not exactly enthusiastic.

Once he'd walked off, she leaned close to her friends. "I may be dead in a few."

SCOTT HUGGED PAIGE and shook hands with her boyfriend.

"If you ever want to give a friend a cheap cruise, look me up," Paige said over her shoulder as they left.

"I'll do that," he said, picking up the soft drink he'd set on their table and finishing it off.

He watched his colleague leave. Not for any reason other than he knew Mercedes was waiting for him across the way and he was experiencing the wildest mix of feelings ever. Among them was trepidation at facing her.

He hadn't expected to see her again before he went to Galveston to board the ship. Hadn't expected to see anyone but Rafe, of course, but yesterday, when she and Gemma had both left, he'd thought that had been the last of it. He knew he hadn't handled Mercedes with any tact, but he hadn't known what else to do.

Lucky him, now he had another chance.

He glanced toward the gulf and wondered what would happen if he just sprinted toward it, dived in and made a getaway. He scoffed and called himself a chicken. Not to mention, a liar. Though he was nervous about facing Mercedes, he also was thankful for it more than he was comfortable admitting. Just ten more minutes with her. Or an hour. Time to say a proper goodbye, but any way you looked at it, goodbye was going to suck.

He turned and walked to her and her friends.

"Hey," he said, smiling. "Ready?"

"Faith and I are going to walk to Silver Sands," Nadia said. "We're going to crash there tonight so we don't need to drive."

They each hugged Mercedes as if they were going on a long trip, too.

"We have our phones," Faith said pointedly to Mercedes.

And then he and Mercedes stood there alone. A few others were still scattered across the patio, some of whom had come for his party and some who were just bar patrons who hadn't left yet. Derek Severson, a firefighter as well as the owner of the Shell Shack, was closing up the tiny thatched-roof structure for the night.

"Would you like to take a walk?" he asked, ready to get out of the bright lights.

Mercedes acted suddenly shy, averting her eyes and nodding. "Sounds good. Beach?"

"Of course. Have to have one last walk on the beach." They started toward the stairs. "I wonder if I'll miss the beach."

"At least you know you won't miss the ocean."

They were quiet for a few minutes as they headed north. She'd slipped her shoes off and they walked at the water's edge, the waves soaking them up to their ankles from time to time. Each time they did, the water was sucked through his beach shoes as it receded. He gave all his concentration to the sensation, too overwhelmed otherwise to sort through everything roiling through him. After a while, he took her hand without thinking about it, only realizing he'd done it when he felt her fingers squeezing his lightly.

As the time without conversation stretched, so did the tension between them. Things were going to have to be said, and soon. But he still didn't know what or how.

"Tonight was unreal," he said, choosing a relatively safe topic.

"You really were surprised?" Mercedes asked.

"Completely. I had no idea. Rafe is a sneaky dude."

"Lots of people showed up. You're a popular guy."

He laughed, mostly because he wasn't sure what to say. He got along with everyone at the station just fine, but to have them go out of their way just for him…that affected him like he wouldn't have guessed. "You know…" Letting the words hang, he shook his head. "I'm actually going to miss this place a little."

"You sound shocked by that," Mercedes said, looking up at him as they walked along.

"It wasn't part of the plan. At all." He pulled his gaze from the sand in front of their feet to take in the dark but beautiful scene around them. They'd come farther than he'd realized. To their left and ahead a few hundred feet was the last hotel on the shore. They were just about to the city-limits line, to the deserted dunes, a few miles south of where he'd taken her crab hunting, among other things.

The gulf was relatively calm tonight, the steady roar of waves a familiar backdrop. The air was thick and damp and smelled of sea life. There wasn't a soul in sight around them. He took a mental picture to save for later.

"I never realized there were so many decent people in my life here," he said, having trouble explaining his thoughts. "If you'd asked me ahead of time if I wanted a goodbye party, I would have said hell no, because I wouldn't be able to name five people I thought would show up."

"Guess you were wrong," she said with a tentative grin. She was acting odd tonight. Almost as if they barely knew each other.

"Leaving San Amaro wasn't supposed to be hard."

"No? Just drive across that bridge without any qualms? No looking back?"

"I've wanted to get away for so long. There was never any doubt how easy it would be, if I could just find the right place to go and thing to do. The scuba job is perfect. But…"

"You've lived here a long time."

"Yeah."

"So…" Mercedes stopped walking and turned toward him as he halted, too. Her gaze was pointed toward the ground as she pushed her hair behind her shoulder. Pursed her lips as she took a deep, shoulder-raising breath. "Why don't you stay?" she finally said in a voice barely audible over the waves. Her unsure eyes sought his.

He was about to answer, when she touched his chest to silence him.

"I know you don't love your job, but what if you could find something else around here?"

"I don't—"

"Because I think there's something kind of awesome between us. Something we haven't given a chance yet."

He wrapped his hand around hers, still resting on his chest, and he felt his own heart pounding.

"Mercedes—"

"No. Let me finish," she said, determined. She took her hand away. "I know I'm kind of hard to deal with, since I spend a lot of time taking care of my grandma. That'll probably get a little worse again when Charlie moves out. But Gram thinks a lot of you." She shook her head. "I'm doing this so wrong. Scott? The thing is, I…love you. And I don't want you to leave."

She loved him?

Maybe he could love her, too, but…

He had to admit, what she offered, the way she made it sound was tempting.

Scott broke eye contact and took several steps away, his back to her.

Walking away from her now was tough. But if he stayed, he would never be happy. And maybe even more important, he wouldn't be able to keep her happy.

The hatred and anger in Gemma's eyes was still fresh in his memory. He never wanted to see that in Mercedes's eyes, directed at him. Though walking away tonight was going to blow big-time, it would only be worse if he gave them both a chance to care more.

He walked back to where she still stood watching him.

"I can't." His voice came out hoarse. Thick. "I'm sorry, Mercedes. I have to go tomorrow."

She pressed her lips together and dropped her gaze. He counted the rises of her chest as she breathed…twice. Three times. She nodded.

"If anything could make me stay, it would be

you," he said, fighting the urge to take her hands in his, knowing touching her would only make it even harder for both of them.

As if she sensed his urge, she took a step back and nodded again. "Mercedes." He kicked at the sand with one foot, his eyes downcast. "I spent the day on the couch, recovering from a bottle of whiskey. Again. You thought I was bad the last time? That was nothing. I went all out. Just about did myself in."

Mercedes's gaze didn't waver. "It's okay, Scott. People make mistakes. You pick yourself up and try again."

He shook his head. "No. I need to get away. Make a fresh start."

She stared at him for several seconds and there was so much in her eyes, so much sadness that he didn't want to see. "I'm not enough to keep you here," she said, or he thought she said. It was so quiet he couldn't be sure.

"No. I'm not enough."

Her eyes popped open. "You could be," she said sadly. "If you'd let yourself."

If only it was that damn easy.

She stepped to him, rose on her toes and pressed a kiss to his lips. Scott instinctively caught the back of her head and prolonged the touch of their lips for a few seconds before she ended it.

Mercedes stepped around him and walked in the direction of the Holiday Inn.

"What are you doing?" he called after her. "I'll take you home."

Without looking back, she shook her head. "I'm calling my sister to pick me up at the hotel. Goodbye, Scott."

He watched until she disappeared around to the front of the building, the crushing pain in his chest increasing with every step she took. When she was gone, he turned back to face the endless, dark gulf. Standing there on the shore, he felt tiny, no bigger than a gnat in the general scheme of the universe.

MERCEDES AVOIDED GOING into the blindingly bright hotel, instead finding a bench outside, far from the main door and any street lamps, to wait for Charlie.

She couldn't help thinking her life at this moment would make one heck of a country song.

That's as far as she let herself go in thinking about what had just happened. She pulled out her phone and started an absorbing game of solitaire, her jaw clenched so hard it ached. It was mindless, and that was just what she needed. Keeping herself from giving in to tears was an all-out effort.

Headlights turned around the corner and

came toward her, the only sign of life she'd seen. Strange for summer on the island, but she supposed this hotel was out of the way, being the last one on the beach. She was grateful for the privacy as she fought her battle.

Charlie pulled up to the main circle drive in Mercedes's car. Mercedes's hideaway was halfway down, toward the end of the hotel. She stood and stepped out of the shadows, waving at her sister. Charlie eventually noticed her and pulled forward.

When Mercedes got in the car and closed the door, Charlie stared at her expectantly. Still, Mercedes fought, though she wasn't altogether sure why. Maybe she was afraid that if she started crying, she wouldn't stop.

"Want to talk about it?" Charlie said in a gentle voice that said she had a pretty good guess of what had happened.

Mercedes shook her head, looking straight ahead. Several more seconds ticked by as if Charlie silently debated saying more. She didn't, though. She put the car into Drive and headed home.

On the way, Mercedes sneaked a peek at her sister. Her hair was pushed back from her face with a cloth headband. She wore a long-sleeved tee and…

"You're wearing your pajamas?" Mercedes

asked. If Charlie slept in sweats and a tee it'd
be one thing, but her sister was a pajama snob
and always insisted on cute little sets. Mercedes
could only see the bottoms—barely, because they
were so skimpy—but she recognized the light-
weight set.

"When your sister calls in the middle of the
night sounding like her cat got run over by a car,
you don't stop to pick the right outfit." Charlie
smiled sadly at her as she turned on to their street.

Emotion—more emotion—engulfed Mercedes.
"Thank you for coming to get me."

Faith and Nadia had told her to call if she
needed them. She was eternally grateful she had
them as friends, but right now, she just wanted
family. And home.

They pulled into the carport and sat there in
the heavy darkness. Mercedes tried to summon
the energy to get out and climb the stairs to her
bed. She opened the car door and moved before
her sister talked more.

She didn't want to talk.

She didn't want to do anything.

Charlie seemed to understand that and they
went up the stairs of the dimly lit house in silence.

Mercedes changed into her own pajamas. She
pulled her blankets back and stood there, her stubborn strength wearing thin. Instead of climbing

into bed, she opened her door and walked down the dark hall to her sister's door. Knocked lightly.

The tears came before she could get the door open all the way, and they didn't come slowly or easily—they rushed out of her, as did the sobs, and once again, she found herself curled up on her sister's bed. Taking small comfort in her sister's embrace.

CHAPTER TWENTY-EIGHT

AFTER CHECKING INTO a dirt-cheap hotel room, Scott had gotten back in his car without an agenda.

He'd ended up at a waterside park, just down from the busy harbor, where he and his father had come when he was a kid. Watching the ships come and go had always given Scott a thrill, and his dad had indulged him by driving him here frequently, even though it was a good thirty minutes from the neighborhood they'd lived in.

Scott hadn't even been aware he'd still known the way, but here he was. He climbed out of his car, for which he still needed to arrange long-term storage, and strolled toward an empty bench by the water.

Though it was early evening—he'd gotten a delayed start from San Amaro this morning after such a late night—there was plenty of boat traffic.

Every single craft that passed, large or small, commercial or private, took him back in time. When he'd been six or seven, he and his dad had started a game of making up stories about where some of the ships were heading, what they were carrying, who was on board. They'd spent hours coming up with tales, getting so involved that they'd lose track of time and get lectured by Scott's distraught mom when they finally got home. He and his dad had always weathered her storms as a team, hiding their amusement until she was done, then laughing silently when she'd run out of steam.

Nostalgia washed over him, lodged a lump the size of a cantaloupe in his throat. Those had been happy times. Scott had been a different person then. One who imagined tales of adventure and high stakes and yet who always had happy endings for his tales. So much so, his dad had ribbed him for it and often teased him by making his own stories contain pirates and explosions and sinking ships. He'd done it good-naturedly, as an ongoing joke between them.

He missed that man.

Over the past years, he'd been convinced that man had never existed, but sitting here now, remembering…it wasn't so black-and-white. The father who had sat here in this very park next to him, whiling away hours at a time, laughing, questioning, sometimes teaching—that hadn't been faked, Scott realized. The love and companionship had been as real as the tugboats that chugged by. It was harder to see his dad as the terrible person Scott had built him up to be since that moment when he'd learned the truth. His dad's big mistake, as he'd called it.

People make mistakes.

He could still hear Mercedes's voice from last night. He squeezed his eyes closed at the thought of her, at the memory of the look in her eyes when he'd told her he couldn't stay.

He'd made a mistake two nights ago by taking a drink, a single first drink that had snowballed into an entire bottle. And while that wasn't the only reason he couldn't be with Mercedes, she'd been willing and ready to overlook that mistake when he'd confessed. There wasn't a doubt in his mind that she would have stood behind him and done everything in her power to help him not fall off the wagon again.

People make mistakes.

He'd made multitudes in his lifetime and had been forgiven countless times. And yet, he was still making his dad pay for his screwups.

Was it helping anything? No.

Had alienating his dad, cutting him out of his life for more than ten years, made anything any better for Scott? Hell, no.

His life had gone downhill since that day when he was eighteen. He'd let it. Let the anger and pain eat away at him day by day.

He'd been mired in negativity and determined

to hold on to the anger for all this time…why? To make his dad pay for his mistakes? If Dale Pataki had paid, it wasn't because of Scott's being too mad to even talk to him. Scott was the one who had paid. Was still paying today.

It was time to make some changes.

EVIDENTLY, HIS OLD MAN hadn't gone conservative in his driving over the years.

Not forty minutes after Scott had ended the call, his dad pulled into the parking lot in his black truck. Scott had moved from sitting on the bench to leaning his elbows on the chain-link fence that ran the length of the park along the el-evated waterline. The park had just about cleared out, as it was nearing the dinner hour. He watched a private yacht that was big enough to house the entire San Amaro Fire and EMS departments and their extended families glide slowly by on its way out to open waters.

His dad eventually made his way across the grassy park grounds to join him at the fence.

"Thought you might be in some kind of trou-ble," his dad said, wiping sweat from the back of his neck.

"No trouble. Didn't mean to worry you." Their conversation had consisted of him asking if his dad could meet him at the harbor park and his dad responding that he'd be there right away.

"What's going on, Scott?"

Question of the hour. He'd had nearly sixty minutes to rethink things but had no qualms, or even wobbles of confidence, that this was the right thing to do.

"What you're doing for Gemma is good," he began. "Thank you."

"I should thank you. She's my responsibility, not yours, and yet you took her in when she couldn't come to me."

"Somewhat against my will, believe me," Scott said.

A tense silence descended on them as Scott tried to figure out what it was he wanted to say. "Been thinking a lot today as I get ready to move on to the next thing."

"Gemma said you're taking a job on a ship."

"Start Monday. How's it going with her?"

His dad waved his head slowly from side to side. "We're doing okay, believe it or not. Took a couple of days, but we've aired things out."

"Aired things out? Sounds loud."

"Got that right. That girl has a fire in her, doesn't she?"

"She's got something. Fire, courage, attitude." Scott watched two young guys working on a fishing boat as it headed back to shore for the day. "All qualities that will help her. She's going to need all the help she can get."

"She's going to stay on for a while. I'm going to help her with the baby."

Scott snapped his head toward his dad in surprise. "I'd say you've made some progress then."

"Baby steps." His dad absently took a roll of antacids out of his pants pocket and popped a tablet into his mouth. "You didn't call me out here to chat about Gemma, did you?"

"No." Scott hesitated. "I've been out here for a few hours. Thinking. Remembering. We used to have some pretty good times."

"That we did. Should've written down some of the stories we made up." He shook his head and chuckled. "We got pretty outlandish with a few. Remember the alien pirate?"

Scott cracked a grin. "With the appetite for young fishermen? I remember." Scott studied the callus on his left index finger as if he'd never noticed it before. "I won't pretend to understand what went on all those years ago when you met Gemma's mom, Dad."

His father sobered so suddenly it was as though a button had been pushed.

"I guess it's occurred to me that I don't need to understand it. God knows most people wouldn't understand some of the decisions I've made. Things I've done." He paused. "Mistakes I've made."

"We all make 'em."

Scott nodded. "I've been making you pay for yours for nearly eleven years. It takes a lot of energy to hang on to something like that. Seems to me that energy could be put toward something more constructive."

His dad turned to look at him. Waited.

"I'd like to leave with us on better terms," Scott continued. "It's past time."

His dad exhaled suddenly, as if he'd been holding his breath. "I'd like that, Scott. More than I can put words to. I'll say it again, I'm sorry for all the pain I've caused you."

"I'll never agree with what you did, but it's in the past."

The corners of his dad's mouth quivered emotionally. He stuck his hand out for Scott to shake. "Peace?"

"Peace." They shook. Scott took in a long, slow breath of relief. He knew he'd done the right thing, knew Mercedes would approve. He didn't know why that mattered to him, but it did.

"I admire you," his dad said. "Always have. You're more of a man than I'll ever be."

Scott looked into his father's eyes and saw he meant what he said, whether Scott believed it or not. "I don't know about that."

"You make a guy proud. Always have. All these years, though I didn't know a thing about what was happening in your day-to-day life, I've been damn proud of who you are. What you do for a living. How you stand up for your principles."

"Maybe if we'd been in touch, you wouldn't be so proud. I've handled a lot of things pretty badly."

"Nah." His dad leaned his elbows on the table. "All little stuff. Not important. What's important is the man you are today. You forgave me for some pretty big stuff." He nodded once. "You're a good guy, in spite of your old man."

They stood there watching the marine traffic for several more minutes without saying anything else, but the silence now was peaceful. Companionable. Scott finally understood what people meant when they said a weight had been lifted off their shoulders. He felt as though he was lighter. He drew in air and imagined there was more room inside him for it now that the resentment and the anger of years and years had been cast aside.

"So now what?" Scott asked.

"Come with me. I've got something to show you."

Scott didn't immediately respond. Go with him? "Where?"

"A surprise. You'll see when we get there."

"You want me to ride somewhere with you?"

"I suppose you could follow in your car, but it'd be a waste of gas."

Scott would have preferred to drive his dad. With some trepidation he couldn't explain, he asked, "You'll bring me back here?"

"Whenever you're ready."

Scott watched him for another five seconds and finally nodded once. "Let's go, then."

CHAPTER TWENTY-NINE

As Dale pulled into a hospital parking lot, Scott's imagination took off. "Is it Gemma? Is she okay?"

His dad couldn't hold back a smile. "She's just fine." He turned off the truck and opened his door. "Come on."

Scott didn't speak again, realizing his dad wasn't going to answer questions. The man's mood was anything but grave, so he didn't figure there was cause for concern.

When they took the elevator up to the Labor and Delivery floor, he angled a look at his dad. "You said she's okay."

"Yep."

"Did she have the baby?"

His dad continued walking, then paused outside a patient room. The door was closed. He knocked lightly and listened for a response. Scott was pretty sure it was Gemma's voice that told them to come in.

Pushing the door open, his dad led him into a dimly lit room. Gemma lay at a forty-five-degree angle on the bed, the TV hanging from the ceiling showing some reality show.

"Scott?" She clicked the TV off and sat up, looking between him and their father.

"Hey," he said, genuinely glad to see her. Even happier she hadn't scowled or yelled at him yet. "What's going on?"

She looked questioningly at their dad.

"I didn't say anything," the old man told her.

Scott dropped his gaze to her middle. "You… Did you have the baby?"

"No, I took the pillow out of my shirt."

He glanced back at her abdomen for a second.

"Yes, I had him. Last night."

"Where is he?" Scott asked. "Is he okay?"

"He's…tiny. He'll be here for a little bit, until he can learn to eat." She swung her legs over the side of the bed. "Want to see him?"

"Of course I do."

"He's in the NICU but I can visit him whenever I want to." She was careful getting up, probably sore.

He waited for her to lead the way.

"You coming, Dad?" she asked, and hearing her address him that way threw Scott for a loop. Just for a second.

"You two go. I'll stop by to see him again before I leave for the night." In spite of his refusal, his face beamed with grandfatherly pride.

Gemma and Scott walked side by side down the hall, in the opposite direction from where Scott and their dad had come in.

"My water broke when we were eating dinner yesterday," she said, the hint of a grin on her face. "Dad was kind of mortified but he tried to hide it."

"That'll put a damper on any meal. So he took you in right away?"

"I've never seen an over-fifty dude move so fast. He was terrified. I was, too, but watching him kind of took my mind off things a little."

Scott could only imagine. He'd seen his share of freaked-out men with their wives or other family members in labor. With good reason. "Everything went okay? What time was he born?"

"In the end, everything worked out. He was born at 7:47 p.m. We got to the hospital just before seven."

Scott whistled. "Little bugger came fast."

"Too fast for an epidural," Gemma said indignantly. "I'm telling you, they should make teenage girls watch an uncensored birth. Not a doubt in my mind that would cut the number of teenage pregnancies in half."

"Pretty rough, huh?"

She looked at him in disbelief. "Rough?" She shook her head. "The first five minutes after my water broke were rough. It went downhill from

there. I swear to God, no human should have to
go through that without drugs."

"But you made it. And it was just a couple of
hours. For some women, labor can last for days."

Gemma opened the door to the outer room of
the intensive care nursery, smiling as she looked
through the window at the babies. "I made it. And
he's awesome."

"Back again?" one of the nurses said, addressing Gemma with a warm smile.

Gemma nodded. "This is his uncle."

It took several seconds and seeing Gemma's
thumb indicating him for the truth of that statement to sink in. Belatedly, he nodded and forced
something resembling a smile.

"Come on," Gemma urged him, washing her
hands. He joined her at the sink and scrubbed
with soap. She was through the door before her
hands were dry.

She transformed into a different person before
his eyes as she headed for the bassinet in the far
corner. She walked lighter, and not just because
she no longer had a baby in her. He was pretty
sure she wouldn't be able to stop grinning if she'd
tried.

"There he is," she said in a syrupy voice. "How's
my little man doing?"

Inside the clear bassinet was a tiny little dude
whose head seemed too big for his body. A lamp

warmed him, but he appeared to be in good condition for a preemie, at least by sight. Gemma reached in and touched his nickel-size hand. The baby grasped her finger and Scott felt something in his world shift.

"Hey," he said to the baby, his voice hushed. "Look at you."

"Meet Samuel Scott Lawrence," Gemma said proudly.

Scott blinked. Maybe twice. Looked at her to gauge her sincerity. "Samuel Scott, huh?"

She nodded, meeting his gaze.

"Is that a coincidence?"

Gemma elbowed him. "Idiot. Of course not. His middle name is in honor of his fabulous grumpy uncle."

A smile slowly spread across Scott's face as he let that sink in. He couldn't think of what to say. He just stared at his miniature semi-namesake, awed as the small one stirred and opened his eyes.

"Is that okay?" Gemma asked nervously.

"Hell, yeah."

She elbowed him again. "Small ears!"

"Sorry," Scott whispered. "I'll have to work on that." He followed Gemma's lead and gently touched Samuel's arm with the back of his index finger. "Wow. He's so…"

"Tiny?"

"Amazing. Congratulations, Gem. You did it."

"Thanks." She stared at her son, her eyes full of love. "I know you've always thought I'm crazy for wanting to keep him myself but…" She shook her head, overcome by emotion. "He's mine to love."

Scott turned his attention to her instead of Samuel. "And he'll always love his mom."

Nodding, she said, "If I treat him right, yes. And I'm going to treat him like a prince."

"He's lucky to have you." The sentiment was genuine. During the month that Gemma had stayed with him, he'd become certain of several things, and one of them was that she'd loved that child before he was born. Though he'd never met Gemma's mother, he was willing to bet that she wasn't the most loving mom on the planet. Gemma seemed determined to be different. "Have you told your mom yet?"

She straightened and all joy disappeared from her face. "Dad made me call her. She's coming tomorrow to see her grandson."

"What if she wants you to come home with her?"

Gemma shrugged. "She can want all she wants." She averted her gaze. "I'm going to stay with Dad. Until I'm ready to try it on my own. He seems… I don't know. He seems like he wants to help. Like he really cares, for once."

Scott was silent for a bit. "I think maybe he always has cared. He's just now starting to figure out how to show it."

"Gotta grow up sometime, I guess. Scott?"

He tore his eyes away from the squirming little guy. "Yeah?"

"I'm sorry. For being so pissed at you for calling him."

"I only did it because—"

"Because what else could you do?" she finished. "I was more pissed at my situation, when you get down to the truth. Pissed that I was out of options."

He nodded and squeezed her shoulder. "I get it. It's okay. Mercedes pled your case for you and that's pretty much what she said."

"I talked to Mercedes a while ago."

He didn't want to care. Didn't want to think about her. Not yet. Not until he was three thousand miles off the coast, settling into his new life. Then maybe he could handle it.

"She told me what happened. How you left it."

Scott acknowledged that by raising his brows and focusing his attention on the baby's cheek. He ran his finger lightly over it, and Samuel turned his head toward him.

"Nothing to say for yourself?" she asked quietly.

"Nothing to say."

Still watching him, Gemma tilted her head. "I stand by my belief that it could've worked between you two. If you'd just… I don't know. Tried."

"You look exhausted. Don't you think we should head back to your room?" he asked, straightening.

Gemma laughed halfheartedly. "I see how you are. Fine. Lucky for you, I am tired." She turned to Samuel. "Good night, my little rock star. I'll see you soon." She bent down and kissed his tiny hand, an awkward feat thanks to the heat lamp. "Love you to pieces, Sammy."

Scott again caressed the baby's cheek. "Nice to meet you, Samuel Scott Lawrence. I have a feeling you're a pretty lucky dude. See you later."

As he and Gemma headed back toward her room, she asked, "When do you think you'll be back?"

He'd made no plans to come back. Sure, he probably wouldn't spend the rest of his life on a cruise ship, but that's all he knew. And suddenly, in terms of her little boy, his nephew, that didn't seem quite soon enough. At that rate, Sammy would be in high school before he saw him again. "I don't know," he said, "but you gave me a pretty damn compelling reason to visit."

CHAPTER THIRTY

MERCEDES BARELY NOTICED the strange noise coming from the hallway. In truth, she hadn't noticed much in the past twenty-four hours besides the physical ache in every cell of her body. She'd been sitting here on the couch ever since dinner, thinking she should go work on the new campaign she and Morgan Billings had discussed, but unable to convince herself to move.

When Gram burst into the living room in a motorized wheelchair, a high-pitched scream of surprise escaped from Mercedes.

Gram came to a stop a couple feet from her and chuckled.

"What in the world? Where did that come from?" Mercedes asked.

"Your sister insisted on buying it."

"She bought that?" Mercedes jumped up and walked around the chair she and Gram had drooled over two years ago. It was the top of the line and the price tag had been several times more than their budget. "She just…bought it?"

Gram was all grins as she attempted to act as if

it was too extravagant. Her satisfaction was plain to see, though. "Apparently the girl has money to burn."

Charlie appeared in the doorway then. "I don't know why you two didn't mention this to me before."

Mercedes exchanged a look with Gram. "We... didn't think of it, I guess." She checked out the controls at Gram's fingertips. "You like it?"

Gram nodded, her eyes damp. "This will free you up."

"It's a little independence for Gram," Charlie said, coming into the room. "She'll of course still need help getting in and out of it, but she can move around the main floor by herself now."

"I've never minded wheeling you anywhere, Gram. You know that, right?"

"Of course, sweetie. But this will make me feel better, not having to call you just to move."

"That was so thoughtful of you, Charlie," Mercedes said, and suddenly tears filled her eyes, as well. Again. She turned away, trying to hide.

She was happy for Gram, that she'd feel a little less like a burden, yes, but the tears had nothing to do with anything going on in this room. They'd been just under the surface all day, waiting to rush out at the slightest wavering of her control.

Stupid tears.

"Happy to do it," Charlie said, as if spending

so much money was no big deal. "Selena's coming over in a while to discuss some business stuff. I need to run to the store to get a couple things. I'll be back in a half hour."

Her back still to her sister, Mercedes nodded. Managed to squeeze out "That's fine" without her voice betraying her. Her head ached with the effort of hiding her tears, but poor Charlie had been subjected to her crying enough for one lifetime.

She heard Charlie kiss Gram on her way out and Gram said goodbye.

Mercedes battled the ridiculous tears. She tried to brush them away, but it was like shoveling pebbles out of the way before an avalanche. She lowered herself to the couch and covered her face helplessly.

She heard the buzz of the wheelchair and the next thing she knew, Gram's hand rested on her leg, patting her every few seconds.

"Charlotte told me your Scott left town," Gram said.

Mercedes could only nod for several seconds. Then she managed to clarify. "Not my Scott."

"You fell in love." There was no question in Gram's words, so Mercedes didn't reply. "Thank goodness."

Mercedes's head snapped up in shock. "He doesn't feel the same, Gram. I asked him to stay and he left anyway."

Her grandma nodded and frowned. "That's unfortunate and I'm very sorry about it. Nothing quite compares to the agony of having one's heart broken."

Agony. That was a good word.

"Why did you say 'thank goodness' then?"

Gram breathed in deeply, lifted her chin and stared Mercedes down. "I've been worried about you, Sadie. For some time now."

"What? Why?"

"You're such a dear, caring girl to devote so much of your time to this old woman. I was afraid you were using that as an excuse not to have your own life."

"I have a life." She sniffed and took the tissue from the front pocket of her shorts to dry her face once again.

"You have a good life. Friends, job. But Sadie, you've not had a serious boyfriend once since you moved in."

"I've never had a serious boyfriend, Gram. It's not because of you. Although…yeah. I have some things I'm trying to work through. To not be so scared."

"As I suspected."

"Asking him to stay was a huge thing for me." She studied Gram's bony, veiny hand on her leg, running her fingers over the back of it. "And look where it got me." The lump in her throat swelled up again, and she closed her eyes. She was so tired of feeling this way. It had been less than twenty-four hours, but crying was getting so old.

"I'm sorry, sweetie. It hurts. May have been a century ago, but I've been there."

The thought of Gram young and in love made Mercedes smile. "Surely no man left you hanging."

"There was one," Gram said, her voice distant as she seemed to go back in time, remembering. "I would've done anything for him. Thought the world revolved around him. He broke my heart."

"Really? So what'd you do?"

"I waited for him to get his head screwed on straight."

"Did he?"

"He came back and asked me to marry him in 1947."

Mercedes let that sink in. "Grandpa?" she asked, astonished to discover the marriage that had lasted for so many years until her grandpa's death had such a precarious start.

Gram grinned. "Men can be slow. Maybe Scott will get his head screwed on straight and realize you're the best thing that ever happened to him."

"I don't think so, Gram. But I do know one thing. I'm tired of crying. I think Charlie's afraid to be alone in a room with me." She managed an embarrassed laugh. "I'll be okay."

Her grandma took her hand. "Cry if you need to, Sadie. No matter what, I'm proud of you. I know going to Scott took courage."

Mercedes nodded, but her heart wasn't really into it. Working up the nerve to ask Scott to stay had been monumental. But what good was courage and risk when she only ended up feeling like this?

CHAPTER THIRTY-ONE

Scott had always thought he was emotionally wrung out after a twenty-four-hour shift of non-stop EMS calls. Turned out being a paramedic had nothing on real life some days.

As he took the elevator up from the lower-level hospital cafeteria, his hands filled with pretzels, mini donuts and a highly caffeinated, full-of-sugar soda, he amended that thought. If today had been a work shift, then all the calls had had happy endings. Even if getting to those endings had been draining and stressful.

The elevator doors opened on the main floor and a large man with his hands full got on and quickly took up more than his share of space.

"Sorry, man." The guy was barely visible behind a large bouquet of roses, three gift bags with tissue poking out and a gigantic white teddy bear. He shuffled the bear under his elbow and Scott got a better view of him.

He looked as if he could be a professional wrestler. He had a good three inches and a hundred pounds of muscle and broadness on Scott. His arms were heavily tattooed, a humorous contrast with the fluffy bear. A small hoop hung from one ear, and he wore a thick silver chain around his neck.

The beefy guy glanced around the flowers to check which elevator buttons were lit up. He nodded in satisfaction. "You going to Labor and Delivery, too?"

"Yep." Scott couldn't take his eyes off all the loot.

"You stocking up on junk food for your wife?"

"This is all for me. Going to visit my...sister." It was the first time Scott had called her that out loud. He was surprised at how okay it felt to say it.

"I know what you're thinking," the guy said contritely. "I went overboard."

"I don't know," Scott said, grinning. "Did you bring something for everyone in the wing?"

The guy laughed. "It's all for my wife. Well, the bear is technically for my brand-new daughter, but she'll have to grow into it."

The elevator seemed to move at a snail's pace. Scott tuned in to make sure it was, in fact, still moving.

"I'm not going to apologize to anyone, man," Beefy Guy continued.

"No," Scott said, hiding his amusement.

"It's just that..." The guy shrugged with one

shoulder. "I've got the best woman in the world. And now the best baby girl. I feel like I've got everything a guy could ever want." He lifted the hand that held the gift bags. "Even if that little package there is going to put me in the poorhouse for the next five years."

"You got her some bling?"

"A ring. Diamonds and sapphires. Her favorites."

"Nice."

"Call me whipped or whatever, man." The beefy guy's voice was lower, conspiratorial. "I can own that. When you've got an amazing woman, you can't take her for granted. You've got to do whatever you can to keep her."

Something about his words made Scott uneasy, and he checked to see which floor was lit up. One more floor to go. He tapped his fingers against the elevator wall, itching to get out. At last the doors slid open and he did his best to exit at a normal pace.

"Take it easy," the guy said.

"Have a good one."

When Scott reached Gemma's closed door, he paused. The man's words seemed to hang in the air. Taunt him. He shook his head, as if to get rid of them, and opened the donuts. Instead of heading into her room, he wandered down the hallway with no particular destination in mind.

When you have an amazing woman...

Mercedes was an amazing woman. As Gemma had pointed out, she was lightness and caring to Scott's dark selfishness. She was always giving, without questioning. Her mind automatically jumped to the positive side of everything but not in a can't-handle-the-bad-stuff way. She was the strength of her little family, he'd figured that out even in the short time he'd spent with each of them.

Scott had spent half a lifetime holding on to all the bad stuff. He hadn't always been like that. The kid version of him, the one who spun tales with happy endings at the harbor park, had been happy. Focused on the bright side of everything.

It wasn't tough to figure out when he'd changed. When his family had fallen apart, he'd lost himself. He'd let anger and a grudge the size of the Gulf of Mexico rule him. That blackness he'd let grow had colored everything—his relationships with others, or lack thereof, his job...

Though emergency medicine included a lot of death, there were countless stories where he and his colleagues had been able to turn things around for a patient. Greg Wolf, the newlywed dad-to-be popped into his head. He hadn't even recognized Greg, still couldn't remember a thing about the call that had saved Greg's life. How many other calls like that were there, that Scott had buried in order to focus on the ones with tragic ends?

Then there were the less obvious ones, like Brad Gilbert's son. Though Scott hadn't been able to save Elliott's life, according to Brad, Scott's best efforts had helped him find peace. Whether Scott agreed with or understood Brad's assessment or not, he'd apparently had a positive effect. But all he'd seen was the negative.

Day after day.

His job had been intense, and losing a patient would never be easy to swallow, but maybe Rafe was on to something with his talk about perspective.

It was easier to see the negative, but the positive had been staring him right in the face.

When he'd confessed his failure at abstaining from alcohol the other night, Mercedes hadn't thought twice about it. Hadn't backed away. All she'd done was encourage him. Offer him hope.

And he'd walked away.

Idiot.

Gemma had accused him of running away from those who needed him, just like his dad. Well, it was time to stop running. It appeared his dad had kicked the habit and Scott was going to, as well. Mercedes didn't need him, but she'd said she wanted him. He hoped his stupidity and stubbornness, his inability to recognize the best thing in his life, hadn't blown his chances with her.

If she'd let him, he was going to spend a life-time doing whatever he could to keep her. But first he had to go get her.

MERCEDES WAS PUSHING her horse and she knew it.

They'd been out for almost two hours, and she hadn't had much use for a relaxed walk or a gen-tle trot. It seemed they couldn't gallop enough, though, for Mercedes to work out her anger.

She'd spent a good twenty-four hours wallow-ing and sniffling around. When she'd woken up this morning, she'd transitioned to mad. Ticked that Scott was too chicken to give them a chance. Pissed that he'd fallen off the wagon. Irate that she'd finally, for the first time in her life, gotten up the nerve to love somebody—let alone tell him she loved him—and he'd walked away.

Charlie had suggested something about the various steps of grieving. Mercedes didn't know the steps or their order and didn't care. She just wanted to burn off all the emotions and get back to her even-keeled life.

How could you grieve someone who'd never been yours in the first place?

Winded, she slowed Nutmeg as they reached the end of a meadow. "You are so getting an extra treat when we get back to the stables," Mercedes said, rubbing the horse's neck.

As her breathing slowed, she thought she heard another horse coming toward them through the woods. Exactly what she didn't want. She'd come out here on a Sunday morning to be alone. Without waiting around to see if she was right, she turned Nutmeg around and ordered her to gallop back across the meadow.

She and Nutmeg were three-quarters of the way across the meadow, nearly to the trees on the other side, when she thought she heard a yell. Without turning around, she urged Nutmeg to go faster, to no avail. The horse instead slowed, going against Mercedes's commands for the first time ever in all the years she'd ridden her. Proof that she had indeed pushed Nutmeg too hard. "Sorry, girl."

"Mercedes!"

She blinked. Frowned.

She knew that voice.

It took more courage than it should have to turn around and verify that it was, indeed, Scott.

He was really there, sitting atop Serrano, slowing to a trot thirty feet away. She stared, her voice failing her, her emotions such a wild conglomeration she couldn't decide how seeing him made her feel. Mad, because she had been all morning and it was tough to put the brakes on it—and seeing his face wasn't enough to assuage her. Hopeful because, well, he was here. Concerned because he was supposed to be getting ready to be on a ship the next day, sailing away. Afraid that this was going to end even more painfully than the last time they'd parted.

He dismounted and walked toward her and Nutmeg with long, purposeful strides, his face unreadable. He wore jeans, a black T-shirt and a pair of new-looking black boots. And a black cowboy hat.

"Nice hat," she finally said as she swung her leg over Nutmeg and slid down to the ground.

He broke out into a slow smile, as if he knew his dimples were her biggest weakness. "It's not a Stetson, but it'll do. You're a tough one to track down."

"Gram basically forced me out of the house. What are you doing here?"

He stepped closer. "I thought maybe you'd want to see this." He dug in his pocket and took out his phone.

When she realized it was a picture of Gemma's baby, she pulled it close. Gemma had texted her photos, but Mercedes couldn't get enough. This one was of Scott holding Sam in the crook of his arm. The juxtaposition of the hard-living tough guy with the tiny, brand-new boy brought tears to her eyes.

She wiped them brusquely away, repeating to herself yet again the promise she'd made to herself. No more tears.

"Beautiful picture," she said, handing it back. "I hope to drive up to see them next weekend," Mercedes said. "Aren't you supposed to be heading for a ship somewhere?"

"I made a mistake."

A mistake. Wrong start date? Wrong city? She looked at him in confusion.

"I turned down the job on the cruise ship."

"You turned it down."

"Because I'm an idiot."

"You turned it down because you're an idiot?"

"I came back because I'm an idiot. Mercedes…" He shoved his hands into his front pockets, shook his head.

She closed her eyes, tried to close out any hope his words awakened. Her heart felt bruised, raw. It wouldn't take much to make it ache again.

"You left, Scott." Mercedes looked to the side, out over the miles of land that stretched below them. "You walked away."

"I've done a lot of dumb things in my life, but that one's at the top of my list."

She battled the hope trying to surge inside her with everything she had. "That was less than two days ago. What could possibly change in two days?" She swallowed, fighting to keep her voice steady.

Scott took her hand in his, weaving their fingers together. "Let's see. In the past twelve hours, I made peace with my dad, made up with Gemma, met my brand-new nephew, quit my job before starting it and drove all night because even with all that, something still isn't right."

She met his gaze, trying to absorb what he'd told her. "You and your dad?"

"I forgave him."

"That's great, Scott. Gemma said she's getting along okay with him, as well."

Scott nodded. "It's not a big happy family yet. Might never be. But at least we're all talking. Trying."

"You drove all night?" she asked as she sorted through what he'd said.

"Haven't slept since Friday night. So if I botch this up, I'll try to blame it on exhaustion."

"Botch what?"

He brushed his knuckle along her jaw. "Telling you what I came to tell you."

"Okay…?" Her heart thundered in anticipation.

"I came back because of you."

God, that sounded good, but…

"You quit your paramedic job, Scott. You left because you needed to escape."

"It wasn't the place I needed to escape from. It

was my frame of mind. The anger I've been har
boring for so long. I've let that go."

"Just like that?"

"Just like that after more than ten years." He
brushed her hair back and looked earnestly into
her eyes. He was more unguarded than ever be
fore. Open. Vulnerable.

"Have you really thought this through? You're
okay with staying here? Because I'm kind of com
mitted to the island."

"I thought it through for six and a half hours in
the car. I'm committed to being where you are..
if I'm welcome."

"You are, but..."

"But?"

"What are you going to do for a career? I don'
want you to feel forced to go back to the job you
hated."

"I made some calls this morning. Nothing offi
cial, but it looks like I'll be able to get some part
time hours teaching paramedics classes."

"And the rest of the time?"

His lips curved upward, faintly displaying his
dimples. "When I got here, I talked to Maria and
her husband. Apparently they liked my idea o
opening another stable on the island. They've
been researching things like land, regulations, po
tential market. We're just in the beginning stage

of talks, but I might manage the stables on the island for them."

"That sounds good, Scott. Really good." She was losing the battle. Hope was bubbling up twice as fast as she could find reasons to crush it. "All this in twelve hours, huh?"

"All this because of you. Because I love you, Mercedes."

Forget the battle. Hope had pretty much washed away everything else inside her now. Blood rushed out of her head and into her chest. She wasn't sure, but she might have actually swayed on her feet. She closed her eyes and let herself relish the moment. The tears were back, but this time she didn't wipe them away. Because they were good tears.

"I love you, too."

Mercedes slid her arms up his chest and around his neck, then planted a slow, expressive kiss on his lips because she couldn't think of a better way to tell him how she felt. He pulled her closer and the kiss went on for so long that her horse snorted, making both of them laugh.

"I'd invite you to my place to celebrate, but I don't have a place," Scott said in a sexy, gravelly voice.

"You can come to my place, but our midday celebration will have to consist of tea and cookies with Gram. A rousing round or two of Scrabble.

And maybe if I'm lucky—" she leaned close to his ear, whispering "—you can rescue me later, Mr. Paramedic."

"If that means what I'm thinking, I'll be happy to rescue you every day. For the rest of my life."

* * * * *